PRAISE FOR THE WORKS
OF MARCUS MAJOR

A Family Affair

"Engaging . . . [a] tale that explores the erosion of trust and commitment among the members of an African-American family."
—*Publishers Weekly*

A Man Most Worthy

"Irresistible . . . interesting twists and turns . . . an entertaining and insightful novel . . . [a] sexy, witty, and wise offering from one of today's most gifted talents—an author worthy of the kind of success this wonderful new novel is certain to bring."
—*Booklist*

"A story that will tug at even the toughest of hearts."
—*Tri-State Defender*

4 Guys and Trouble

"Entertaining, hip, and charming. Crafted with a sense of style, insight, fun and a twist."
—*Publishers Weekly*

"A delightful story."
—*Booklist*

"Kenya and Amir"
in Got to Be Real

"Superbly handled."
—*USA Today*

"An entertaining urban fable."
—*Publishers Weekly*

continued . . .

Also by Marcus Major

A Man Most Worthy
4 Guys and Trouble
Good Peoples

ANTHOLOGIES
Got to Be Real
Mothers & Sons

MARCUS MAJOR

a family affair

New American Library

New American Library
Published by New American Library, a division of
Penguin Group (USA) Inc., 375 Hudson Street,
New York, New York 10014, USA
Penguin Group (Canada), 10 Alcorn Avenue, Toronto,
Ontario M4V 3B2, Canada (a division of Pearson Penguin Canada Inc.)
Penguin Books Ltd., 80 Strand, London WC2R 0RL, England
Penguin Ireland, 25 St. Stephen's Green, Dublin 2,
Ireland (a division of Penguin Books Ltd.)
Penguin Group (Australia), 250 Camberwell Road, Camberwell, Victoria 3124,
Australia (a division of Pearson Australia Group Pty. Ltd.)
Penguin Books India Pvt. Ltd., 11 Community Centre, Panchsheel Park,
New Delhi - 110 017, India
Penguin Group (NZ), Cnr Airborne and Rosedale Roads, Albany,
Auckland 1310, New Zealand (a division of Pearson New Zealand Ltd.)
Penguin Books (South Africa) (Pty.) Ltd., 24 Sturdee Avenue,
Rosebank, Johannesburg 2196, South Africa

Penguin Books Ltd, Registered Offices:
80 Strand, London WC2R 0RL, England

Published by New American Library,
a division of Penguin Group (USA) Inc. Previously published in a Dutton edition.

First New American Library Printing, January 2005

3   5   7   9   10   8   6   4   2

NEW AMERICAN LIBRARY and logo are trademarks of
Penguin Group (USA) Inc.

New American Library Trade Paperback ISBN: 0-451-21400-5

The Library of Congress has cataloged the hardcover edition of this title as follows:

Major, Marcus.
A family affair / Marcus Major.
p. cm.
ISBN 0-525-94768-X (alk. paper)
1. African-American families—Fiction. 2. Philadelphia (Pa.)—Fiction.
3. Adultery—Fiction. I. Title.

PS3563.A3923F36 2004
813'.54—dc22   2003056490

Set in Sabon
Designed by Lenny Telesca

Printed in the United States of America

For my aunt
Sandra Faye Earley
1952–2003

a family affair

chapter 1

On the way to his seat in the den, Leonard Moore threw a playful punch at his youngest son, Myles, hitting him square in the chest. He drew his fist back, impressed.

"Hey," Leonard said as he settled onto the couch next to Amir, "your brother has been working out."

Amir took a sip of his soda and scoffed. "He should have plenty of energy to work out." He eyed Myles contemptuously. "*Some* of us have to do real work."

Leonard laughed and looked proudly at Myles. "Tell him, son, you work hard. Not only are you a teacher, you're a writer."

"Aaah, oh." Amir set the glass back onto the coffee table, "I almost forgot, this man here is a wordsmith," he said grandly.

"Do you want me to tell you what you are?" Myles asked smartly. He picked up the remote off the arm of the chair and turned to the other NFL pregame show.

"Uh-oh, 'Mir," Leonard said playfully, "you better calm down before Myles puts it on you."

Amir found the notion preposterous. "I don't care how much this cat swells up, Pop. He'll always be *little* brother to me." Amir cracked his knuckles showily.

Myles had long ago perfected the practice of ignoring Amir, but Leonard laughed so loudly that it made Myles chuckle. Ever since they were kids, their father loved pitting them against each other. Myles just shook his head as he concentrated on what the commentator was saying about the Raiders-Chiefs game to be played later that day.

"I don't know, 'Mir," Leonard said, enjoying himself too much to let it go. "He's a big dude."

"Puh-lease," Amir said, "what's he gonna do, Pop? Backspace me to death?" Amir lifted his leg up defensively and cringed. "Put me in the dreaded parentheses?"

Leonard was now roaring. Margaret Eva Moore came into the den, quickly surveyed the room, and walked over to the coffee table, where she slid a coaster under Amir's drink.

"Don't y'all have anything better to do than mess with Myles?" she asked.

"Sadly, Mom, they don't," Myles said. "It's the only respite they have from their monotonous, inconsequential tedium of an existence."

Amir's eyes widened. "Duck, Pop! He's gonna big word us to death." Amir lifted his forearm. "Thesaurus-shields up!"

Even Myles and his mother were now laughing. She eyed Leonard's near empty glass.

"You want something else to drink, Lenny?"

"Yeah, Peg," he snarled, "I would like to have something else to drink, but you won't let me have a beer in my own house."

His father's tone, Myles noticed, seemed unnecessarily nasty. He looked over at Amir. Apparently, he didn't think much of it because he was busily munching on a handful of potato chips. Myles looked up at his mother.

She let Leonard's rudeness go. "So would you like iced tea, juice, or soda?" Peggy asked patiently.

Before Leonard answered, he noticed Myles' gaze on him.

When he spoke this time, the surliness was gone. "No, Peg, I'm fine."

She turned and walked back into the kitchen. After waiting a minute or two, only to not look so obvious, Myles finished his soda, got up, and walked out of the room in search of his wife. Peering out into the backyard, Myles spotted Marisa and his cousin Jasmine sitting at the wooden picnic table. They were watching his twin eight-year-old nieces put on a karate exhibition. Myles chuckled at the seriousness etched on Deja's and Jade's faces as they went through a series of martial arts moves on the mat.

Marisa applauded enthusiastically. Jasmine, keeping in line with a proper teenager's sense of blasé regarding everything in the world, mustered a few claps. Myles also noticed that Jasmine was following her dictum of wearing the most provocative clothing allowed. Half of her back was showing because of her low-slung jeans and her tight blouse. Although she had recently turned seventeen and was on the cusp of womanhood, it seemed to Myles that only a minute ago Jasmine was the twins' age.

She was also on the cusp of giving her aunt Peggy a heart attack. Since Jasmine's mother had had another relapse and was locked up on drug charges, Jasmine was living with Myles' parents. Despite the fact that Myles tried to warn her, she tested Peggy often. His mother was a sweet lady and all, but she was always a short trip away from blacking out when it came to disrespectful children. Apparently, from what Myles had been hearing of late, Jasmine wasn't heeding his warning. Maybe because she didn't believe him. Maybe because she didn't think she was still a child, but rather an adult on equal footing with her aunt.

If that was the case, she was in for a rude awakening.

"Not bad, not bad," Myles said as he stepped out into the backyard. "There were some areas that need improvement, though."

"You know karate, Uncle Myles?" Deja asked, catching her breath.

"What?" Myles looked around dramatically. "You betta ask somebody!"

So Jade did. "Does Uncle Myles know karate, Aunt Marisa?"

"Um, no," she replied.

"You betta ask somebody else," Myles railed. "I'm a *master*. In fact"—Myles looked around—"too bad there are no cinder blocks for me to break into two." He cracked his knuckles like Amir had done earlier.

"I'll find one, if you like," Jasmine offered smugly.

"Of course," Myles continued, keeping his attention on the girls, "since you two are just starting, I know y'all don't want any of me. If you did, I would teach you a thing or two . . . or three or four."

"Oh, really?" Deja asked.

"Yeah, really."

"Well, don't sing it, bring it," Jade said.

Myles began slipping out of his boots. "Well, I'm not in competition form, but I suppose I can wing it."

"And when they break your arm, I suppose we can sling it," Marisa chimed.

Myles stepped onto the mat and faced the twins. Smiling, he bowed grandly to them. Their response was fixed determination.

"All right," Myles said, "let's do this. . . ."

Fwoomp!

"Get up, come on . . . get up."

Having missed the mat while taking his pratfall, Myles

was laid out in the backyard next to a pile of leaves. He opened his eyes a sliver.

His nieces, Deja and Jade, were standing menacingly over him with their fists clenched, looking like miniature versions of Charlie's Angels. Myles peeped the snarls on their faces. They looked ready, willing, and more than able to dispense more beatdown. They had the unmistakable "this is what happens to niggas who loud talk us" look on their faces. Their desire for him to get up was with that idea in mind, not out of any concern for his well-being.

Myles gave an exaggerated eye twitch and moaned. Then he opened his eyes and looked at Jade. "Mommy, can I go back in the water? It's been an hour since I've eaten."

Jasmine rolled her eyes. "On that note . . ." She got up and walked into the house.

"What?" Jade asked Myles.

"You said I can go back in the water," Myles insisted. "I ate my peanut butter and jelly over an hour ago."

Myles noticed that Deja had eased slightly out of her fighting stance, but Jade wouldn't relent. She was ruthless.

"She's not your mother," Deja said cautiously.

Myles turned his head toward her and looked at her wide-eyed. "Mommy, there's two of you?"

"She's not your mother either, and you're not at the beach," Jade said. She took a step toward Myles.

Myles flinched. He thought he was about to catch a Lugz in his midsection.

"Now, you was talking a lot of stuff before," Jade continued. "You ready to back it up?"

Myles fought the urge to correct her "was" with "were" and instead propped himself up on his elbows and scowled at her in puzzlement. Then he grinned knowingly.

"You're just joking with me, Mommy," he said confidently. "If we're not at the beach, then how come I have all these pretty birds flying over my head?" Myles sat up and grasped at the air. "I'm going to catch one for myself. Tweet-tweet little birdies, tweet-tweet."

The twins laughed.

Marisa joined them on the mat.

"Grandma?" Myles asked, eyeing her. "I thought you were in Georgia."

Marisa ignored him. "Girls, stop beating up your uncle. Your mother wants you inside." She nodded in the direction of the kitchen window. Kenya was visible through it, motioning for the girls to come in.

"Okay, Aunt Marisa."

The girls bowed toward their vanquished foe.

"You were a very worthy adversary, but we had to teach you a harsh lesson," Deja said.

"Yeah," Jade added, wagging her index finger like a pint-size Jackie Chan. "Next time, be more cautious with your words."

Myles nodded softly, his face full of contrition. Lesson learned.

"You better check on him," Jade said to Marisa as she made her way to the house. "He's talking crazy."

"Will do," Marisa said. "And thanks for taking it easy on him."

Jade looked back over her shoulder. "We believe in mercy."

Myles watched his nieces go into the house. He looked up at Marisa. "Tell me, wife, when did the 'mercy' occur? I must've missed that part."

Marisa shrugged. "They said they showed you mercy. I see no reason to believe they didn't."

"Oh, you don't?" Myles asked. "I guess you missed that glancing kick in the general vicinity of my balls?"

"No, I caught that," Marisa said.

"Thank God I did, too," Myles said, "or at least partially deflected it, or we might've had ourselves a situation out here."

"So, is everything down there still functional?" Marisa asked coyly. She kicked at a stray leaf with her boot.

Most definitely, Myles thought as he eyed his wife, redefining outdoorsy-chic in her open flannel shirt, soft turtleneck, and jeans. And it was stiffening at that moment.

"Why don't you come down here and find out?" Myles asked.

Marisa tossed her hair back and laughed. "You know, I have half a mind to take you up on your offer, just to see what you would say when your mother came out here swinging her broom."

"That's easy," Myles said. "I know exactly what I would say."

"What's that?"

"Mom! Stop beating on Marisa. I know she's corrupting me, but she can't help it. She's scandalous!"

"Shut up, mama's boy," Marisa said. After he put his boots back on, she helped him up. Myles brushed himself off. Marisa slipped her arms around his waist as they slowly began to make their way to the door. "If she only knew how eager to be corrupted your freaky ass is."

Myles instinctively looked toward the house to make sure they were out of earshot.

Marisa cackled. "Look at you. Mama's *boy*."

"So why did you marry me?"

"Because I like jewelry," Marisa replied, casually looking at her ring, "and because you begged me."

"Uh-uh, *Cubana,* that's not how I remember it at all," Myles corrected. "It was *you* who asked me."

"You sure about that?" Marisa asked, peeking slyly at him out of the corner of her eye, "because I seem to remember it differently."

"Yep." Myles gave her ass a squeeze as they made their way into the house.

In the kitchen were Kenya, Jasmine, and Peggy. Jasmine and Kenya were sitting at the table, where Kenya was wrapping the leftovers. Peggy was standing at the sink, her arms forearm deep in suds. She was washing the dinner dishes by hand and then setting them aside in the second sink. Next, she would load them into the dishwasher for a second washing. She felt that was the only way they got truly clean.

Myles heard the twins' excited voices coming from the den, where they were recounting the high points of their backyard ass-kicking demonstration to their father, Amir.

"I don't know why you're souping those girls' heads up, Myles," Jasmine said as Myles and Marisa sat down at the table. "You're gonna have them out here in the world thinking they can really hurt someone with that karate."

Peggy looked up from the dishes at the sound of someone coming down the steps. She heard the jingle of keys and then the sound of her husband's voice coming from the den.

"You heading out, Pop?" Amir asked.

"Yeah, I got a couple of things I want to take care of. I want to pick up some things for the shop for tomorrow."

Peggy noticed his voice seemed a little louder than necessary. Like he was saying it loud enough for her to hear in the kitchen. At that moment, their eyes met through the doorway. As though she'd asked him to, he headed for the kitchen to tell her himself.

"Pop-pop," Deja said from the den, "we took out Uncle Myles in the backyard."

"You did?" Leonard asked, disbelieving. "Jade, y'all put it on your uncle?"

"Yep," Jade said, "we put it on him."

"See?" Jasmine said. "Now they're telling your father how they punked you."

Myles smiled. "Nothing wrong with them having a little confidence. It's a good thing when little girls believe in themselves. Isn't it?"

"Yeah," Jasmine said grimly, "but in the real world, there are no friendly uncles to take a dive. The real world hits back."

Though her back was to Jasmine, Peggy could hear the pain in that statement. Most seventeen-year-old girls have a limited purview of the real world. Jasmine knew too much of it, Peggy thought as she loaded a platter into the dishwasher.

She felt the main issue with kids today was that they needed a proper adult in their lives to stay on them. Children act like they don't want supervision, when in fact, they crave it. They equate it with caring. But too many kids had adults in their lives trying to tell them what to do whom they didn't respect. A child isn't going to listen to an adult who can't even take care of themselves properly. That's why Jasmine was having such a hard time of it. Why she now lived there with her aunt and uncle. Because Jasmine's mother—Peggy's younger sister, Dee—had failed her.

"Peg, I'm gonna head on over to Home Depot and pick up some things."

Peggy turned around to face her husband. He was wearing a Hilfiger parka that Amir had left over at the house a long time ago and long since forgotten about. It looked ridiculous on him. She thought a man his age had no business wearing it.

"Your family's all here, Lenny."

Leonard shifted his weight and reflexively checked his watch. "I know, Margaret Eva, but if I don't get to the store soon, it's gonna close. And then when will I be able to go tomorrow? I'll be in the shop all day."

That answer had come a little too smoothly for Peggy's taste. A bit too practiced. Like it had been rehearsed in front of a mirror while he was putting on that parka. Leonard seldom called her by her birth name. Peggy wondered whether his use of it had been a calculation or a misstep—for the purpose of distraction or due to nervousness.

She wasn't the only one who thought he was acting strangely. Marisa looked at Kenya, Myles, and Jasmine. If, like her, any of them found anything unusual about Leonard leaving a Sunday family gathering to go to the hardware store, they weren't letting on.

Peggy gave a slight nod to her husband and then turned back to the dishes.

"Myles, if you and Marisa are gone by the time I get back, you have a safe trip," Leonard said. "Don't let leadfoot here speed, Marisa."

Marisa kept her tone neutral. "I won't, Mr. Len."

"All right, Dad. See you later."

"You coming up again next week?"

"We'll see," Myles said, looking at Marisa. "We don't know yet."

"Okay. See everybody later," Leonard said from in the hallway as he left out of the front door.

Jasmine looked at Myles and snickered. "You don't know if you're coming up next weekend until Marisa tells you if you're coming up. Then you'll know."

With that remark, Peggy forgot about her husband's odd behavior and raised an eyebrow. Out of the mouths of babes.

Myles was probably also waiting for Marisa to let him know when he was going to be a father. Peggy knew Myles was ready for children. So what was the hold up?

"Oh, you got jokes?" Myles asked. "What's wrong with me asking my wife if she wants to come? Do you want somebody making decisions for you like you don't have a voice?"

Jasmine motioned toward her aunt. "It happens to me every day."

"And you want it to stop once you're an adult, right?" Myles asked.

Marisa added, "There's nothing wrong with us discussing things, listening to each other and deciding together, is there, Jas?"

More than anybody else in the family, Marisa's opinion resonated the most with Jasmine. Her ready acceptance of something being true if it came out of Marisa's mouth used to surprise Peggy. By now she was used to it.

"For you there isn't," Jasmine replied smartly. "You get to do the deciding. He does the listening."

"Ha!" Amir cackled from the den.

Myles looked toward the doorway. "We don't need to hear from the peanut gallery. Like you're running things in your marriage anyway."

"I handles mine, brah, you best believe that," Amir said.

Marisa, Myles, and Jasmine looked at Kenya.

"The beauty of it is, I let him think that he really does," she whispered. "What's that old saying? 'If you want to grow your own dope, plant a man.' "

All three Mrs. Moores and Jasmine laughed.

"She's talking about you, dog," Myles called out.

"Don't get it twisted, Kenya!" Amir said. "Don't make me come in there."

"Don't listen to him, babe," Kenya said, laughing. "I know you're the king."

"Exactly," came the satisfied reply, "and I'm a just ruler, too. Justice prevails throughout my kingdom."

"See. What I tell you?" Kenya circled her finger around her ear.

Remembering the original topic of discussion, Myles reached over and gave Jasmine a pinch on the cheek. "Whatsamatta, my precious baby cousin?" he cooed. "You want me to let you win at something?"

Jasmine brushed his hand away. "Stop it."

"Go get the Connect Four out of the pantry," Myles said teasingly, again pinching Jasmine's cheek.

"Cut it out."

Myles hesitated. "Candy Land?" He shrugged his shoulders. "Okay, but don't you think you're a little old for it?"

Marisa and Kenya laughed. Jasmine tried not to.

"Go somewhere with that, Myles," she said. "I don't need you to let me win at anything. And neither do the twins. It'll only gonna get them in trouble."

Marisa joined her mother-in-law at the sink and exchanged polite smiles. Marisa began rinsing off the dishes that were in the second sink and loading them into the dishwasher.

Peggy looked at her daughter-in-law as she knelt down and began putting the knives in the dishwasher. That's not where she would have put them, but she decided not to say anything. She knew Marisa was making an effort to reach out to her. They weren't exactly close. Not nearly as close as she and her other daughter-in-law, Kenya. Or even her and Jackie—Marisa's friend and Kenya's business partner. Where was Jackie anyway? She and Carlos sometimes came over for Sunday dinner. She wanted to see the baby.

"Where are the Roques tonight?" she asked to no one in particular, knowing that Kenya, Myles, or Marisa were all capable of answering.

"She and 'Los had a family thing to go to, Mom." Myles said, "I think Jackie's aunt is having a birthday party."

"Snnnxxx . . . snnnxx . . ."

"Wake up."

Carlos had dozed off in Jackie's aunt's basement while waiting for the Eagles game to start. The big meal he had consumed earlier had acted like a sedative.

"Honey, get up."

"Huh, wha—*como?*"

Carlos opened his eyes to see his wife standing over him.

He quickly glanced around to gather his surroundings. The television was tuned to ESPN and was showing highlights of the early games. Jackie's teenage nephew Roberto was at the other end of the couch snoozing.

"We need someone to go get some more candles," Jackie said.

Carlos stared vacantly at her, then adjusted the pillow. "Okay. Well, I wish them Godspeed and good luck."

"Carlos," she said impatiently.

"How did I get elected, Jackie? There's a house full of people here."

"Our car is at the end of the driveway," Jackie replied.

"Yeah, that's because we're *guests,* Jackie. Let our *hosts* go to Pathmark and get the candles."

"You're weren't worried about civility when you were gorging yourself on that *lechon asado* upstairs." Jackie had one arm folded at her waist and the other dangling. In her hand rested the car keys. "You looked awfully familiar then, didn't you?"

"I'm a *guest*. That's what guests do. They arrive and eat people out of house and home. Besides, this is a party, isn't it?" Carlos emphasized again and closed his eyes.

"Yeah, you look real festive down here snoring away with Roberto. I don't know how you can sleep on such a full stomach anyway."

Carlos looked over at Roberto. He was snoring peacefully, with his hands resting on his stomach. "Well, we were both having a ball until you came down here."

Jackie playfully kicked him in the shin. "You're a *puerco*, you know that?"

"Even more reason why I can't go. How can I be expected to drive with these hooves?" he said, waving his hands in the air.

"Come on now, get up." Jackie said with exasperation. "CJ needs to be fed, so I can't go."

"And you shouldn't have to, wife," Carlos said, his voice full of compassion. "You're a guest, too."

Carlos noticed Jackie's jaw setting. He tried appealing for mercy.

"I don't know my way around Camden. I don't even know where Pathmark is," he protested.

"Now you're gonna play dumb?"

Carlos shrugged his shoulders and looked as dim-witted as he could to signify that he wasn't playing.

"That's pathetic," Jackie said, shaking her head. "Feigning stupidity to get out of having to do something. Is your laziness so powerful that you would rather have others think you're an idiot than do something you don't want to?"

"You have no idea," Carlos said, tugging at his belt. "We're all lions at heart. We just want to lounge and rule while the women go out and do the hunting, gathering, and baby minding."

"Sad. Truly sad," Jackie said. "Fine. Roberto will go with you." Jackie looked at her nephew. "Roberto!"

"Snnnx—huh, wha—*como?*"

Carlos was grousing to himself as he looked for a parking spot near the entrance of the Pathmark on Haddon Avenue.

As soon as people in the house found out he was going to the store, it had become an event. All of a sudden everybody and their mama-sister-uncle needed something picked up. What had started out as a trip for some candles had transformed into his having a frigging list of shit in his pocket to get.

Who in the hell had ever heard of trying to put ninety damn candles on a cake anyway? Only Jackie's crazy-ass family would be so extra to attempt it—or to bake a cake big enough to hold ninety candles. He hoped they were gonna give poor Aunt Doris some help blowing that bonfire out. Once you get a certain age, the shit is supposed to be symbolic, isn't it? You throw a couple of candles on there and say, *Feliz Cumpleaños! Happy Birthday, Old Girl!* May you have many more. Though in your case, it's highly unlikely. . . .

Carlos looked at the clock in the dashboard. Look at that. He was probably going to miss the start of the Eagles game. And he was uncomfortable because he had eaten too much. And . . . dammit, it's cold out here.

Carlos considered the best way to do this errand. He decided to rip the list in half and send Roberto to get half of the stuff and he'd get the other half to save time.

He found a spot reasonably close and wheeled his Maxima into it. Carlos carefully began ripping the sheet of paper into two.

"What are you doing?" Roberto asked.

"Tossing half this shit out," Carlos replied casually. "If they're not lucky enough to be on the half I keep, oh well."

Roberto looked at him wide-eyed. "Word? Oh, shit."

"Stop cursing, *pendejo,* before I tell your mother," Carlos said. "Come on."

He and Roberto got out and made their way to the store.

"All right, neph. Here's how we're gonna do this." As he handed him one of the pieces, it flapped in the wind. "You get the stuff on your list, I'll get mine, and we'll meet at the checkout."

Roberto looked at his list and stopped abruptly. "Yo, no way! I'm not getting these."

Carlos laughed. "Hey, they're for *your* sister." He looked over his shoulder at his nephew. Then it was his turn to stop suddenly.

"What the—?"

"What's wrong?" Roberto asked.

Across the parking lot, across the street, Carlos saw Mr. Moore walking up the steps of the Oasis Motel. Carlos knew it was him; he recognized the blue parka that Mr. Moore was fond of wearing. He was with some woman. She was bundled up so Carlos couldn't make her out, but he could tell by her lively step that it definitely wasn't Mrs. Moore. The pair disappeared into one of the rooms.

"I'll be damned," Carlos mumbled, forgetting about the cold.

"What's up?" Roberto asked, turning around and following Carlos' gaze.

"Nothing. Let's go get this stuff so we can get back to the game."

They walked into the entrance, with Carlos stopping to take one more glance back over his shoulder. He shook his head.

"I'll be *damned.*"

chapter 2

Peggy looked at the digital clock when she heard the front door open—12:17. She had told herself that she wasn't waiting up for Leonard, but noticed that she wasn't in too much of a hurry to get to bed either. She finished wrapping her hair with the scarf, turned off the light in the bathroom, and walked into the bedroom. She sat down on the edge of the bed, slid out of her slippers, and flexed her toes.

When she heard the clatter of pots in the kitchen, she walked out into the hallway to the top of the stairs. "Leonard, this child up here is trying to sleep. Don't come in here making all kinds of noise this time of night."

"Actually, all I hear is your yelling, Aunt Peg," came a voice out of a bedroom.

"She has to get up for school tomorrow."

"Tomorrow's Saturday."

"And if you want to see it, then I suggest you go to sleep, Jasmine," Peggy snapped.

She waited at the top of the stairs to see if Leonard was going to answer her. When Peggy realized he wasn't, she thought about saying something else to him to elicit a response, but instead went back into her bedroom and closed the door. She sat on the edge of the bed and picked up her crossword puzzle off of the nightstand. Peggy leaned her head back and massaged her neck. Leonard used to give great massages. For many years he offered his hands willingly. Now she had to ask, which she hadn't done for a long time. She had gotten tired of him saying no. Of making excuses about being too tired or his hands being too sore. Of frowning his face up like the thought of rubbing his wife's body repulsed him. So she had stopped asking.

Lord knows, Leonard getting excited over seeing her naked body had been a ship that had long since sailed. Like most couples, the frequency with which she and Leonard made love had declined as they aged, but there had still been intimacy. There had been weekend trips to the Poconos. Cuddling in bed watching James Bond movie marathons. Strolls along the boardwalk in Atlantic City.

That all changed a few years ago, around the time when she was going through the change in life. It was subtle at first, but soon it became obvious—at least to her, she didn't care how many people he tried to make think she was crazy—that Leonard no longer regarded her as a viable option to fulfill his needs. As a viable woman, period.

During the rare instances now that they had any physical contact, it was forced, hurried. Like Leonard was fulfilling an obligation that when he was done with, there would be peace in the valley until time for the arduous chore came back around again. He was a little better about putting up a front as far as going out with her to dinner or to social functions. But she knew it was still a front, nonetheless.

Forty-five minutes later, when Leonard came into the room, Peggy could smell the stench of cigarette smoke in his clothes. She and Leonard had quit smoking almost twenty years ago. Why a person who didn't smoke would want to be around a bunch of smokers was beyond her. Again he was wearing Amir's old parka, looking ridiculous.

"Heaven forbid you come home without stopping in Starks Bar."

"I had a beer." Leonard slid off his parka and slung it over the back of a chair, ensuring that it, too, would now smell like stale smoke. "You don't want me to have it in the house."

Her husband had always drank. When the boys were young, he would keep beer in the house and have a beer or two on Sunday while watching football on TV. It hadn't bothered her. One six-pack would last him a couple of weekends. For the last few years, though, her husband had been drinking more. And had started to drink hard liquor.

So when Jasmine had come to live with them, Peggy had asked him to stop keeping alcohol in their home. She knew Jasmine was rebellious by nature and didn't want her getting hold of any. Peggy had appreciated her husband's willingness to go along with her request. Now she realized why he had been so eager to do so. It allowed him to drink all he wanted outside the home, plus the freedom to do whatever else his sixty-going-on-thirty ass wanted to do.

And those clownish niggas down at Starks Bar. Lenny was definitely in the right element if he wanted to act a fool. She heard stories from the younger women in her salon about all kinds of shenanigans going on there. Wet T-shirt contests. Rump-shaker contests. A bunch of tired old men sweating over women half their age, and no doubt paying dearly for the right to do so.

"When you get pulled over for DUI, I hope you call one of your drinking buddies from Starks instead of me, Lenny."

Leonard ignored her and went into the bathroom. When she heard a disgusting hacking sound, she decided she'd had enough. She didn't want his stinking ass in bed with her. She put on her bathrobe, picked up her crossword puzzle, and went into Amir's old room.

The next morning, Jackie came through the front door of the rancher that served as the group home. After hanging her coat up in the foyer closet, she spied Kenya in the small sitting area off the main living room. Spread on the coffee table in front of her were requisition forms, payroll sheets, and expense reports.

"Hey," Jackie said.

"Hi."

Jackie noticed Kenya's coffee mug.

"Is that fresh?"

"Wha-yeah . . . um-hm."

Jackie walked down the long hallway past the kids' bedrooms to the small room in the back, which served as the administrative office. All five of the bedrooms were empty because the kids and three of the staffers were on a trip to the aquarium, then a Sixers game.

She wondered what was bothering Kenya, but decided it could wait until she had gotten herself a cup of coffee and said hi to the home's nutritionist, Diane.

Minutes later, she walked into the living room, sat down in the oversize burgundy wingback chair next to Kenya, and took a few sips of her steaming cup of coffee.

"You can leave all that, Kenya," Jackie said, motioning to the pile of papers in front of her. "I'll finish it and log the data into the computer."

Kenya half nodded but didn't say anything. Jackie wondered if she had even heard her because she continued doing the paperwork.

"Diane is a great hire, Kenya," Jackie said, continuing to

eye Kenya over her mug. "Not only is she a great cook, the kids seem to like and respect her."

"Yeah."

Jackie sat her coaster down. She was through being ignored. "What's wrong?"

Kenya finally looked up. "What do you mean?"

"Did something happen last night to piss you off?"

Kenya had just got done working the third shift—the overnight shift. She had done so unannounced, for she wanted to catch the overnight crew in their natural state. Since they had opened the home several months back, she or Jackie rarely worked overnight.

Kenya nodded at Jackie.

"It's Charles. I came here at one a.m. last night and he's sitting in the living room watching *SportsCenter*. Jan was out doing the shopping, and Darlene was cleaning the staff bathroom—"

"So no one was watching the hallway?" Jackie interrupted.

"Exactly," Kenya said. "That's what Charles was supposed to be doing."

Jackie settled back in her chair and absorbed the information. Charles was competent. Good with the kids, but lazy. And not watching the kids' hallway at night was the big no-no. The girls' bedrooms were on one side and the boys' bedrooms were on the other. A staffer sitting at the desk in the hallway was the only way to ensure that there was no hanky-panky going on among the teens at night.

Jackie drew a deep breath before she asked her next question. "Did Darius take advantage of it?" Jackie asked.

Their eyes met. Jackie knew that was a source of Kenya's concern as well.

Kenya shook her head. "No, doesn't look like it. He was asleep, luckily."

Jackie exhaled. Darius was a seventeen-year-old who was under their care. Jackie and Kenya's facility was designed to deal with children whose families, for whatever reason, were no longer able to adequately provide a positive environment for them, until such a time when the home situation was stabilized. A guardian could sign the kids in or the kids could be sent to them via a court order.

It also served children as an alternative to a juvenile detention facility, if a judge deemed that a structured home experience was preferable to incarceration.

Jackie and Kenya and their staff provided counseling on-site, both for the child individually and collectively with the family.

Darius had come via a court order. He didn't know who his father was and his mother was strung out and turning tricks, last anyone had heard. Darius had been living with his grandmother until she passed, five years ago, and that's when he really took a downturn as far as behavior.

Theft, assault, and vandalism were all in his dossier. He also had anger-control issues and had been unable to finish high school because of them. He had disrespected countless teachers. Arrangements were made for him to attend night school. Unable to conform to that either, he finally got his GED.

One thing Darius had little trouble doing was attracting girls. He embodied so many of the things a young girl could want: handsome, dangerous, sharp, exciting. Both of the sixteen-year-old girls there, Melissa and Candace, had crushes on him and were seemingly just waiting for the chance to slip him some booty in a bid to one-up the other. Kenya and Jackie had instructed the staff that under no circumstances was Darius ever to be alone in any setting with any of the girls.

With the hallway unguarded, all Darius had to do was sneak into the girls' bedroom and tap one of them on the shoulder for a clandestine meeting in the bathroom. Or commit their mischief right there in the room, if they didn't mind an audience.

"I know it's a bit boring, but really, how much effort does it take to sit in a hallway?" Kenya asked with agitation.

Jackie glanced toward the hallway. "And if he wanted to watch TV, he just could've moved the desk to the end of the hall. He can see the living room TV from there."

"I guess he wanted to be comfortable." Kenya said, "He was splayed out on the couch like he didn't have a care in the world."

"What did he do when you walked in?" Jackie asked. "Jump up?"

Kenya's eyes widened angrily. "No. He treated it as if I was overreacting, like he had everything under control. And took his time getting up." Kenya rested her foot on the edge of the table and scratched her knee though her jeans. "I know how important it is to have a male staffer on the premises, especially overnight, but girl, I tell you, I wanted to fire his ass on the spot."

"You could've," Jackie said. "Not watching the hall is damn near a fireable offense. Besides, we don't have to put up with any man not understanding that we're running this. Our careers are on the line here in this venture—not his. He'll just move on to another situation and think of ways to get over on his next boss."

Kenya nodded in agreement. "Don't I know it. If midnight to eight wasn't such a tough shift to fill, he would've been gone last night. In the meantime, we can try and find someone else. Maybe one of the subs is looking for more hours."

"I'll make some calls today," Jackie said. She noticed Kenya's face started to look a little more relaxed. "How are the twins?" she asked, changing the subject. "You think they're okay this morning without their mommy there when they wake up?"

Kenya smiled. "When I left last night, Amir assured me that he had everything under control."

"He didn't mind losing his wife for the night?" Jackie teased.

"A little, I'm sure. But he knew I was coming by here to check up on the staff, and believe me, he's all for that."

Jackie grunted in agreement as she picked up her coffee. "Carlos is the same way. He's always reminding me that I have to crack the whip, how we can't trust anybody." Jackie took a sip. "I don't know why they think everyone is trying to get over on us."

Kenya gave her an ironic look. "Probably because they are always trying to get over on us."

"Ya know," Jackie agreed.

Kenya glanced at her watch. "Knowing Amir, the girls are probably right now settling down to a nice healthy breakfast of chocolate cake and singing songs of joy about it."

Jackie smiled. She thought about the comedy bit that Kenya was referring to. "Bill Cosby is one funny man, isn't he?"

"That he is."

"By the way, how come you didn't go on the outing with the kids?" Jackie asked.

They heard the sound of the back door opening and closing.

"That's why," Kenya said tiredly, nodding in the direction of the noise. "Darius decided he wanted to go off-site this morning without permission, so I'm making him rake up the leaves in the backyard."

Jackie sucked her teeth. "Where did he go?"

"Half mile up the road, to the Wawa. He said he was thirsty." Seeing Jackie's puzzled expression and anticipating her next question, Kenya continued. "He said we didn't have what he wanted in the kitchen."

"So rather than get something else, he decides to just leave without permission." Jackie shook her head in resignation. "Why is he so willful?"

"That's Darius," Kenya said, shrugging her shoulders.

They heard Darius approaching. He appeared in the doorway, perspiration beading on his forehead. "Hey, Jackie."

"Hello, Darius."

"Are those leaves raked yet?" Kenya asked with annoyance.

"Yeah, yeah, raked and bagged," Darius said. "I guess you didn't get that notice, I know how paperwork can get lost. Anyway, the former president signed an executive order regarding such undue labor . . . I think it was called the Emancipation Proclamation, or something."

"We need to familiarize ourselves with that," Jackie said smartly. "Meanwhile you can familiarize yourself with house rules. One of the most important is not leaving the site without permission."

Darius wiped his brow and shrugged. "I was thirsty."

His nonchalance pissed the ladies off.

"Why didn't you just ask someone to run you to the store?" Kenya asked.

"You might have said no," Darius replied. "Then I would have looked really defiant going anyway, right?"

"That's some convoluted logic you have, Darius," Jackie said. "If we said no, why isn't the proper choice then to just do without it?"

Darius paused for a moment as he pondered that. He then

gave Jackie a knowing look. "You've obviously never had a Snapple Prickly Peach before."

"Was that juice you just had to have worth raking all those leaves?" Kenya asked.

"Um-hm," Darius assured her, "it was banging. Besides, a little exercise never hurt anyone." He rolled his neck with the casual arrogance of youth. "Raking is good exercise."

"And missing the Sixers game?" Jackie asked.

"I'm gonna use the quiet around here to get some reading done," Darius said. "I'm working on *Manchild in the Promised Land*." He eyed the two women. When he saw the intent on their faces, he knew he'd better throw them a bone.

"Look, Kenya and Jackie, my bad. I know I shouldn't have gone off the property."

"What angers me," Jackie said, "is that you have far too much sense for this kind of behavior. You know the hell we would catch if something happened to you off facility grounds."

"Indeed." Kenya studied Darius. "For all your consciousness-raising efforts and the talk of the need for people of color to be self-motivated, why would you risk the livelihood of two sistas? You've known us long enough to know what we're about. What we're trying to accomplish here."

Jackie decided to drive the point home. "And you've been in the system long enough, and you're certainly perceptive enough, to know the difference between folks who are poverty pimping and people who have a sincere interest in affecting people's lives positively," Jackie said. "Kenya and I aren't getting rich off this enterprise. There are a lot easier, less stressful ways for us to make a living than what we're trying to do here."

Darius' gaze dropped to the carpet. He had known the ladies for years, particularly Jackie. She was his original case worker when he first entered the system.

"In a few weeks when you turn eighteen, you will have all the freedom you want," Kenya said.

Darius' eyes lifted and flashed in anger. "And you can't wait for that, can you, Kenya? You're probably marking the days off somewhere on a calendar."

Kenya knew Darius had misunderstood her. In a calm voice, she said, "No, what I'm saying is that you will soon be able to make the decisions without so many restrictions because you will be an adult." God help us all, she thought.

"And your lives will be a whole lot easier, too, won't it?" Darius accused Jackie.

"Actually, yes." Jackie said, "Because we trust that as an adult, you will be productive and happy—because you're talented and sensible. Knowing that you're doing well will make our lives easier. We are looking forward to that."

That successfully deflected Darius' rising fury. Jackie knew he didn't want to feel uncared for by Kenya and her. She always found it amusing how the biggest problem children always had feelings made of glass.

Darius glanced at the clock on the wall. "Well, I'm gonna take a shower and go to my room."

"To read, right?" Kenya asked.

Darius nodded.

"Because I thought maybe you wanted to go to the mall with Aaron when he came in to pick up his check."

Aaron was one of their younger male staffers. He worked there part-time while he worked on completing his master's at Rowan University.

Kenya saw the look on Darius' face. Gotcha, she thought.

"Aaron called this morning and asked if it was okay," Kenya explained to Jackie. "Said he and Darius had talked about it a few days back."

Jackie chuckled and regarded Darius shrewdly. "So that's

why you didn't want to go to the Sixers game." Jackie knew Darius disliked being on outings with the whole group. Felt like everyone they met could tell they were "group home rejects."

"Mm-hmm, girl." Kenya folded her arms. "He thinks he's slick. Thinks he's just gonna hop in Aaron's Jeep for a fun-filled afternoon away from us."

"Well, I don't see any reason why he can't go—oh dear," Jackie said, pressing her palm against her cheek. "I forgot about the unsupervised jaunt to the Wawa."

"It's positively tragic, isn't it?" Kenya asked.

"Hold up, I was punished for the trip to the store. The yard is spotless." Darius smiled widely and raised his index finger. "Remember, we don't hold grudges around here. Once it's done with, it's done with."

"Oh, but that raking can hardly be considered punishment, can it?" Jackie asked. "That's merely 'good exercise,' right?" Gotcha, Jackie thought.

Chagrined, Darius slowly nodded. He recovered quickly, however.

"I'll leave my fate in you ladies' capable hands," he said. "Whatever you decide, I know it will be just."

"We'll let you know after you get done with your shower," Kenya said.

Darius headed down the hallway. "I'm not weary, I'se sick of trying . . . ," he chanted.

"That's not exactly helping your cause, Darius," Jackie warned him.

Darius pulled an abrupt about-face. "By the way, I'm not trying to tell you ladies how to run your business, but you might wanna do something about that cat Charles."

Setting aside Darius' impertinence for a second, Kenya was more concerned as to the reason he was saying it. "Why?" she asked.

Darius leaned against the doorway. "Late last night I got up to make a bathroom run, and dude was snoring away on the couch." He shrugged expressively. "A person with less character than I might've taken advantage of the lack of supervision and visited one of the young ladies on the other side of the hall." He was the picture of wide-eyed innocence. "I wouldn't want two motivated, kindhearted sistas like yourselves to get in trouble behind something like that. What if a teen turned up pregnant while under your care? I shudder at the thought of what that would do to your careers."

After waiting a moment, just to see the lumps in Jackie's and Kenya's throats form to an acceptable size, Darius turned and headed to the shower. Gotcha, he thought.

After hearing Darius go into his room, Jackie slowly shook her head at Kenya. "Break out that calendar and mark off another day, girl."

While Aaron was still poring over CDs in the jazz section, Darius paid for his selection and exited the Sam Goody record store in the Echelon Mall.

His haste to leave the store had little to do with a distaste for jazz and everything to do with the two girls sitting out on the bench in the mall area checking him out. Out of the corner of his eye, Darius had seen them enter the store as he was standing in line to pay for his CD. He had also seen one of the girls hit the other on the arm to get her attention and motion toward him, so he knew they liked what they saw. The two girls then scurried back out of the store to the bench in the mall area. Darius knew what that action was all about. They realized he was about to leave, and they wanted to get a better look at him and to give him the opportunity to converse with them.

As Darius approached the pair, he decided to focus his attention on the girl on the right. She wasn't as built as the other girl. Nor was she blatantly giving him come-hither signals, like her friend. But something about her sparked Darius' interest.

Without asking, Darius sat down on the bench next to the flashier girl.

"Excuse *you*," the other girl said.

He ignored her. "Hi, I'm Darius," he said. "And you be?"

"Danae," came the reply.

"Hi, Danae." Darius looked past her shoulder. "What's your friend's name, Danae?"

"Jas—"

"Jas leaving," Jasmine stood up and walked into the store.

"Pe-ace." Darius needled, trying to elicit a response as his eyes followed Jasmine—tight jeans, matching jean jacket, spotless red-and-white Nikes, smooth hazel skin, and ponytail—all the way into the store.

Jasmine hesitated for a step, then continued walking into the record store, clutching her purse.

Danae was happy to have Darius to herself. "She needs to make an exchange 'cause her cousin brought her the wrong CD. Where do you live?" She poked her chest out, intent on drawing even more attention to her body than her low neckline already had.

"Camden." Darius never told people the truth about his living arrangements. Besides, in another few weeks it would be true because he'd be living with his cousin Malek in Camden when he turned eighteen.

"Oh, yeah?" Danae said, perking up even more. "What part?"

When Darius saw that reaction, he figured he was dealing with a silly suburban girl. One who was bored, looking for a little excitement, and probably believed that every male in Camden was some thugged-out, moneyed-up criminal. And no doubt excited about the fantasy of playing Beyoncé to his Jay-Z.

Perhaps he should tell her about his juvenile arrest record. That should really get her panties wet, Darius thought. His eyes searched the store for her friend, Jasmine. He wondered if she was as silly as this one.

"What part?" Danae repeated.

"South," Darius answered. "Where you from?"

"Lawndale—but I'm really from north Philly," Danae assured him. "I don't know why my moms moved us out here to this corny place."

"Maybe she wanted a better environment for you." Darius said flatly. "A place where you don't have to have your grit on twenty-four seven. A better quality of life. Ain't there less stress living in south Jersey than in north Philly?"

"Less excitement, too," Danae said. "It's corny like *that*."

And of course that should take precedence over everything else, Darius thought. His eyes glazed over. Where was her friend?

Aaron came out of the store and approached the bench. "Hi," he said to Danae.

"Hi."

"D, I'll be in the Waldenbooks."

"All right, yo," Darius responded.

That was why Darius liked Aaron. He could've blown Darius' cover. Said something to reveal to Danae his role and Darius' subordinate position. But he saw Darius was talking to a young lady, didn't want to embarrass him, and instead treated him like they were on equal footing.

Darius looked back into the store. Jasmine was now at the register.

"You got your own spot?" Danae asked.

Damn, this girl didn't play around. She just skipped right over asking whether he had a ride.

"No, I live with my cousin."

"Is that him?" Danae asked, nodding toward Aaron.

Darius decided to have a little fun. "No, that's my parole officer." He pointed toward his sneakers. "I'm due to get my electronic ankle bracelet removed today."

Danae's eyes widened. "Uh-uh. Let me see it."

"I'm just kidding. He's just a buddy of mine."

"I didn't believe you." Danae tossed her hair off her shoulder. "Do you go to Camden High?"

"No, I'm done with school."

"Oh." Convinced now she was dealing with an older man, Danae crossed her legs, trying to appear more sophisticated.

"What exactly does 'done' mean?" Jasmine asked sharply. "You dropped out?"

Darius suppressed a smile. Jasmine was now standing in front of them clutching her Sam Goody bag.

"Why do you care?" Darius asked.

Jasmine snorted. "I don't."

Seeing her look so unperturbed and nonchalant, Darius felt his skin tingle. He wished she was standing closer. He bet she smelled good.

"You ready to go?" Jasmine asked Danae.

Danae tried to give Jasmine a "what's your hurry" look, but Jasmine took out her cell phone anyway.

"Who you calling?" Darius asked.

"Why do *you* care?" Jasmine asked.

"I'm just saying," Darius said, leaning back on the bench, "that I think I know your boyfriend, that's all."

"You couldn't, because I don't have a boyfriend," Jasmine said.

"Do you want one?" Darius deadpanned.

Jasmine looked at him. His face was as serious as a tax audit. She did her best to conceal how much he flustered her, and tried to appear bored instead.

"Yeah, one day," she said.

Danae didn't like one bit that Darius' attention had swung in Jasmine's direction. "I am ready to go, Jas." Danae stood up.

"I'm about to call Uncle Lenny to pick us up," Jasmine said, turning on the phone.

"May I see what you bought?" Darius asked, looking at Jasmine's bag. He noticed her reluctance. "Come on." He held out his bag and looked up at her seductively. "I'll show you mine if you show me yours."

Jasmine handed him her bag and took his. They both looked in each other's bag. Darius smiled.

"What?" Danae asked, clearly impatient.

"We got the same thing," Jasmine explained. "The new Roots CD."

"Great minds think alike," Darius said. After taking one more look inside, he closed Jasmine's bag and handed it back to her.

"Great minds don't drop out," Jasmine retorted.

"I never said I dropped out, Jasmine," Darius said. "*You* said I dropped out."

A long beat passed as they gazed at each other. "Well, at least you have good taste in music."

"As do you," Darius said.

"What's the big deal?" Danae asked, agitated. "The Roots are a local band. Everybody has them."

"Do you like Jazzyfatnastees, Vivian Green?" Darius asked Jasmine.

"Do I?" Jasmine asked, her eyes lighting up. "Those are my girls!" This time she was truly impressed. "So you appreciate good music, huh? I had you figured as strictly a hip-hop head."

"Sometimes there's more to people than meets the eye," Darius said. "Like, if someone met you, they can plainly see you're fine as hell. But only by getting to know you could they tell that you're as smart as you're pretty."

Blushing, Jasmine looked like she wanted to crawl into the bag. She couldn't think of anything to say in response.

"Do you want *me* to call your uncle?" Danae asked, mad about being ignored.

Jasmine relented and made the call.

What a pain in the ass Danae is, Darius thought as Jasmine was talking on the phone. Just because I don't want her.

Jasmine clicked off the phone. "My uncle says he will pick us up in front of the food court entrance in ten minutes."

"Well, that's all the way at the other end of the mall. Let's go," Danae started walking away.

"I gotta go," Jasmine said, smiling at Darius.

He stood up. "All right, I'll check you out later."

Jasmine's eyebrows furrowed in puzzlement. She hesitated for a moment.

Darius knew she was wondering why he wasn't asking her for her phone number.

"If it's destined to be, I'm sure we'll speak again," he said.

Jasmine shrugged. If he wanted to put it in fate's hands, so be it.

"Bye," she said.

"Later."

As Darius watched Jasmine catch up to Danae, Aaron walked over to him.

"You ready to go back to the home, Darius?" Aaron asked, smiling slyly.

"Yeah. Can I get that pen, Aaron?"

Aaron took the pen out of his shirt pocket and handed it to him. Darius scribbled down a phone number on his palm. The one he had gotten off Jasmine's exchange receipt.

chapter 3

Carlos was sitting in the office in the rear of Amir's barber shop. As he waited for Amir, he was checking out his haircut and freshly manicured goatee in a handheld mirror.

He put down the mirror and looked at a photograph of Amir, Myles, and their father. The picture looked about fifteen years old. The three of them were wearing identical barber uniforms, and Myles and Amir were flanking their proud father outside his shop in Lawndale.

Carlos heard a loud burst of laughter emanate from the shop. Seconds later, the door swung open and Amir joined him in the office.

"What's going on out there?" Carlos asked.

"Ibn came into the shop." Amir chuckled. "He was telling us about another one of his sordid escapades."

"That cat is wild."

"Who you telling?" Amir said, taking the seat behind the desk. "That fool's life would make Hugh Hefner blush." Not that his past was much better, Amir thought. He had lost count of how many women he had bedded by his junior year in college. If he hadn't met Kenya, he might still be running around like Ibn.

"What's up?" he asked Carlos.

Carlos set the mirror down. He made sure the door was closed, then faced Amir again. "It's about your father."

"What about him?"

"I saw him stepping out on your moms."

Amir's forehead creased, not sure if Carlos was being funny. But he quickly realized Carlos was deadly serious.

"When?"

"This past Sunday night."

Carlos saw Amir's mind processing, trying to recall if he could account for his father's whereabouts that past Sunday evening. When Carlos saw the growing look of concern on Amir's face, he knew that he couldn't.

"Where?"

"At that motel across the street from the Pathmark."

"The Pathmark in Camden or the one in Lawndale?"

"The one in Camden."

"Who was the female?"

Carlos shrugged. "I don't know."

"You don't know, because you don't know her?"

"Well, she looked young—she was walking kind of spry—silly, girly like. Ya know, like she was excited that she was about to get some dick."

Amir's mouth turned down. "How close were you to them?"

"I was in the parking lot across the street."

"At the Pathmark?"

"Yeah."

"Well, hell, 'Los," Amir said, placing his palms flat on the table, "how can you be sure it was him? You're at least a hundred yards away, at night—did you have your contacts in?"

"I thought your sister-in-law was the lawyer in the family," Carlos said evenly.

"Did you see his car in the parking lot?"

"No."

"You didn't drive around to the back to see if it was back there?"

Carlos began fiddling with a brass globe paperweight. "I didn't really want to find out, Amir." He set the paperweight down and searched his friend's face. "You know what I mean?"

Amir leaned back and studied Carlos. "You must not be too concerned about it. Waiting a whole week to mention it—and waiting until after I've cut your hair today to tell me."

"Hey." Carlos stroked his chin. "I wanted your hand to be steady when cutting my shit."

Amir looked annoyed and Carlos quickly added. "Look, Amir, you know I love Ms. Peg. She treats me like a son." Carlos shifted in his chair and recrossed his feet. "But you are her son. I just didn't want to make it bigger than you wanted to make it."

Amir did understand. "What you're saying is, you don't know whether I'm as big an asshole as my father is, so you're feeling me out."

"Bingo." Carlos raised his shoulders in a shrug. "And now that I see you doing your damnedest to dismiss the notion entirely—"

"Wouldn't you, if it was your father?"

"I'd expect it. I know my father *is* an asshole. It's known throughout the family, as evidenced by the existence of my ten-year-old half brother."

Amir had almost forgotten that Carlos had a young brother, Emilio. "Your moms forgave that?"

"It wasn't easy. My mother was humiliated. My father was ashamed of himself. *Desgracia*," Carlos muttered, shaking his head. "But now Emilio is accepted by everyone."

"Really?" Amir asked. "I know you see him, but I didn't know your mother and the rest of the family did, too."

"What are they gonna do? Hate the kid? It's not his fault. Once my mom chose to forgive my dad's indiscretion, she had to accept the baggage that came along with the indiscretion— not that I'm trying to call Emilio baggage. You understand what I'm saying."

Amir nodded. "What about Emilio's mother?"

"That *puta*? Please. She's not welcome in the home." Carlos sighed. "*Mi madre* is a kind woman and all, but she ain't a blessed saint. Emilio's blameless—his mother isn't."

Amir coughed out a halfhearted chuckle, but his mind was busily whirring. "Did you tell Myles yet?"

Amir knew how tight Carlos and his brother were. He and Carlos were friends through Myles.

Carlos shook his head. "I haven't seen him since I saw your father—"

"Allegedly saw our father," Amir corrected.

"Okay, counselor," Carlos said, his palms held out, backing off the touchy subject.

Amir looked out into the shop's back alley, adding up all the impressions he'd had lately about his mother and father. He knew his parents weren't particularly close these days. He knew that she sometimes slept in his old bedroom. He had heard his mother complain more than once about his father staying out late. And now Carlos was saying he'd seen Pop with some female heading into a motel room.

"You think your mother knows?" Carlos asked.

"I don't know. She never said anything," Amir answered.

"You think I should tell Myles what I saw?"

Amir gave him a skeptical look. "'Los, you think that's a good idea? You know how Myles gets."

Carlos shook his head.

"Let me do some investigating and find out what's going on."

Carlos didn't like the sound of that. "'Mir, that's my best friend. If he finds out that I knew and didn't tell him, he'll kill me. I know this, because if the shoe was on the other foot, I'd kill him."

Amir waved his hand. "No, no—I'm gonna tell him. Just let me handle it my way. Okay?"

After some hemming and hawing, Carlos gave a slight nod of acceptance. It wasn't something he was particularly looking forward to doing anyway.

Neither was Amir. But it was incumbent upon him to get to the bottom of this.

Marisa reached over and picked up the phone. "Hello?"

"Marisa?" Peggy asked surprised.

Marisa wondered why Ms. Peg was surprised that she was answering the phone in her house.

"Yes, Ms. Peg."

"I'm surprised to catch you home," Peggy said. "Usually when I call Myles in the early evening, you're not there."

And that means what? Marisa wondered. That I'm lacking because I'm not here waiting for my husband with his slippers in my hands when he gets off work? Marisa hadn't realized that Myles and his mother had such a set routine as far as phone conversations either. She bet Ms. Peg got her sly little digs in during those conversations with Myles: *What time does Marisa get home?* *So you have to fend for yourself every night as far as dinner?* *When are y'all ever gonna find time to have some children?*

"Well, it's not like I'm running the streets. Weekdays, I'm on the radio doing my show during evening rush hour, from four to seven. But since it's Saturday, I'm home."

Peggy didn't appreciate her tone. Did she say that she was out running the streets? And did this woman just presume to tell her what day of the week it was, like she was stupid? Hell, from what she could gather, Marisa was usually out doing something on weekends, too. She decided not to go there. She didn't call to speak to Marisa any—

Peggy's thoughts were interrupted by the sound of loud music coming from upstairs. The bass was reverberating so loudly, the chandelier in the dining room began to shimmy.

"Hold on, Marisa." Peggy rose from the table and walked over to the foot of the stairs.

"Jasmine, turn that noise down or turn it off!" she yelled.

The music continued to blare.

"I know you hear me, girl. Goddammit!"

This girl had got her to cursing, taking the Lord's name in vain. Just as Peggy put her foot on the first stair to go have it out with Jasmine, the music was turned off.

Peggy turned and headed back to the dining room. "I'm gonna seriously hurt that girl."

Marisa really liked Jasmine. Though she was related by blood to the Moores, Marisa knew Jasmine was nearly as much of an outsider as she was. From what Myles had told her, Jasmine's childhood had been far from stable. Her father was a ghost and her mother, Dee, was an addict. Myles told her that Ms. Peg had been trying to convince her sister to turn custody of Jasmine over to her for years. Jasmine's mother had resisted, therefore Jasmine had bounced around from home to home, school to school, living like circus folk. Her aunt and uncle's house was the closest thing she had ever come to a settled home situation. But Ms. Peg's rules and regulations were probably akin to prison for someone who was as used to freedom as was Jasmine.

"I'm getting tired of her little yuck attitude around here,"

Peggy continued, mumbling more to herself than Marisa. "That's why I told her to go upstairs—so I wouldn't have to look at her face."

"What's wrong with her?" Marisa asked.

"Humph. It would be quicker to tell you what's *right* with her."

"What did she do?" Marisa asked. "Maybe if I talked to her . . ."

Marisa's voice trailed off. She realized from the silence on the other end that Ms. Peg wasn't amenable to that proposition. Marisa shifted gears. "Listen to me. You did call to speak to Myles, didn't you?"

Peggy laughed weakly. "Yes."

"He's in the basement," Marisa said. "I'll go get him."

Go ahead and pop a blood vessel, Marisa thought, as she headed out of the kitchen. All Ms. Peg wanted was someone to listen to her as she talked about how crazy Jasmine was. She wasn't interesting in actually addressing and resolving any problems.

Who the hell does Ms. Glamourpuss think she is? Peggy thought as she waited for Myles. She's gonna tell me how to raise a child—though she hasn't had one of her own yet? Please. Just because Myles hangs on your every word like you're some kinda sage, don't think I need to hear it. I ain't a man under your spell.

Marisa was beautiful, that much couldn't be denied. Too beautiful, in fact, Peggy thought. She always wondered how much of her son's love for his wife was tied up in her looks.

Wife? Those matching rings on their fingers aside, who knew if they were even married? Peggy hadn't been there to see any ceremony, nor had anybody else. They had eloped. It had taken Peggy a long time to get over that. Not being able to see her youngest son get married. In fact, a part of her still hadn't got over it. She had taken it as a slap in the face.

When Kenya had married Amir, she, Kenya, and Kenya's mother, Carol, had a ball planning the entire event. Shopping for the just right wedding dress. The best band, the perfect reception hall, the classiest limos. She appreciated how much Kenya had included her, sought out her advice in the planning of the event. It had really brought Kenya and her together.

But Ms. Thing obviously couldn't be concerned with such matters. So all she had gotten from them was some pictures of them standing with some Rastafarian "reverend" on a beach in Jamaica. Some wedding photo.

Besides her daily radio gig, Marisa had her own weekly talk show on television as well. Peggy knew that she was very successful and as such, Marisa had a lot of people at her beck and call. And as hard charging as Marisa was, Peggy had little doubt she had any trouble letting people know who was the boss. Peggy couldn't help but question if Myles and Marisa's home life was an extension of her job. Whether Myles was just another person in her life to do her bidding. Hell, he was pretty much on her payroll. The extravagant spread they had could hardly be sustained by Myles' teaching salary.

And here it was going on four years of marriage and still no word of impending grandchildren yet? Peggy wondered if Marisa was not only too wrapped up in her career to take time off for a baby, but also too self-centered to want to be a mother. As any parent will tell you, once a baby is born, the baby becomes the boss. The baby dictates to the parents. The parents lives have to change to suit the baby.

Of course, it's worth the trade-off and then some, because there is nothing in the world like the unconditional love a child has for her mother. Nothing comes close to that kind of love. Well, maybe when the Holy Spirit moves through you, but other than that, nothing else. And like she said, nothing else of *this* world.

Peggy had a feeling that Marisa might not ever get to experience it because she couldn't get past the thought of being dictated to by anybody, even her own child. And that was sad. And selfish. Because she would be denying Myles the opportunity to be a father. And if ever a man was cut out to be someone's daddy, it was Myles.

"Hello?"

Myles' voice snapped Peggy back to the present.

"Son, let me tell you what your crazy cousin had the nerve to do . . ."

chapter 4

Amir pulled his truck into the rear parking lot of the one-story brick building that served the dual purpose of being his father's barber shop and his mother's beauty salon. The only car in the lot was his father's Lincoln.

Amir had come early because he knew his father would be here alone, and he wanted to find him alone. This wasn't a task he was looking forward to, but one he knew he should do. He drew a deep breath and stepped out onto the gravel.

"Yo, Pop."

Leonard regarded Amir strangely as he entered the shop.

"What are you doing here?" he asked. He was standing at the barber counter cleaning his clippers over the sink. "You having flashbacks or something? You have your own shop to mind."

Amir smiled as he took off his coat and hung it on the coatrack.

"Or are you here to steal what's left of my customers you haven't already stolen?" Leonard asked. "Damn, son. At least have the decency to do it from Camden. Don't come here and solicit in my face. You're already on the verge of sending me to the poorhouse."

"Poorhouse? Come on, Pop." Amir settled into one of the customer seats. "All those years of free labor you got from me and Myles—I know you got a couple of yachts somewhere."

"Free?" Leonard repeated, snapping his head back. "I had to feed you two cats for all those years. Have you ever seen Myles eat?"

Amir laughed. "True. You have a point there."

"I'm about to ask you for a chair at your shop," Leonard continued. "So I can work for you. At least that way I can see my old customers again."

"Your customers?" Amir mocked. "The only reason the young heads were coming here was for me." He crossed his boots at the ankle. "I would think you should be happy."

"Happy?"

"Yeah? With the demographic shift. Now you've got your shop back. A place where you and the other old men can play checkers and argue over who is better-looking, Lola Falana or Pam Grier."

"Very funny," Leonard said. He turned back to the counter and picked up another pair of clippers.

His father was a couple of inches shorter than him. He was balding from the temples and kept his hair cut low because of it. His shoulders were not as broad and he had a slight paunch. Amir saw a newspaper on one of the chairs and knew his father must've just finished reading it, as he did every morning. He was still wearing his reading glasses, which made him look every bit of sixty-two years old.

Amir wondered what he would look like at age sixty-two. Not much of a clue stood in front of him because he favored his mother.

Leonard finished with his clippers and set them down. He rinsed off his hands in the sink and turned back to Amir. "So what's going on?" he asked as he wiped his hands off on a towel. "Something on your mind?"

Amir swallowed. "Yeah." He motioned for his dad to have a seat.

Leonard's face bespoke bafflement as he sat in his barber's chair. Amir wondered if it was real or feigned.

Leonard rested his forearms on the armrests and looked at Amir expectantly.

Amir wished that he had chosen a barber's chair to sit in as well, so he could be on an equal level with his father. This conversation was going to be hard enough without his father peering down at him like this.

"You taught me to be a straight shooter, so I'm gonna come right out and ask," Amir said quickly. "Are you stepping out on Mom?"

Leonard straightened in his seat. "Did I hear you right?" he asked tightly. "Did you just ask me if I was cheating on your mother?"

Amir nodded coolly. At least, he was trying his best to project coolness. In reality, his body was warm and itchy with discomfort.

Leonard opened his mouth and shook his head. "Well, ain't this a grand way to start off a week."

"Look, Dad," Amir said. "I'm coming to you because somebody told me that they saw you going into a motel with a woman."

Leonard shifted in his seat. "Who said that?"

"Just somebody," Amir replied.

"Who?"

"Just somebody, Pop," Amir repeated.

"And I'm asking *who*," Leonard replied, his voice growing angrier. "Why do you have more regard for 'just somebody' than me? Who is it?"

Amir exhaled. "It isn't about having more regard for anybody else. I just don't think it matters who said it."

"It matters to me," Leonard answered curtly. "Wouldn't you want to know?"

Amir didn't respond right away. He wanted to make sure he had his father's eye before he did. "I'd wanna know who said it—if it was a lie. Otherwise, it doesn't matter who it was. I'm in the wrong regardless. Getting mad just because someone saw me do wrong would be pointless."

"Well, it's not pointless to me," Leonard said, rising out of his chair.

Amir realized his father wasn't going to let it go, so he made up a name. "Damon saw you."

Leonard's face contorted. "Who the hell is Damon?"

"A young cat that used to come in here from time to time," Amir said. "Drives a blue Honda, goes to Rutgers?" Amir added to lend authenticity to the mythical character.

After trying in vain to recall Damon, Leonard gave up. "Well, if I don't know him well enough to even remember him, I don't see how he could know me well enough to know it was me going into some motel."

He snatched off his reading glasses and threw them onto the counter. He placed his palms on the countertop with his back to Amir.

"So it wasn't you?"

Leonard turned to his son. "Isn't that what I said?"

Actually, you never did deny it, Amir thought.

Leonard seemed to read Amir's mind. "No, it wasn't me," he said with annoyance. Amir wondered if he was more bothered that he had to unequivocally deny it or because he was having this conversation in the first place.

Amir stood up. He was ready to get the hell out of there.

"All right, then," he said as he collected his coat off the

rack. He reactively patted his pocket to make sure he had his keys. "If I don't see you before then, I'll see you for Sunday dinner at the house."

Leonard grumbled a reply as he walked over to the front window and changed the sign from Closed to Open.

Amir tried to think of something to say to lighten the mood, but couldn't find anything. "Bye." He headed toward the back door.

He had taken two steps before his father's voice stopped him in his tracks. "You know, I would've expected something like this from Myles," Leonard said quietly.

Amir looked over at his father. He had his back to him, peering through the large window at the passing traffic.

"What? What do you mean?"

Leonard shrugged nonchalantly. He casually strolled over to his barber's chair and took a seat as Amir waited for a response. "I would've figured that you would know better."

"Better?" Amir asked.

Leonard gave him a blank stare. "I would've thought that you would already know how things are, that's all." A sly smile formed at the corners of his mouth. "You of all people."

The sound of the back door opening came before Amir could respond.

"Look who's here."

"Hey, Amir."

Amir replayed his father's words in his head. *"Already know how things are?"*

"What are you doing in this neck of the woods?"

Amir finally looked away from his father at the older men who had entered the shop together.

"Hello, Mr. Ruffin. Mr. Davis."

"You feel like giving me a shave?" Mr. Davis asked, rubbing the scruff under his chin.

Amir smiled. "My father will take care of you. I gotta get to Camden and open my shop. How are you doing?"

"We're fine, boy, but not as well as you, though," Mr. Ruffin said, patting Amir's back. "Your father tells us your shop is doing very well. Always bragging on you."

"Yeah, it's doing okay," Amir said.

"Chip off the old block, huh?" Mr. Davis hung his scarf on the wooden coatrack.

Amir glanced over at his father. He had a smock in his hand and was preparing the chair for Mr. Davis.

"Yeah, something like that," Amir said. With that he turned and walked out of the back door.

chapter 5

Peggy started the dishwasher, turned off the kitchen light, and joined Jasmine and Leonard in the den. They were sitting on the couch together watching *Everybody Loves Raymond*. Peggy sat on the loveseat.

It was nice to have her husband home and Jasmine not locked up in her room. They rarely watched TV together. Though she had to admit, Leonard had been going out less frequently the past couple of weeks. She hoped the trend would continue.

"I'm gonna fry some chicken tomorrow," Peggy announced.

"Mmm," Leonard said. "On a Friday? What's the occasion?"

Peggy shook her head. "None. Well, Myles and Marisa are driving up tomorrow after work. Plus, Kenya said that she and Amir might drop by."

Leonard rolled his eyes at Jasmine. "I knew it couldn't have been just for us."

"She don't care about us," Jasmine said, playing along.

"Y'all need to stop," Peggy said good-humoredly.

Leonard turned his attention back to the show. "Ya know, I've noticed something. How come in all these sitcoms the women have so much sense and the men are idiots?"

Peggy and Jasmine looked at each other, then laughed.

"I'm serious," Leonard continued. "Think about it. In every sitcom the woman has all the sense and the husband is childish, henpecked, clueless, or foolish. Ever since I can remember, with *The Honeymooners*. Why does the man always have to be a clown?"

"I think they call that reality TV, Uncle Lenny," Jasmine said.

While Peggy fell out, Leonard hit Jasmine with a pillow.

"Very funny," Leonard said, trying not to laugh.

"It's not true anyway," Peggy said after her laughter subsided. "I can think of a bunch of shows where the woman acted the role of dingbat."

"Hon," Leonard said glibly, "they weren't acting."

Now it was Leonard's turn to howl. Peggy rolled her eyes. The phone rang.

"Answer that, baby. It's probably Lucille Ball calling to tell Lenny to shut up," Peggy said.

Jasmine reached over on the end table and picked up the receiver. "Hello?"

"Hi, may I speak with Jasmine?"

"Speaking."

"Hey, Jasmine, this is Darius."

"Who?"

"Darius . . . from the Echelon Mall a few weeks back."

Wow, Jasmine thought. Now this is a surprise. "Oh, hey, what's up?"

Peggy could tell from Jasmine's body language and the care with which she wasn't saying a name that she was talking to a boy. Jasmine noticed Peggy's eyes on her and left the room.

Once in the dining room, Jasmine spoke. "How did you get my number?" she asked, making sure to sound more curious than angry.

"It was a gift. From the man upstairs. I dropped to my knees and he delivered."

"Oh, God just blazed it into your mind, huh?" Jasmine asked.

"No, a detective lives upstairs from me," Darius explained. "He tracked your number down for me. I don't want to talk about what I was doing on my knees to get it."

Jasmine laughed. This Darius was okay. She decided to go upstairs for more privacy.

As Jasmine walked up the stairs, Peggy looked at Lenny. "That must be someone she really likes. He gets the privacy of the boudoir."

Once in the room, Jasmine lay across her bed. "Come on, how did you really get my number?"

"I got it off the exchange slip in the bag when you bought the Roots CD," Darius explained. "Do you mind?"

Actually, yes. What the hell took him so long to call, then? Since their meeting, Jasmine had been back at the mall the next couple of weekends hoping to see him again.

"Well, you sure took your sweet time about calling," she said.

Darius had wanted to call her earlier. But while he was staying in the group home, it wasn't feasible. Their calls were monitored. He could've used a pay phone, but then how would he have explained that to Jasmine? Him not being able to give her a phone number to call him. The operator coming on to ask him to deposit more change. No, thanks.

Yesterday, he had moved out of the home and in with his cousin, and calling Jasmine was one of his first orders of business once he settled in.

"I'm shy. I had to get up the nerve." Darius explained.

"Yeah right." Jasmine remembered how he plopped down

on the mall bench uninvited. He was too good-looking and too smooth to be shy.

"Let me make it up to you," Darius said. "How about I pick you up from school tomorrow? We go get something to eat?"

Whoa. This guy was quick.

"I don't know you like that," Jasmine said, taking pains to make sure she didn't say it too roughly. After all, she did want to get to know him.

"Then how you gonna get to know me?" Darius asked.

Jasmine thought it over for a second. "There's a pizza shop two blocks up from my school. Tomorrow, why don't you park your car at my school and we can walk there together?"

"Cool," Darius agreed.

"All right, tomorrow, three o'clock, at the main entrance to my school." Jasmine was having trouble concealing her excitement. She decided she had better get off the phone before she turned giggly and stupid. "I'll see you then."

"Wait," Darius said. "I don't know what school you go to."

"Why don't you ask the man upstairs?" Jasmine teased.

"Oh, now you got jokes?" Darius replied. "What school you go to, girl?"

"If it's destined to be, I'm sure you'll find it," Jasmine said mockingly.

Darius suppressed a laugh. Damn, he could really get into this girl.

"No problem. I'll just come to Lawndale—town ain't but so big anyway—and ask around. Someone is bound to know your home address. I'll just show up at your house, stereo blasting, pants sagging, representing. '*Yo, fam. Is that fine-ass Jasmine up in this piece?*'"

Jasmine couldn't even laugh, or blush. The scenario was too horrifying, even in jest.

"No, don't do that, unless you never want to see me again," Jasmine warned. "I go to Highland High School. You know where that is?"

"Yeah." Darius wasn't exactly sure, but it could be in south central Baghdad—he'd still find it by three o'clock tomorrow.

"See you then," Jasmine said.

"Oh, you can count on that."

Peggy happily strummed her fingers on the steering wheel along with the Temptations' "Can't Get Next to You" as she drove through pre–rush hour traffic. She was on her way to Pathmark to buy the chicken she had promised Leonard and Jasmine. As picky an eater as Jasmine was, even she threw down when it came time to eat some of Peggy's fried chicken. Besides, Myles and Marisa were coming up tonight, and Myles' ability to put away her chicken was legendary.

Peggy was still humming along to the Temptations as she entered the store. Growing up, her favorite Temp was David Ruffin. Like so many other young girls, she liked the flashy one, the bad boy.

As she pushed her cart up and down the aisle of the supermarket, she found herself putting much more in the cart than the chicken and seasonings that she had originally planned to get. The green mint tea that Jasmine especially liked. The lemon cookies that the twins favored. The beef jerky that for reasons unfathomable to her Leonard liked to gnaw on.

While she was checking out the flavored waters, she heard a high-pitched laugh behind her. When she turned around, she saw Danae's mother and another woman at the end of the aisle. The other woman hurriedly disappeared from view, but she and Danae's mother made eye contact. Her expression went from silly, to embarrassed, to composed.

"Hi, Peggy."

"Hi," Peggy replied, returning her wave. She was furiously trying to remember this woman's name. If her name was as memorable as her style of dress, she would have no problem. She was wearing a fuzzy pink sweater at least two sizes too small and two buttons too open for her ample cleavage. It was too short as well, as it revealed her pierced navel. Vanessa Lewis? Yes, Vanessa was her name.

She and her daughter, Danae, had recently moved to Lawndale from Philadelphia. Maybe that's why Jasmine and Danae first hit it off, seeing how they were both Philly girls recently transplanted to the suburbs.

Peggy had heard of some strange happenings at Danae's house. Vanessa came into the salon occasionally. She had immediately struck Peggy as immature—which was further proven as far as she was concerned by the way Vanessa acted when she saw her just now.

And no sooner than Vanessa would leave the salon, the other ladies would start clucking about her. Whispers about what she did for a living. About the number of men they had seen coming to and from her house. The boisterous parties. Vanessa must have had Danae when she was quite young because she didn't look more than a minute past thirty.

Oh Lord, here she comes. It was like once she realized Peggy had seen her, she felt obliged to talk to her.

"Hi, Vanessa. How are you?"

"Hey, I'm fine," Vanessa replied. Her eyes danced everywhere except in the path of Peggy's.

Peggy was relieved that she had called her by the right name, but still thought her behavior strange. And what about that loud laugh she had heard? Was that meant for her?

"How is Jasmine?" Vanessa asked.

"She's fine," Peggy replied. "She made the honor roll again. She's been really concentrating on her schoolwork."

"Is this the brand detergent you use, Vanessa?" a voice asked from behind Peggy. She turned around and saw the woman who'd been with Vanessa earlier.

"Excuse me," she said to Peggy, far too late and too brusquely for it to be sincere.

"Yeah, Stacy, that's it . . . Tide with the bleach . . . ," Vanessa replied, all of a sudden looking uncomfortable.

Peggy was ready to leave anyway. "Okay, Vanessa, well—"

"Stacy," the other woman said as she stuck out her free hand, blocking Peggy's exit.

Peggy took her hand. "Nice to meet you. Peggy."

Vanessa spoke up. "You know Danae's friend Jasmine. Peggy is her—"

"Grandmother?" Stacy offered as she put the detergent in the cart.

Vanessa's eyes looked like saucers, like she couldn't believe what her friend had just said.

Peggy had had enough of these two. "No, I'm not her grandmother—I'm her aunt. Though I'm certainly old enough to be her grandmother. Nice meeting you." She glanced at Vanessa. "It was nice seeing you again. I hope to see you at the hair salon soon."

Peggy pushed her cart off down the aisle. She never could understand why people felt that age was something to be ashamed of. Wasn't it inevitable? It wasn't something like weight, or hair, or clothes—something you could control.

And she didn't know this Stacy person, or what her issue was—nor did she care. With her funny-looking self. She had a cute enough shape, but she was nowhere the head turner that Vanessa was. Hell, Peggy thought, I may be twenty-five, thirty years older than you, but I still look better than your short, elfin-looking self.

She didn't have time to worry about it. The store was rapidly filling up with people getting off work, and she still needed to get some Crisco. If she didn't hurry, she was going to be stuck in a long checkout line.

As she rounded the corner to enter the next aisle, she heard a loud voice say, "Guess she gotta go buy her Depends."

Peggy was certain the voice belonged to that Stacy person. She stopped the cart and began to go back and ask that child what her problem was.

Then she caught herself. God don't like ugly.

And if God didn't like ugly, He had already shown what he felt about Stacy.

Darius and Jasmine were in a booth at Damico's eating pizza.

"How's your friend?" Darius asked.

"Danae? She's cool." Jasmine had decided not to tell her about her date with Darius. At least not until she had a better idea of what she was working with. Instead, she had told Danae she was going to the library. Jasmine knew she wouldn't be interested in going there.

Jasmine wasn't sure why Darius was asking about Danae.

"Why? You want me to hook you up with her?" Jasmine asked as she picked off a piece of mushroom and ate it.

"Why would I want you to do something like that?" Darius said, sprinkling Romano cheese onto his slice.

Jasmine shrugged. When she and Danae were out together, Danae usually drew most of the attention from men because of her curvaceous body. "You brought her up."

"I was just making conversation. Don't get it twisted. I've never been into the video-ho type myself," Darius continued.

Jasmine nearly choked. "Excuse me?"

"What?" Darius asked innocently. "She sure was dressed the part when I met her."

"Don't be calling my friend a video ho, that's what."

Darius wasn't one to back down. "How about modesty-challenged?"

"How about we drop the subject, period." Jasmine said firmly, wiping her fingers with a napkin.

Darius took a sip of his soda to hide his amusement. He had been trying to generate a response and liked that Jasmine would stand up for her friend. He appreciated loyalty. He set his drink down. "I was just making conversation."

"Well, I can think of whole lotta things we can talk about instead."

"Like what?"

On the walk over there from the school, Darius had told her that he was eighteen, the '95 Nissan Sentra that he had arrived up in belonged to his cousin with whom he lived with. She decided to start there.

"So that's your cousin's car back at the school?"

"Mm-hm," Darius replied. "He doesn't use it, though. His name is Malek. I live with him. He runs an auto-repair shop in Pennsauken."

"How long have you lived with him?" Jasmine asked.

Darius didn't feel like going into his experience with foster care and group home living. So he lied.

"Not long. I lived with my grandmother in Camden until she died, and for the last few years I was living down South with some relatives. When I turned eighteen, I decided to come back up here." Darius took another bite of his pizza.

"Your parents?"

Darius lifted his shoulders and turned up his palms.

"Why didn't you finish school?"

Darius swallowed and wiped his lips. "School isn't my thing."

Jasmine furrowed her brow. "I don't know anybody who *likes* it—"

"Then why do you go?" Darius interrupted.

"Because I have to."

"Why?"

"Because you need your ticket punched in this society," Jasmine said. "It's all about credentials. Diplomas, degrees, certifications, licenses—you know, credentials."

Darius nodded. "I understand what you're saying. I don't want you to think I'm putting down learning. I read constantly. It's just that I'm interested in education, not indoctrination. I just couldn't sit through school anymore, so I got my GED instead."

"Was it because it's boring to you?" Jasmine asked, curious.

"More than just that," Darius rested his elbow on the table. "I got tired of hearing *their* view of things. Like the founding fathers, for instance. The facts that men like Jefferson and Washington owned and enslaved Africans and raped African women take precedence to me over anything else they did in their lives." He scowled at the thought. "I had teachers tell me that I shouldn't let that 'cloud my judgment' and that I have to 'view them in the context of the time they lived.'" Darius snarled with disgust. "That's some bullshit, right there. I wonder if they would be as understanding if it was their ancestors."

"So you challenge them on it," Jasmine said.

Darius eyes widened. "If you challenge them, you're being disrespectful, or insubordinate. And then there's that weird dynamic between black males and white female teachers," he pointed out. "A lot of times I saw fear in their eyes like they thought I was gonna rob them or rape them. And that would really piss me off. How you gonna teach somebody if you're afraid of them? How you gonna teach somebody adequately if you've already judged them to be a criminal?"

Darius was a little gruff, Jasmine thought. A lot of bass in his voice. Wore his hair in cornrows, and had deep, dark, chocolate skin, which reminded her of Amir's. Tall and lanky, but with square shoulders and taut muscles.

Jasmine wondered how much Darius had brought on himself. He didn't seem to be the type to worry too much about dispelling any negative notions someone might have about him. She liked the fact that he didn't care.

"Well, anyway," Darius continued, "so I got my GED and I'm enrolling in Pennco Tech when the next classes start in a few weeks."

"What are you gonna study?"

"Automotive technology," he said proudly. "I want to be a mechanic like my cousin. When I'm not in class, I'll be at the shop working for him."

Jasmine nodded impressed. He was a lot deeper than she had thought.

"So do I pass the test?" he asked.

"What test?"

"Am I good enough to get to know a nice suburban girl like you better?" Darius grinned.

Jasmine liked his smile. He should smile more often. With his cute self.

"Please," she said, "I'm a city girl. I'm just living with my aunt and uncle in Lawndale because my mother can't stay clean long enough for me to get through school."

"Your father?" Darius asked.

Jasmine imitated Darius' gesture from earlier. "MIA."

"Well, since our people have failed us, I guess it's up to us to raise ourselves, huh?" Darius said.

Not if my aunt Peggy has anything to say about it, Jasmine thought.

The Moore family had just eaten a Friday night dinner of fried chicken, mashed potatoes, and string beans. Leonard, Amir, and the twins were in the den watching *Monsters, Inc.* The rest of the clan was still in the kitchen. Peggy and Marisa were at the sink rinsing off dishes and loading them into the dishwasher.

Peggy and Marisa were making an effort to be warm with each other, but both were still wary. Peggy could sense Marisa's nervousness. She knew that Marisa didn't think she liked her and was committed to making an effort to help Marisa feel more welcome. The last thing she wanted was to be at odds with a daughter-in-law. Peggy had raised her sons to believe that once a man chooses a wife, his wife should come before anyone or anything else—except God. And since this was the woman her son chose to marry, it was incumbent upon her to find a way to get along with her.

At the table, Kenya had just told a story about how she had beat Myles in chess a while back, and had done it so soundly that Myles had to lie down, his head was hurting so badly.

Myles looked at Jasmine and nodded his head toward Kenya. "Some people don't see the importance of being factual, but you might as well get a start on it now. When you're in college, your professors are gonna expect you to."

Jasmine shrugged her shoulders. "Who said I was going to college?"

"What?" Kenya and Myles said in unison. Kenya stopped halfway to the refrigerator with a plate of leftover string beans. Peggy shook her head. "Would you listen to this child?" she said to Marisa.

"College isn't for everybody," Jasmine continued. Not necessarily meaning it, but thinking about what Darius had said earlier.

"How would you know if you haven't ever been?" Kenya asked.

"I've been to school and I don't like it," Jasmine replied, remembering the heat with which Darius had said it. "When I'm done with high school, I'm done with books."

"So that's it?" Myles asked. "You're swearing off books forever like it's nicotine or something? You're kicking any and all things literary?" He snapped his thumb in the air like he was summoning a waiter. "Garçon, garçon, garç—yes. Can you please put me in the no-reading section. It's quite irritating in here. All these people around me with their blasted reading material . . ."

". . . exposing me to all their secondhand knowledge." Kenya chimed in. "Don't they know a sista is trying to quit learning?"

Myles grinned at his sister-in-law. "How about her being in a car, and—you know like Spider-Man has that spidey sense that tingles when something bad is going to happen?"

"Right, right," Kenya said with anticipation.

"Picture Jaz riding with her friends and saying, 'Uh-oh, ladies, we're lost, and my' "—Myles paused and sniffed the air—" 'my "ignorance intuition" is acting up. Danger must loom ahead—Oh no, it's a library! I'm blinded!' " Myles shielded his eyes.

Kenya continued with the scenario. "And her friend's saying, 'We're gonna take her home and show her some rap videos. Put on some UPN. She'll be all right, she'll be all right . . .' "

Kenya and Myles howled. Marisa and Peggy exchanged looks to see if the other was laughing.

Jasmine was the only one not amused.

"I never said I wasn't going to read again," she explained, refusing to back down. "But it'll be books that I want to read. Like Sista Souljah." She gave Myles a wry look. "Maybe I'll read yours, if you ever get published."

"How is the writing coming, Myles?" Peggy asked, wanting to get Jasmine calmed down.

"Right now I'm concentrating on teaching, Mom. I'm going to get back to my book in earnest this summer. I only have a couple of more chapters to go."

"That's good," Peggy said.

"Be sure and send me your rejection letters, Myles, so I can wallpaper my room," Jasmine spread her arms grandly. "A testament to your failures."

"Jasmine!" Peggy dropped her sponge, turned around, and glared at her.

"Dag, Aunt Peg," Jasmine mumbled. "I was only kidding."

"Well, I'm not amused," she said, continuing to glower. "Okay?"

"Leave her alone, Mom," Myles said, deflecting the tension. "She's only showing out because she misses me. Ever since I moved to Maryland, she doesn't know what to do with herself."

Jasmine made the okay sign with her finger and thumb and rolled her eyes again.

Peggy sighed. "That child . . ."

"She doesn't mean anything by it, Ms. Peg. It's just her way."

Peggy shook her head. She hoped Marisa was right, but truth be told, she was worried for Jasmine. She could be so ugly at times. And with the amount of ugliness she had seen in her short life, she had a lot of negative inspiration to draw from.

"So you're just interested in fiction then, Jaz," Kenya asked, bringing the discussion back to the original subject.

"No, I didn't say that," Jasmine said, leaning back in her chair. "But it will be what I want to read. Not a bunch of stuff about pilgrims and ancient Rome and witches standing over pots and knights battling monsters coming out of caves—then battling the monsters' momma. How does any of that have any bearing on my life?"

"I thought you liked school," Myles said. "You get good grades."

"I get good grades because it comes easy to me. That doesn't mean I like it. "

It sure does come easy, thought Peggy. Jasmine got her book sense from her mother, who was always top of her class when she was in school. Unfortunately, she was worried that Jasmine might have also inherited her mother's poor decision-making gene when it came to life choices. Why was she even sitting here talking this nonsense about not going to college? It bothered Peggy to no end that her sister hadn't done something more with her life. She had squandered opportunity after opportunity and her God-given intellect by getting involved with the wrong men and then doing drugs. And since Jasmine was staying with her while her mother was in jail, she would be damned if she was going to let history repeat itself on her watch.

Peggy handed the last pan to Marisa to rinse off and turned around.

"Do you all know that Jasmine just scored a 1340 on her SATs?"

"Wow." Kenya whistled.

"That's great, Jaz," Marisa said.

"That's higher than I ever got," Myles added.

Jasmine, embarrassed by the release of the information and eager to divert the attention, looked at Myles with her face twisted. "Since when are you the yardstick for greatness?"

"Hah!" Amir roared from the hallway, on his way to the bathroom.

"So I don't even know why this is a topic of discussion," Peggy continued. "This child right here will be going to somebody's college—you can believe that." She eyed Jasmine squarely. "God did not bless you with your smarts for you to waste them."

After a beat, Jasmine's eyes went from her aunt's to the tabletop. Also dropping was the decibel level of her voice as she mumbled something unintelligible.

"Jaz," Kenya warned.

"Don't tell her anything," Peggy said as she took off her apron. "Thanks for the help with the dishes, Marisa."

"You're welcome, Ms. Peg."

"And to just offer to help without being asked. Imagine that." Peggy gave Jasmine a cutting look before she left the kitchen and went into the laundry room.

Once Marisa had finished drying her hands, she took the lone remaining seat at the table in between Jasmine and her husband.

"Jaz, college is the greatest time of your life," Marisa said. "I've yet to meet a person who has gone who hasn't thought so. You can't compare it with high school. Oftentimes, high school is the most difficult period of a person's life. It was for me, anyway. And college is also the opportunity to find yourself, be exposed to a wide array of choices and find out what interests you. And whatever you choose to do as your life's work, everybody in this house believes you're going to be something special. That you're going to leave your mark on the world. College is merely the first step to finding and claiming your rightful place."

Jasmine looked at Marisa and nodded, letting the matter drop. She wasn't even sure if Darius was right, and had just said it to get a rise out of everybody.

Leonard was sitting at the bar sipping a beer, watching the sports highlights of the day on the television hanging above. He was about to join Pete, Chucky, and some of the rest of the fellas in the billiards room in the back when he felt a familiar hand in the small of his back.

"I saw your housefrau today."

"My what?" Leonard asked, turning.

"Your *old* lady," Stacy said as she slid on the stool next to Leonard. "At first I thought it was your mama."

"You saw my wife?" Leonard asked, anxious. "You didn't say anything to her, did you?"

Stacy ignored him and spoke to the bartender instead. "Mr. Lenny wants me to have a Long Island iced tea, Charles."

Leonard studied Stacy's face. He knew she was deliberately ignoring his question, hoping to make him squirm. He decided he wouldn't give her the satisfaction. He finished his beer and got up.

"Where you going?" she asked, surprised.

"Home."

"All right, all right." She laughed. "No, I didn't say anything to your precious wife." Stacy motioned to his stool. "C'mon, Mr. Lenny, keep me company."

Lenny sat back down. He didn't know whether Stacy had really fallen for his bluff or whether she was just humoring him.

"Dayum," she said, "Mr. fuckin' sensitive." Stacy took a

sip of her drink and crossed her legs. When she put her drink down, she put her hand on Leonard's thigh.

Leonard nervously glanced toward the door.

Stacy laughed. "What? You don't think the people in this bar know what's going on between me and you?"

"Not unless you told them," Leonard said, eyeing her suspiciously.

"Yeah, right," Stacy snarled. "I notice you don't mind those pool-playing Negroes in the back knowing you're fucking me. Or how does Chucky put it, 'hitting those young skins.'"

That's exactly how Chucky put it. Nevertheless, Leonard removed her hand. "I invited my sons here, tonight," he explained. "There's a chance they might show up." Leonard was especially wary of Amir checking up on him. Truth be told, they hadn't had a whole lot to say to each other since their conversation at the shop several weeks back.

Leonard had been cooling it since then—staying at home for the most part. Except for a quickie last Tuesday afternoon, his only contact with Stacy had been by phone.

Stacy's eyes widened. "Ooh, I hope it's that too-fine oldest son of yours. I'd love to put something on his chocolate ass."

Leonard felt a pang in his chest. Damn, if it wasn't jealousy. He ignored it the best he could and picked up the fresh beer Charles had placed in front of him.

Stacy placed her hand on his shoulder and leaned into him. "Maybe we can have a threesome."

Leonard gave her a nasty look. Stacy leaned back and laughed.

"I'm just playing with ya, daddy. You know it's your dick only that I covet." Stacy turned her stool to face him and straddled it so that her legs were spread wide. "In fact, I'm getting wet right now thinking about you slipping me a stiff one. Mmm, makes my mouth water."

Leonard smiled slyly. Stacy leaned in close.

"We still getting together tomorrow night?"

"Yep. You want me to get a room, right?"

"No need for that—meet me at my spot." Stacy said. "We'll be alone. I put my roommate out."

Leonard's eyebrows raised. "Yeah."

"Yeah, she was working my nerves." Stacy said, taking a sip of her drink. "So I told her she had to go."

Leonard figured that she could afford to do that with all the bread that he had been laying on her. She was a needy thing. But the pussy was so good that he couldn't complain too much.

"Besides, I had to make room for you," Stacy said matter-of-factly, "for when you leave your wife to come live with me."

"That's not gonna happen, Stacy," Leonard said firmly. He thought he saw hurt register in Stacy's face. So he decided to throw her a bone, to imply that it was purely for practical reasons he was sticking around. "It's cheaper to keep her."

"But wouldn't you like to be able to fuck me anytime you wanted?" Stacy whispered in his ear. "Um. You could wake me up at three a.m., flip me over, and put that thick snake of yours to work . . . or when I'm in the kitchen, you can bend me right over the sink . . . anytime you wanted."

Leonard felt his penis stiffen. He couldn't wait until tomorrow.

chapter 6

Peggy couldn't get back to sleep.

Leonard had just come home an hour earlier, smelling like a bar, and crawled into bed with her. Unlike before, Amir's old bedroom wasn't an option because Myles and Marisa were staying in there. So she had to put up with his stinking ass.

Around eight o'clock that evening Leonard had excused himself. At least he didn't lie this time. He told the family he was going to grab a beer and even invited Amir and Myles to join him.

Peggy didn't know what that rigmarole was about, other than to give Leonard some cover. *("I invited the boys to come with me.")* Leonard knew damn well that the boys didn't drink.

Granted, Peggy knew that Leonard's nights out had been infrequent of late. And there were no young children at home that needed minding, so she was free to go out to a movie, a show, or out to dinner with a friend, if she chose to. But she didn't know what was in that bar that would justify it in Leonard's mind to skip out on evenings with his family like this. His son and his wife were spending the night. His other son's family was here. Would it have killed him to stay his ass at home? Is he so far gone that he just doesn't care how this shit looks?

Leonard's loud snoring was starting to anger her. While smothering his ass with a pillow did hold some appeal, she knew she would regret it in the morning. Peggy decided to go downstairs, watch some late-night television, and fall asleep on the couch.

As she got to the bottom steps, she heard soft giggling coming from the kitchen—no, the dining room. What the hell . . .

"Jasmine?" Peggy turned on the dining room light. Jasmine was stretched out on the dining room carpet with—no, she *didn't* have one of her good pillows off the living room sofa down on the floor. Jasmine squinted and shielded her eyes.

"Who are you talking to this time of night?"

Jasmine sat up and looked at her like she was a hemorrhoid the size of a coconut. Peggy hated when she gave her that "why do you exist, you pain in the ass" look.

"Dag, Aunt Peg, nobody."

"Nobody, huh?" Peggy said. "So you're sitting there talking to the dial tone?"

Jasmine grimaced. "Danae, okay?"

Peggy hated even more when she lied to her. Danae wasn't inspiring this kind of stealth. "Get off the phone and go to bed."

Jasmine was incredulous. "Why? I don't have school tomorrow."

"It's one thirty, that's why."

"I'm seventeen years old," Jasmine argued.

"That supposed to mean something to me?" Peggy asked. "If you want to use my phone tomorrow or ever again, you better get off of it now."

As Jasmine loudly sucked her teeth, Peggy wanted to throttle her.

"C'mon now, respect your peeps, Jaz, I'll see you tomorrow," Darius said.

"All right." Jasmine eyed Peggy with contempt. "'Cause I *gotta* go." She clicked off the phone and brushed past Peggy to put it back in the kitchen.

"And put my pillow back where you got it from."

Jasmine silently brushed back past her, picked up the pillow, and walked into the living room.

"And you ain't gonna sleep all day tomorrow, either. You got enough energy to stay on the phone all times of night, you got enough energy to help around this house."

Jasmine put the pillow back and mumbled something under her breath.

Peggy wasn't sure what she said but she thought she heard the word "husband." "What was that? What you say?" Peggy approached her.

Jasmine smiled wickedly. Looked so evil that it startled Peggy.

"I said good night, Auntie."

Peggy watched her go up the stairs.

Peggy was sitting on the green sofa in the family room watching the morning news when Jasmine came down the stairs.

It wasn't Jasmine's first time downstairs that morning. Peggy had slept on the couch in the den, and the sound of Jasmine's bustling about had wakened her. She had shocked the hell out of Peggy by getting up at the crack of dawn and emptying the dishwasher, taking out the trash, and even cleaning the downstairs bathroom. Would wonders never cease?

"See ya later, Aunt Peg."

"Where you headed?"

"To the library."

"Okay. Did you happen to notice if Myles and Marisa are up yet?" Peggy asked.

"Marisa is."

Peggy couldn't help wondering if this library trip had anything to do with Jasmine's late-night phone call. She decided not to bring it up, though. Why rehash it when Jasmine was making an effort?

"A trip to the library on a Saturday?" Peggy nodded, impressed. "I'm scared of you."

"Come on now, Aunt Peg," Jasmine said. "You weren't believing Kenya and Myles' nonsense about me and books, were you?"

"No, I know better." She looked at her niece. "Jasmine, why don't you at least take a breakfast bar out of the cabinet with you? You're looking so thin, lately."

Jasmine set her knapsack down, turned, and headed into the kitchen. Peggy heard her rifling through a cabinet. Seconds later she was in the foyer, putting the bar in her knapsack.

"You get more nutritional value out of it if you actually eat it," Peggy chided.

"I know, I know. I'll eat it at the library." Jasmine adjusted her knapsack and buttoned her blue pea coat. "Bye," she said as she opened the front door.

"It's cold out there. Do you want me to drive you?" Peggy asked.

"Yeah, right," Jasmine said. "You know you don't wanna get up from your toasty spot."

"I know that's right," Peggy said chuckling, "but I will."

"No, thanks, Aunt Peg. It's not that cold. I can endure it for four blocks."

"Okay, baby. Call me on my cell phone if you need a ride home."

Peggy shifted on the sofa and looked through the blinds as her niece trudged down the path. Such a pretty girl, looked so much like her mother did at the same age it sometimes startled her. She just hoped that Jasmine made better decisions than her mother, Deidre. Dee had wasted so much potential on foolishness and had too much intelligence to be sitting in some prison in Pennsylvania behind drugs.

Peggy prayed that when she got out this time that her baby sister would stay clean. She knew one thing: Dee wasn't going to have an easy time rebuilding her relationship with her daughter. Jasmine was so angry with her, she didn't even want to go visit her. Peggy didn't force her to go either because she couldn't blame her for her attitude. It can't be an easy thing for a daughter to see her mother in prison. Especially a mother who has let her daughter down so many times because of her weaknesses. All Jasmine had ever wanted was to be able to admire her mother.

In fact, anger would be better. Jasmine was apathetic. She just seemed *through* with the whole situation.

Jasmine and Darius sat in one of the library's small, third-floor study rooms. They had a number of magazines laid out on the table in front of them. When Jasmine leaned over to pick up last month's *Essence,* Darius sneaked a peck onto her neck.

"Excuse you," Jasmine said, sitting back into her seat.

"You're right, my bad," Darius said. "I hadn't meant to do that."

Jasmine shot him a puzzled look.

"I meant to do this." Darius leaned over and cradled Jasmine's jaw. He softly kissed her earlobe and planted soft kisses all along her neck. He nuzzled appreciatively and pulled back, allowing his fingertips to trace tenderly along her chin as if each second he touched her skin was precious.

Jasmine's body was warming up. But she was determined to keep her cool. She didn't want to come off as young acting and naïve. Especially because Darius seemed so experienced and assured.

She picked up *Essence* and began casually thumbing through it. She felt Darius' eyes on her. She wondered if he could see her nervousness. Hell, she wondered if her skin was melting off of her body, because that's how she felt.

"What do you think of this hairstyle?" Jasmine asked, pointing to an ad in the magazine. "I'm thinking about getting something similar."

Darius barely gave the magazine a cursory glance. "I think you would still be fine as hell even if you were bald-headed with a week's worth of stubble on your head."

Jasmine looked over at him. "Yeah?"

Darius licked his lips. "No doubt."

The lip licking had done it. Jasmine practically poured onto his lap, locked on his mouth, and tried to extract the wetness from his lips.

Darius tilted his head for a better angle and stroked her neck and back.

When Jasmine had the urge to straddle him, she knew she had to stop herself. The room had a glass window, where anybody happening by could peer in. The last thing she needed was someone who knew the Moore family seeing her dry humping in the library.

Making far more of an effort to get back to her chair than necessary, Jasmine righted herself in his lap, making sure her ass rested squarely on his crotch. She writhed slightly as she scooped up some wayward magazines from the far end of the table. Once she felt Darius' burgeoning erection, she got up and slid back into her seat.

Darius chuckled.

"What?" she asked innocently.

A librarian passed by the window, pretending she wasn't snooping. Jasmine was glad she wasn't still on Darius' lap.

"What?" Jasmine repeated.

Darius smiled slyly. "Nothing." He picked up a car magazine and started flipping the pages. Jasmine could tell by the way he was sitting that he was uncomfortable, and would be until his erection subsided.

Good, Jasmine thought. She wasn't going to be the only one hot and bothered.

Amir fastened the smock around Carlos' neck, then started combing his hair. "You want the same ol', right?" he asked.

"Yeah." Carlos cocked his head toward another customer who was waiting his turn, Ibn, and decided to imitate something he always said. "Why mess with perfection?"

Ibn put down the magazine he was reading and looked at Carlos. "Hm?"

"What?" Carlos said.

"What do you want, Carlos?" Ibn asked. "You're the one that called my name."

"I didn't call you."

"Oh." Ibn shrugged his shoulders and turned his attention back to his magazine. "I thought I heard you say 'perfection.'"

Carlos and Amir started laughing.

"I never thought I'd meet a guy more arrogant than this guy," Carlos said, jabbing his thumb at Amir, "but you take the cake."

"He takes the whole bakery," Amir said, turning on his clippers.

Ibn laughed. "Come on, fellas, it's just an act."

"Stop lying, Ib," Willie said from the other chair. "You know you pattern your life after Gorgeous George."

Ibn's face lit up. "Well, Gorgeous George was a stud, no doubt."

"Who?" Carlos asked.

"Gorgeous George was a wrestler during the fifties," Willie explained. "When I was a kid, wrestling was big—it would be on the TV during prime time. Families used to watch it together."

"Times sure have changed," Amir said, tilting Carlos' head slightly, "Kenya has a fit if she catches one of the girls watching wrestling on TV."

"It was a lot more innocent then," Willie continued. "Anyway, Gorgeous George was a wrestler who used to come to the ring with a bunch of flair, valets, expensive, flashy robes, long blond locks . . . and his ring music was 'Pomp and Circumstance.'"

Amir laughed.

Willie continued. "And his valets would spray his corner with disinfectant, and cologne on his opponents—you know, so they wouldn't offend Gorgeous."

"Da—amn," Carlos said, laughing.

"Yeah, he was something," Willie added. "Now remember, this is during the fifties."

"I saw a biography about Gorgeous George on TV a while back. The man was simply ahead of his time," Ibn said with admiration.

"Yeah, they say he influenced many great showmen to follow. Ali, Liberace, Little Richard . . . ," Willie continued.

"You didn't tell them the best part," Ibn said, nearly

working himself into a froth. "When the referee would try to check him for weapons, Gorgeous would pull back and say, 'Get your filthy hands off of me!' "

As Ibn started howling, everyone else in the shop remained quiet, staring at him. He slowly realized it and his laughter subsided. He straightened up, smoothed out the wrinkles in his pants, and then shrugged as he sat back down. He picked up his magazine again. "You boys obviously lack the class to appreciate a true charismatic showman. That's why it's a dying art."

After Amir finished his hair, Carlos hung around the shop conversing and waiting for Amir to have a break. When Amir had finished Ibn's and another man's head, he headed to his office before Carlos could intercept him.

Carlos peeked into Amir's office door. "Yo, can I talk to you a minute?"

Amir figured Carlos was curious about his father. They hadn't discussed it since that day Carlos told him he had seen him creeping. "Yeah, come in, 'Los. Shut the door."

Carlos draped his leather bomber jacket over a metal chair, then sat down in another one. "How's Kenya holding up being a boss?" he asked. "Pressure getting to her?"

Amir shook his head. "Naw, she seems to want the responsibility. She says she was tired of working under people she thought she was more competent than." Amir gave Carlos a raised eyebrow look. "What about Jackie?"

"Same thing." Carlos said, picking a piece of lint off his knee. "I was worried about how much time the endeavor was going to take her away from CJ, but she does a good job of balancing everything."

"Oh, heaven forbid you have to tend to your son, Carlos."

"It's not that, cockmeat," Carlos replied. "I'm talking about my son spending enough quality, bonding time with his mother—that's my concern. Not whether I have to take care of him. Sheesh! What kind of an asshole do you think I am?" Carlos shook his head with righteous indignation.

Amir was unimpressed by the display. He knew better.

"For you to think that I'm so self-centered that not wanting to tend to my own child would be my paramount concern—you know, lemme set the record straight right here, right now. If I didn't have my mother-in-law around to cook, clean, and pick up after CJ, I would be right on it." Carlos pounded his fist on the desk for emphasis.

They both laughed.

Amir decided to speed the proceedings along. He rose from his seat. "I'm gonna get back out there."

"Wait," Carlos said, "I wanted to ask you about your father, too."

As Amir sat back down, Carlos noticed his sly expression.

"You knew that's what I wanted to ask you about, didn't you?"

"Yeah."

"So why couldn't you just bring it up and save me the trouble of doing so?" Carlos asked.

" 'Cause we're boys, that's why," Amir said. "We should be able to talk about shit without beating around the bush."

Carlos nodded. "I just know it's a sensitive topic."

Amir brushed him off. "Naw. If it was my mother out skanking it up, now that would be a sensitive topic."

Carlos' eyes widened at that prospect. "Ain't that the truth. People may say it's a double standard, but there ain't a son alive who feels different."

Amir leaned back in his swivel chair, idly opening his desk drawer. He eyed the picture of Jade and Deja he kept on his desk. "He pulled a Shaggy."

"It wasn't me, huh?"

"Yep," Amir said, still looking at the top of his desk. "He flat-out denied it. But he was more focused on who the person was who saw him than denying it."

"Did you tell him it was me?"

Amir shot Carlos a dumbass look. "Of course not. That would have made it uncomfortable as hell for you to be around him."

"Yeah, it sure would."

"You, Jackie, and CJ would stop coming around the house . . . my mom would start wondering what's going on . . ."

"Did you tell Myles?" Carlos asked.

Amir put his feet back on the floor and closed the desk drawer. "No."

"Why not?"

"Because my father denied it," Amir explained. "So what's the point? What's Myles gonna do? Interrogate him further?"

Carlos chewed his bottom lip while he mulled it over. "That's all true, 'Mir, but I know what I saw."

" 'Los, I have no doubt that it was my father you saw that night." Amir held up his hand to prevent Carlos' interruption so that he could finish his thought. "I could tell my father was lying to me." Silence fell over the two men. Amir finally rose from his chair and adjusted a calendar on the wall. "And that isn't a good feeling," he mumbled.

Carlos could imagine it wasn't. He almost felt guilty telling Amir about seeing Mr. Moore in the first place.

Amir looked over his shoulder at Carlos. "And do you know what that dude had the nerve to say to me?"

Carlos shook his head.

Amir scratched his chin, then folded his arms across his

chest. "He told me that he would've expected this type of in-quisition from Myles, not from me."

Amir noticed the puzzlement etched on Carlos' face.

"Does that mean that he thinks that Myles would be more inclined to believe something negative about him?" Carlos asked.

Amir sat on the corner of his desk. "Then he said that he thought that I would've already known how things are. Me of all people."

"Wow," Carlos said, exhaling.

"You know," Amir said. "Imagine hearing some bullshit like that from your own father."

"Maybe he meant that—"

"C'mon, 'Los, you know what he meant," Amir said, clearly vexed. "That he's a piece of shit and he assumed that a fellow piece of shit like me would be cool with him being a piece of shit."

They sat there quietly.

"Well, almost every married guy I know cheats," Carlos said. "I guess your pop was just assuming you did, too."

"Yeah, but I don't," Amir said. "I've never fucked around on Kenya—not since we've been married." Amir studied Carlos. "What about you?"

Carlos met his gaze and shook his head. "Nope. Not once. Hell, not even before we were married."

Amir's eyebrows lifted. "Really? I thought I was the only faithful husband in New Jersey."

"Me too," Carlos said, brushing stray hair off of his shirt.

"Oh, really? So that means you thought I was cheating on Kenya? You're as bad as my father."

Carlos sneered. "Well, you thought I was cheating on Jackie, so how are you any better?"

"Hey." Amir shrugged. "I thought it's part of the culture of machismo. One of the benefits of being a Latin stud."

"Rrr-right," Carlos said. "Does Jackie strike you as the dutiful, silently suffering *mujer* waiting for her philandering husband to come home so that she can serve him a nice hot plate of rice and beans?"

Amir laughed. "Nope."

"Act like you know, then," Carlos said. "Shoot, that type of thinking among Latinas has long since passed. Among the Americanized ones, anyway."

Amir mulled over that idea, then asked. "Do you wish you were born a hundred years ago?"

"I stay up at nights thinking about it."

They laughed. Then fell silent again.

"Seriously. It is hard, though, sometimes," Carlos said quietly. "It's *hard* a lot of times—if you catch my drift."

"Who are you telling?" Amir joined in. "I can be out somewhere—anywhere—the gym, the bank, the grocery store, and some fine, thick-ass young trick will start batting her lashes at me—"

Carlos leaned forward. "Giving you that come-hither look."

"Right," Amir continued, "and you know that all she wants to do is bang."

"Exactly," Carlos agreed emphatically. "She's not looking for a relationship, commitment, flowers—"

"Nope. She's just a woman at that freaky 'I'm gonna skank it up for a little while' stage of her life that a lot of women go through."

"A lot of women?" Carlos leaned back in his chair and curled his lip. "Shit, *most* women. Why do you think *Sex and the City* is so popular with them?"

"True dat." Amir thought about it and came to the same

conclusion. "*Most* women. Hell, for all we know our wives went through their phase before we met them."

The two men sat hushed as they pondered that notion for a beat or two. The discomfort it gave them was clearly evident on their faces.

"Anyway, *a lot* of women—," Amir continued.

"Yeah, a lot of women," Carlos agreed.

"A lot of women that I meet give me that vibe that they just want me as a sex partner."

"Hey," Carlos said, nodding, "and why wouldn't they? You're a goddamn good-looking man."

"Thank you," Amir said. "As are you, bro. You're ripped. You keep yourself in tip-top shape."

Carlos rubbed his flat stomach over his sweater. "I do try. I lay off the *empanadas*."

"So women are bound to notice," Amir went on.

"That they are. It's only natural."

Amir's eyes tightened with concentration. "As is the idea of just taking one of those tricks that has lust dancing in her eyes and bending her over a chair. Just hitting it from the back—"

"Flipping her over, dropping a load on her stomach, pulling up your pants and"—Carlos motioned like he was flinging a baseball—"rolling on up out of that piece."

Amir pointed both index fingers at him to let him know he was feeling him.

"Something quick and cheap," Carlos added. "That satiates for the moment but you wouldn't want long-term. Like the drive-through window at McDonald's."

"Right," Amir chimed. "Who wants McDonald's over home cooking? No one would risk losing a home-cooked meal to grab some McDonald's. No one plans to eat at McDonald's weeks or days in advance. Rather, McDonald's is just something you grab because it's quick, available, easy . . ."

"And cheap."

"There you go," Amir said, slapping the table. "And forgettable. Once you eat it, it's gone."

"Quickly."

"When's the last time you heard someone wax nostalgic about some trip to McDonald's for some McNuggets they made back in 1997?"

"Never."

"Yeah, easily forgotten." Amir repositioned his chair so that he could put his feet on the desk. "And it would have no impact on the next home-cooked meal you had."

They looked at each other uneasily.

"Actually," Carlos said, "McDonald's kinda lingers with me." He rubbed his chest and grimaced. "My system has trouble handling it."

Amir nodded slowly. "And if you acquire too much of a taste for fast food, won't you lose your appreciation for home cooking?"

"Yeah, I would think so."

There was again a pause. Then they looked at each other knowingly.

"You're one punk-ass bitch," Amir said, laughing.

"Look who's talking? An appreciation for . . . home cooking," Carlos mocked. "What you can *appreciate* is Kenya not breaking her foot off in your ass."

Amir laughed again. "That's true. I'm man enough to admit it."

"As am I," Carlos said, rubbing his chin. "I honestly think that Jackie would physically try to beat me down."

"I don't think I could pull it off," Amir continued. "I'm not that skilled a liar. She knows me too well."

"Same here," Carlos agreed. "And besides, whether or not Jackie ever found out, there'd always be that fear that she would. And besides, *I* would know."

Amir nodded. "The guilt would bother us because we're not assholes."

"Not to mention the fear of STDs, pregnancy . . ."

"—the girl catching feelings and trying to fuck up your home life."

They both shuddered at the prospect.

"Still."

"It's hard sometimes."

"Yep. When a young, pretty, thick thing is shaking her ass at you like it's an open-ended question or something." Amir sighed and rested his clasped hands on top of his head. "A man gets to thinking things, asking questions."

Carlos stared at the top of the desk, as if it contained an image of such a female. "Like will I ever have another opportunity in my entire life to hit something this fine."

Amir glanced at him. "I see you been there."

"We've all been there," Carlos added. "Well, except for Myles."

"You know," Amir chided, "that guy thinks the sun rises and sets with a flick of Marisa's wrist."

"Yeah, I couldn't imagine having this conversation with him," Carlos said. "That cat probably never even considered the thought of outside pussy."

"How can he?" Amir asked. "The pussy at home got him too whipped for that. He hasn't been married as long as us either."

Carlos considered that idea, then shook his head. "I know we can't have our cake and eat it too, but I kinda like being married, Amir, and would like to stay married." Carlos smiled, though not too brightly, as he didn't want Amir to

85

laugh at him. "I like knowing that there is a woman who thinks highly enough of me to take my last name. To say that she will forsake all others—go without any other man's dick—for the rest of her days. That once she met me, she felt that she didn't have to look anymore."

Amir scrutinized Carlos, then broke up. "Look at your cheesing ass, getting all sensitive and emotional." He picked up the phone off of his desk and handed the receiver to Carlos. "Why don't you just call to say you love her, Stevie Wonder?"

"Shut up, man," Carlos rose out of his seat, his cheeks tinged with embarrassment. "What, I gotta apologize for loving my wife?"

Amir's eyes widened with fascination. "Jesus Christ, now you're sounding like Myles."

Carlos twisted his mouth as he watched Amir laugh at his expense. As he thought about it, he had to admit that his statement had been quite Myles-esque.

Amir let up and came around the desk. He then held his arms out toward Carlos. "I'm sorry, 'Los. Come on, big hug now. I want to be part of you and Myles' We Earnestly Love Our Wives Sensitive Men Club."

Carlos brushed his arms aside. "So, let me see if I got this straight. You love Kenya, right?"

"Damn right, I do. I'd be fucked up if she left me."

"So it's okay to love and appreciate our wives, just not okay to admit so publicly?"

"Not in the company of other men, at least not like how you did it." Amir stretched out his arms. *What, I gotta apologize for loving my wife?*" he asked, imitating Carlos.

Even Carlos laughed this time. "Okay, okay, I got it."

Amir frowned like he was deep in thought.

"What?"

"We are two pieces of shit. We're damn lucky to have our wives."

"You certainly are," Carlos needled. "You're lucky Kenya forgave those shenanigans you pulled when y'all were dating."

Amir couldn't hide his surprise. "How do you know?—Myles' big mouth, right?"

Carlos laughed. "It's a classic story. You reduced to begging." Carlos began mocking him, "'Please forgive me, Kenya.' 'Please open the door and let me in, Kenya.' 'Please marry me, Kenya.' And I bet you're still picking the splinters out your ass from sitting out in that hallway all night."

Amir pointed at him. "See, right there. That's bullshit!"

"Oh, so you weren't sitting in the hallway all night?"

"Yeah," Amir said, not backing down, "but it was carpeted. There were no splinters."

They both laughed heartily.

"Well," Amir said, finally, "that's ancient history."

"You were almost ancient history," Carlos said. "You're lucky Kenya gave you another shot."

"True," Amir agreed. He looked at his watch. "You wanna go grab something to eat?"

"Cool. As long as it isn't McDonald's," Carlos chuckled.

Amir put on his coat and returned to the previous subject. "Dealing with Myles is bad enough, so don't you go syrupy on me, too." Amir scowled as he opened the office door. "Next thing you know, you'll start reading those relationship books that are out there."

Carlos looked at him aghast. "Oh, Jesus, no. Never that!"

chapter 7

Saturday afternoon, Jackie was idling at a traffic light along Federal Street. She and CJ were on their way back from the aquarium, heading for Jackie's aunt's house in east Camden. She turned and peered into the backseat. CJ was gamely fighting off sleep in his car seat. Like he was afraid he was going to miss something.

"You can take a nap, *hijo*," she said, laughing. "We're done with the fishies for today."

As she turned back around, she checked to see if the light was green. It wasn't, but Jackie wouldn't have noticed anyway because something else about half a block up the street had caught her attention.

Jackie saw Jasmine and two other girls walk out of the Timberland store. Now, that's an interesting sight. Jackie was pretty certain that Ms. Peg didn't know that Jasmine was all the way in Camden. She couldn't see Ms. Peg going for that.

The trio of teenage girls were on their way to a red Altima when a man in a black Sentra pulled up to the curb. Jackie watched as Jasmine separated from the other girls and approached the car. The other girls waited as Jasmine began a conversation through the window.

The blare of a car horn behind her let Jackie know the light had changed to green. She pulled off and slowly drove past the scene. She tried to peer into the Sentra as she passed, but the driver's head was turned the other way. Jackie found a spot in front of the Sentra and pulled over. Jasmine was so preoccupied by the conversation that she hadn't noticed Jackie's car.

Jackie debated what to do. She didn't want to embarrass Jasmine in front of her friends. It wasn't like she was going into somebody's house or into one of the college dorms along Market Street. She could very well just be shopping with a couple of friends, one who apparently was old enough to drive. The man in the Sentra had obviously caught sight of Jasmine and her friends and was trying to get with some pretty girls. Both Jasmine and Danae looked older than their ages. The other girl definitely was older, and was also the driver of the Altima as Jackie could see a set of keys she was swinging glinting in the sunlight. As long as Jasmine didn't try to get into the car, then Jackie was contemplating letting it go.

When the Sentra door opened, and Jackie caught sight of the face that stepped out, the hands-off approach was quickly abandoned. She popped out of the car.

"Hey, Jazzy," Jackie said, as she approached the group.

Even though she was wearing a fashionable pair of white faux Fendi sunglasses, Jackie could see from Jasmine's reaction that she had no business being in Camden.

"Hey, Jackie," Jasmine said sheepishly, wondering where in the hell she had come from. Then she spied Jackie's Camry.

Jackie exchanged pleasantries with Danae and introduced herself to Shea—the other girl in the trio. Jackie noticed Greek letters on Shea's shirt and realized she was in a sorority.

Jackie made eye contact with Darius, who had stepped out of the Sentra. Shock didn't begin to describe the look on his face. Jackie was too professional to disclose her relationship to a client in front of other people without permission to do so, so she waited for Darius to reveal their association. She soon realized he had no plan to.

Jackie focused back on Jasmine. "Hey, Jaz, CJ and I are on our way back to Lawndale—why don't you ride with us? You would really be doing me a big favor. I need to run in to the drugstore and don't want to have to bring him in there with me. He's taking a nap—and he's been having trouble sleeping lately, so I don't want to have to wake him."

Jasmine hesitated, but only momentarily. She was smart enough to know that Jackie was offering her a way to save face in front of her friends.

"Sure, Jackie. I can do that." Jackie watched as Jasmine opened the rear door of the Sentra and took out her backpack. This removed any doubt Jackie had as to which car Jasmine had been in. Again, Jackie caught Darius' eye. Again, he was silent.

"Thanks, Jaz, I really appreciate it," Jackie replied.

Jasmine hoisted her shopping bag and backpack and said good-bye to her girlfriends. Jasmine then turned to say good-bye to Darius. She stepped close to him and whispered something in his ear. Darius nodded, but he was still dumbfounded by Jackie's reappearance in his life; wondering how the hell she knew Jasmine.

As they got into the car, Jasmine looked over her shoulder. "Wow, CJ really is sleeping."

"But I'm not going to the drugstore." Jackie checked the flow of oncoming traffic, then pulled out.

"I figured as much," Jasmine said quietly.

"Does Ms. Peg know you're in Camden today, Jaz?"

Jasmine looked out the window. "No."

"I'm guessing from that backpack, she thinks you're at the library, right?"

Jasmine didn't respond.

"Right?"

"Yeah, Jackie," Jasmine said. "I was at the library earlier."

"You're far from it now, though, aren't you? You're rolling through Camden in . . . some man's car. How did you meet him, anyway?"

Jasmine slouched down in her seat. "I met him a while back at the Echelon Mall."

"What's 'a while'?" Jackie pressed. "How long ago?"

"I don't know—last month."

Jackie's mind raced. Darius had just been signed over to adult services. She knew his plan was to enroll in auto-mechanic courses. Last month he was still at the facility. She remembered his trip to the mall with Aaron. That day he had worked her and Kenya's nerves so bad that they just wanted to be rid of him for a few hours.

In the days before he left their facility, Jackie had also heard Darius telling another one of the kids about some fine girl he had met that he planned to get with as soon as he got out. Jackie hadn't given it much thought. With Darius leaving them, it wasn't their problem.

Or so she believed. That notion had come full circle and smacked her in the face. Kenya was going to have a fit when she found out.

"How serious are you and that boy?" Jackie asked.

Jasmine eyed her. "What do you mean?"

"Just what I asked," Jackie said, looking over at her. "You're obviously comfortable enough to hop in his car and ride all over creation. What else are you doing with him?"

Jasmine was embarrassed by this line of questioning. "Nothing, Jackie. We haven't done anything."

Jackie pounded the steering wheel with her fist as she pulled up to another red light. "Listen to me, Jasmine. If you're supposed to be at the library, then your young ass should be at the library! Not getting into cars of men and going to Camden."

Jasmine's eyes widened. She was surprised that Jackie was losing her temper. She had never raised her voice at her before.

"I know, Jackie, but—"

"But nothing," Jackie cut her off. "There isn't shit you can say."

"Why are you getting so upset, Jackie?"

Jackie ignored her and focused on the light. She couldn't tell her the true cause of her worry, so she decided to talk to Kenya first before revealing anything to Jasmine.

They rode in silence until they reached Lawndale. Jackie was about to turn off Warwick Road toward the Moores' home when Jasmine spoke.

"Are you gonna tell Aunt Peg?"

"Why not?" Jackie replied. "I'm sure she'll understand."

"I'm sure she *won't*," Jasmine countered.

The way Jasmine said it made Jackie chuckle, despite her anger.

Jasmine seized the opening. She leaned over and rested her head on Jackie's shoulder. "Come on, Jackie, I won't do it again. . . . No need to get my aunt's blood pressure up. I'll baby-sit CJ for free the next time you and Carlos want to do something. . . ."

They pulled up in front of the Moores' redbrick house. No one was home since both Leonard and Peggy were busy at the shop on Saturday. Jackie knew that Jasmine had been aware of this bit of knowledge when she took her sojourn to Camden.

Jackie looked down at the top of Jasmine's head. This child was so manipulative it wasn't even funny. What's worse is that she was clever about it.

"Jasmine, you have people who care about you. You should know that you can't get away with anything because you have too many eyes on you. The Moores know all of Lawndale and half of Camden. Somebody is gonna spot you when you're doing something wrong."

Jasmine gripped Jackie's arm. "I know, I know . . ."

"All right, I won't tell your aunt," Jackie said, shaking her arm. She definitely was telling Kenya, however. "Now get up. You don't do cutesy well."

Jasmine smiled and gave her a kiss on the cheek. She unhooked her seat belt.

"You gonna come in and lay CJ down?" Jasmine asked.

"No, I have to get back to east Camden. We're expected at my aunt's house."

Jasmine frowned. "You guys were just there."

"I know. But we had to drop off something important here first."

Jackie saw the slickness ease off Jasmine's face as she contemplated that statement. She was now embarrassed and turned her head quickly to hide it.

Jasmine picked up her bag and stepped out of the car.

As Jackie pulled up in the driveway behind Carlos' car, she wondered what he was up to. While she was visiting her aunt, Carlos had called and asked if she could baby-sit CJ this afternoon because he had made plans for him and Jackie. Some surprise.

93

Jackie was more than a little skeptical. She hoped it wasn't some bullshit. Something that *he* wanted to do, like going to some car show or something. Watching Carlos' eyes bug out over a bunch of souped-up, hydraulic-equipped, ridiculously expensive cars wasn't her idea of a good time. And maybe afterward he would rush Jackie through some meal at some inconsequential dive of a restaurant and count that as a day of "taking her out."

She turned the key and walked into the house. The first thing that she noticed was the smell. It smelled clean and soapy—like a freshly showered man. The second thing she noticed is that it was immaculate. Someone had obviously put in a lot of time and effort cleaning. The third thing she noticed was the music playing, Mark Anthony's *Contra la Corriente*. The fourth thing she noticed was the emergence of her husband at the end of the hallway. He was flawless. Skin glistening. Biceps twitching. Hair and goatee freshly groomed.

And the final thing she noticed—and the one with the most lasting impact—was the gleaming white, tight boxer briefs that emphasized his bulge.

Aww shit, Jackie thought.

It was about to get freaky up in here.

Dropping her purse and coat along the way, she walked toward him.

Kenya's nose crinkled. What in the world was Amir doing home on a late Saturday afternoon? Shouldn't he be at the shop?

She felt guilty for being a little disappointed, but she thought she was going to have the house to herself after her morning shift at the facility. With the twins away at karate camp until tomorrow, she had marked this afternoon on her calendar for weeks. A bubble bath, a book, and some peace was all she was looking forward to.

She hoped that Amir would at least grant her that. And please don't let him greet her with the sorry sight of him standing there all helpless and scratching his stomach talking about he was hungry, like he needed Lewis and Clark to show him where the damn kitchen was.

And that he didn't have any of his boys coming over to play poker or watch this week's "must-watch sporting event of the century" and raising a general ruckus in her house. She couldn't be comfortable in her tub with a house full of noisy men downstairs.

Kenya came in through the garage. She laid her keys and purse on the kitchen counter. No sign of Amir. Just as she was about to check the basement, she noticed the sound of water running and peered at the ceiling. Aw hell.

She could tell by the sound that Amir was running a bath. Not his usual shower, but a bath. Of all days.

Kenya made her way through the kitchen and to the stairs—pausing long enough to scoop up her Toni Morrison novel off of the coffee table—and began quickly ascending them, hoping she could talk Amir into letting her have the tub before he got in. The last thing she felt like doing was waiting for him to finish and having to clean it out before using it.

The bathroom door was cracked, so she entered without knocking.

"Babe, can I—"

Amir was sitting on the edge of the garden tub throwing peach-colored rose petals onto the bubbling water. A small table holding two wine flutes and a bottle of champagne chilling in a stainless-steel bucket was set near the tub. Candles were placed all over the room, giving off a peach scent.

Amir was wearing a light blue rayon set that Kenya loved

him in. The sleeves were rolled up on the shirt, and he was now slipping his hands into silk wash mitts. He smiled at her seductively.

"Hi, babe. I figured you would like a nice soak after work."

"You figured right."

The smile fell off Amir's face when he noticed the book.

"Do you want to be alone with your book?"

Sorry, Sister Toni. Kenya flung the book over her shoulder. It landed with a thud on the carpet in the hallway.

"What book?"

They exchanged sexy smiles as Kenya began disrobing.

Jackie and Carlos tussled on the living room sofa. They spilled over onto the floor in a naked embrace, kissing wildly.

Jackie ended up on top. She straddled Carlos, leaned forward and sucked on his neck while he removed her final item of clothing, her bra.

He tossed it aside, ran his fingers up Jackie's back, through her hair and guided her shoulders off of him. Her face now in front of his, Carlos softly cradled her face, stroking her cheeks with his thumbs.

"*Te quiero.*"

"I love you, too," Jackie panted. She was ready to have him inside her. She began maneuvering down, but to her surprise, Carlos grabbed her hips and guided her up his torso instead.

As she hovered over his face, Carlos pulled her down so that her knees were on either side of his head and her *chocha* fell squarely onto his mouth.

"Oh." Jackie focused on the sensation of Carlos' tongue flicking against her wetness. She couldn't imagine anything on this earth more pleasurable until Carlos switched up on her and she felt his tongue pressing against her clitoris with broad, wide strokes.

"*Mierda,*" Jackie moaned as her head limply fell back and her eyes rolled skyward. Carlos was directing her hips with his hands; first slowly rotating them, then gently guiding them up and down.

He doesn't know it yet, but he has done it now, Jackie thought. His ass was going to have to start doing this on the regular. Jackie bit her bottom lip as she felt her body begin to pulsate.

After she recovered from her orgasm, she got up from her perch and stood over Carlos. As she did, she saw him lick his glistening lips.

Damn, if this man don't love him some me, Jackie thought.

She half turned and saw Carlos masturbating. As she saw his hand sliding up and down his shaft, she began to salivate.

Her turn.

Kenya was stretched out on the bed. She was as naked as the day she was born, and without a care in the world because she was in Amir's skilled hands. When he set his mind to pampering his woman, he was without peer.

She lay on her stomach with her eyes closed as Amir lotioned the soles of her feet, the final part of her body requiring such attention after her bath. Amir had decided to go old school with his musical selection. Kenya hummed along to the sound of Teddy Pendergrass' "Come Go with Me." Great choice, because pretty soon she and Amir would both be growling like Teddy.

Amir finished and set the lotion aside. Kenya kept her eyes closed. The next thing she felt was Amir's hands on her hips, lifting her up so that she was on all fours. Kenya didn't resist. She had been horny and ready since Amir had bathed her in the tub, but she was a little surprised. Amir usually allowed more time for foreplay.

When she felt the warm baby oil on her backside, she smiled. She should know better than to doubt her man. She allowed a peek over her shoulder. When she saw the ardent combination of love and lust in Amir's eyes, a feeling of contentment washed over her entire body. She closed her eyes again and caressed her right breast, stroking her hardening nipple with her thumb.

Amir finished oiling her behind, allowing some excess oil to drip down to Kenya's crotch. Then he stepped back so he could admire it in all its luminous, silky glory. Like an artist admiring his handiwork. Without turning around—Kenya had been married to Amir long enough to know what he was doing—she gave him a little show. First, she slowly and subtly swayed her ass from side to side; then she arched and dropped her back. When she spread her knees and began simulation pumping—and heard a grateful moan from Amir—she knew she had him right where she wanted him.

As Amir's mouth explored her from behind, she felt his rock-hard penis brush against her foot. Teddy was now singing "The More I Get, the More I Want." You said a mouthful, Brother Teddy.

Jackie and Carlos had their hands clasped as she rode him. Jackie had him pinned to the floor, and was talking shit as she tried to fuck him senseless.

"You know you can't get enough of this *chocha* . . ."

"Uhhn."

"Can you?"

"No."

"You would be lost without it. Wouldn't you?"

"Lost, baby . . . erg—lost! . . ."

Jackie released his hands. Carlos panted as he began to fondle her behind.

"You worship that *culo* . . . don'cha?"

"Yes."

Jackie placed her palms on his chest and began slowly winding. "I said, you worship my sweet ass, don'cha?"

"Yes," Carlos said, closing his eyes and gripping it lovingly.

She placed her palms on the floor and began working him for real. "Tell, me . . . again."

"I worship your ass, Jackie! I worship your ass!"

"Beg me for it!"

"Gimme that ass . . . Jackie, gimme that ass . . . Oh, please, Jackie!—gurrgh."

Jackie gradually subsided to let Carlos enjoy his orgasm, then slowly stopped altogether.

Carlos opened his eyes and looked adoringly at his wife. He looked so in love that Jackie nearly chuckled. It was a good feeling, though.

Carlos began running his fingers through Jackie's thick curly black hair, letting the curls fall off his knuckles. He hated when she straightened it, saying that *blancas* would kill to have her curly hair, so why was she straightening it to look more like them? And as far as cutting it, well, she did that once and he damn near threw himself on the floor and cried.

Jackie didn't mind. If it made her man happy, then she was cool with it. When she needed a change, she braided it.

"You surprised me today," Jackie said.

Carlos glanced at the wall clock, then back at Jackie. "You surprised that I gave you forty-two minutes of good loving, *chula*?"

Jackie sucked her teeth. "What have I told you about timing it?"

Carlos laughed.

"No, I'm surprised that I got good loving, period."

Carlos' eyes widened. "You saying that it's usually bad?"

Jackie rolled her eyes. "You know what I mean. Cleaning the house, putting them tight drawers on for me. What got into you today?"

Carlos smiled. "Someone reminded me of something."

"What?"

"Que soy un hombre afortunado."

"Damn right, you're a lucky man," Jackie agreed. Then she pouted. "But how could you ever possibly forget that fact?" She motioned to her body. "Look at these magnificent *tetas.*"

They both chuckled.

Carlos moved his hands through her hair to the back of her head and guided her face down so he could kiss her. Jackie turned and gave him her cheek instead.

"Que pasa?"

Jackie crinkled her nose and smiled sheepishly. Carlos now understood what the deal was.

He got up to brush his teeth and rinse his mouth out.

Amir was lying flat on top of Kenya, who was lying on her stomach. He was gently thrusting into her from behind while simultaneously sucking on her neck and shoulders.

Kenya loved this spot. She liked the feeling of Amir's hard pecs on her back. His tight thighs rubbing against the back of her legs. His large hands traveling up and down her arms.

But her pleasure wasn't the main reason she enjoyed this position. They had just finished her optimum position—on her back with Amir holding her left leg in the air—and Amir had sent her into the inner region of ecstasy.

Rather, she liked this position mainly because it excited Amir so much. She liked being pinned down with her husband grunting and smacking in her ear like she was the most delicious thing on the earth. Being controlled, and, she had to admit—if only to herself—being ravaged by her man.

Sometimes she wanted sweetness, tenderness, and gentleness. And sometimes she just wanted to be fucked wildly. Like a smoldering temptress he would kill for.

Amir held her forearms and quickened his pace. Kenya could tell from his excited breathing that he was about to explode. Time for the vixen to make an appearance.

"Fuck me, Amir!"

"Yeah . . . yeah . . ."

"This is your pussy, Amir . . . Ooh, I love your dick, Amir . . . I need your dick to think straight. So fuck me! Please!"

"You need this dick!"

"Yes I do . . . it's all I think about. Shit! It feels so good. God bless your magnificent dick!"

Kenya purred softly and gave him a little wiggle and squirm, knowing what it would do to him.

Sure enough, Amir went pow and collapsed on top of her, kissing her neck and back dozens of times like he always did. In gratitude for being the delicate, fine creature that she was, Kenya liked to imagine. The smoldering temptress persona never lasted long.

After recovering, Amir rolled off her. As Kenya turned over onto her back, Amir took her hand into his.

" 'God bless your magnificent dick?' " he asked.

Kenya winced. "A bit much?"

"Nope. It should be," Amir admitted, "but I like it."

"I bet you do with your vain self." Kenya tapped him on the shoulder. "So, to what did I owe this afternoon delight, anyway?"

"Does there have to be a reason?"

"There shouldn't have to be," Kenya replied.

Amir gave some thought before speaking, choosing his words with care. "Let's just say that speaking to a wise friend today made me realize how much I love my wife—and how lucky I am to have her."

Kenya smiled. "I think you should speak to this friend more often."

Peggy silently watched Leonard take off his watch and set it on his bureau. He had just come home, though he had closed the barber shop four hours ago. Where had he been since then? Apparently, Leonard didn't feel the need to give an explanation.

After slipping off his shoes, he headed to the bathroom.

"Lenny, when did you become so cruel?"

Leonard stopped in his tracks and turned around. "What? What do you mean I'm cruel?"

"You heard me." Peggy looked up at him.

"What do you mean?"

"You're out there doing God knows what, and are brash enough to do it right under my nose. You're cruel because you don't care how it makes me feel."

Peggy paused and held her fist to her mouth, trying to collect herself. It was to no avail. When she spoke again, her voice cracked.

"You don't care what that does to me . . . how that makes me doubt myself . . . or how much I fear for the future because of it." Her shoulders collapsed. The tears started falling between her knees onto the carpet below.

Leonard stood staring at his wife for a couple of beats. He walked over to the bureau, retrieved a handkerchief, and sat next to her on the trunk. He began dabbing at her cheek.

Peggy resisted. But she let go when her husband wrapped his arms around her and squeezed tightly.

"Why have you forgotten me, Lenny?"

"I haven't forgotten you, Peg," he answered somberly. "If it seems so, I apologize. Just know that it's nothing you've done wrong—the fault lies with me."

Peggy looked at him incredulously. "Is that supposed to make me feel better?" She took the handkerchief from him and blew her nose.

"Yes," he said, shuffling his feet on the carpet, "but I suppose it wouldn't."

Peggy willed her tears to stop and took a deep breath. It was time to have at it. "Lenny, are you sleeping around?"

Looking offended, Leonard took his arm from around her shoulder and stood up. "Peggy, there's a big difference between me not being attentive enough—spending too much time down at Starks and stuff—and me sleeping around on you. Relationships go through lulls. People sometimes drift apart. But it isn't always because of another person. Come on."

Leonard walked through the walk-in closet into the bathroom. Seconds later, Peggy heard him gargling.

She had, of course, noticed the indignation in his voice. She exhaled and dug her toe into the rug.

Minutes later, her husband returned to the room walking right past her without saying a word. She heard him fiddling with the CD player on the nightstand near the far wall.

The sound of "At Last" flooded the room. Startled, Peggy looked up. Her husband was standing in front of her.

"Peggy, I love you as much today as the day I married you

thirty-eight years ago." Leonard reached down and took her hands in his and lifted her to her feet.

"What are you doing, Leonard?"

"Playing our wedding song and having a dance with my bride." He wrapped an arm around her waist and pressed her close to him.

"Oh, man," Peggy said, rolling her eyes, but she stopped resisting. She leaned into him and rested her head on his shoulder.

As they swayed, Leonard spoke again, "Remember how I promised you that I would be rich enough to get Etta James to personally sing this song by our tenth wedding anniversary?"

"Um-hm," Peggy replied in a hushed tone. "Yeah, I remember."

"Yeah, well, sorry babe, things didn't go as planned."

She chuckled. "You've done all right by your family, Leonard Moore."

He drew back so he could see her face. "Yeah?" He leaned in and rested his cheek on hers. "Well, maybe I can get her to make our fortieth anniversary."

Maybe *we'll* make it to a fortieth anniversary, Peggy thought, but didn't say. It was not lost on her that Leonard had not flat-out denied that he was sleeping around on her. But she didn't feel like fighting anymore. It had been such a long time since her husband had held her like this. Made her feel wanted.

And even longer since she had some of what was currently pressing up against her waist.

Leonard seemed to have read his wife's mind.

"Uh-oh," he said playfully, "what's that?"

"I don't know," she murmured, playing along. It had been so long since she had seen it, she had thought about having it legally declared dead.

"Let's find out," he said.

He backed her into the mattress and fell on top of her.

"Lenny!" she said, surprised.

"What, Myles and Marisa are still out. And if you're worried about Jasmine hearing us," Leonard said as he unbuttoned his wife's pants, "then I hate to break it to you, but your niece is practically grown. And knows what a man and wife do in the bedroom."

Peggy smiled and wrapped her arms around her husband's neck. "I've missed you."

Leonard gave her a long, passionate kiss on her mouth. "I've haven't gone anywhere, Peg."

As he turned off the lamp, she reached over and turned up the music. She didn't care how grown Jasmine was, no niece needs to hear her aunt moaning.

chapter 8

"Damn, you two have me jealous," Marisa said as she picked at her omelet. "How both of you are gonna get romanced like that yesterday?"

Marisa, Jackie, and Kenya were enjoying brunch at Hibachi on the waterfront in Philadelphia. Jackie and Kenya had just both recounted their encounters yesterday with their husbands.

"Oh, girl please," Jackie said as she cut her waffles, "you're the one who lives with the *enamorado.*"

"You know," Kenya agreed. "Your man is Mr. Poetry writing, let-me-think-of-a-thousand-ways-to-tell-my-lady-how-much-I-love-her-today."

"Well, while I was watching Myles watch TV and scratch himself yesterday afternoon at his parents' house, y'all were getting some booty." Marisa took a bite of her French toast. "Kinda coincidental that both of them would be behooved in like manner. Do you think they planned it?"

Jackie shrugged. "Carlos did get a haircut yesterday, so I know he saw Amir."

Kenya's eyebrows rose. "You know, when I asked Amir afterward what the occasion was, he told me that he had spoken to a wise friend who made him realize how blessed he is."

"Oh, forget it, then," Jackie said. "Carlos isn't that profound."

The three of them laughed.

"Anyway," Jackie continued, looking at Kenya, "before Carlos' pickle tickle, guess who I saw yesterday shopping on Federal Street in Camden—when she was supposed to be at the library."

"Who?"

"Jasmine."

Marisa's ears perked up.

"Get out," Kenya said, "Was she by herself?"

"No, she was with her little friend—I forget her name—and some college girl driving a Altima."

"Lord, Ms. Peg would have a fit if she knew," Kenya said.

That made two of them, Marisa thought. She hoped Jasmine wasn't cutting up.

"Did you say anything to her?" Marisa asked.

"I did more than that," Jackie said. "I put her ass in the car and took her home."

"Good," Kenya said.

"Did you tell Ms. Peg?" Marisa asked.

Jackie shook her head.

"Her lying self has no business running around Camden," Kenya continued.

"That's what I told her when I was yelling at her behind in the car."

"You were yelling at *Ms.* Jasmine?" Kenya asked, amused at the thought.

"Girl," Jackie flipped her wrist, "I didn't even care my child was sleeping in the backseat. I nearly lost it."

"Jasmine brings it out of you," Marisa said. "First of all,

you know how sharp she is, so you're on the defensive because you fear being manipulated. Secondly, you just want to wring her neck whenever she missteps because you hate to see such marvelous potential wasted."

"Ain't it the truth," Kenya said.

"If she wanted to go to Camden, why didn't she just ask someone for a ride rather than pull some deception?" Marisa asked.

Jackie pointed with her fork. "Because she wanted to ride with who she went with."

Kenya shook her head. "The college girl and Danae, right?"

"She didn't ride over to Camden with them," Jackie continued. "Best I can tell, she just met up with them there."

Kenya furrowed her brow and wiped her mouth with her cloth napkin. "Then who did she ride over with?"

"Darius Simpson."

"Wha—?" Kenya dropped her fork.

Jackie nodded.

"Oh, Jesus," Kenya said. *"Darius?"* Her eyes revealed a newfound level of seriousness regarding yesterday's events. "What did you say to him?"

"Nothing," Jackie said. "He pretended he didn't know me and I did likewise. You know I'm not going to be the first one to out a client."

"So you know this Darius because he was in the system?" Marisa asked.

"Yes. And he lived in the home until last month, when he turned eighteen." Jackie answered.

"What's so bad about him?" Marisa asked.

Kenya and Jackie exchanged looks.

"That bad?" Marisa asked. "Lord. Did you tell Jasmine?"

"No," Jackie said. "I wanted to talk it over with Kenya first."

"What is there to talk about?" Kenya asked. "We're gonna tell Ms. Grownass to stay away from him, and beat her down if she doesn't."

"What kind of trouble is this boy?" Marisa asked. She noticed their hesitation. "Look, I know all about client confidentiality," she said, setting down her fork, "but y'all aren't gonna have me worrying and not know what I'm worrying about."

"Darius has a volatile temper—very defiant," Jackie explained. "Has trouble with authority. He's been kicked out of a million schools. We finally encouraged him to just get his GED."

"Besides just being a slick, vindictive, exasperating, all-around asshole," Kenya said, "which I can partly attribute as a defense mechanism to being kicked around the system for so long."

"I would agree with that." Jackie chimed in. "It hasn't been easy for him."

"No, it hasn't been," Kenya agreed. "I wish Darius the best of luck—hope he eventually finds somebody that can deal with all the anger, hurt, and baggage that he's carrying around. But I don't want anybody I love to be the test case."

Marisa nodded. She understood that sentiment.

Kenya went on, "He's been in trouble for car theft, burglary, assault, terroristic threats . . ." She stopped as she tried to think of anything else she might have missed.

"And *very* sexually active," Jackie continued.

"Didn't he once get a girl pregnant?" Kenya asked.

"Yeah, when he was fourteen. She miscarried," Jackie said. "Darius doesn't have any kids that I know of."

"Or that he knows of," Kenya added.

"He's a very handsome boy," Jackie explained to Marisa. "And can be quite charming when he wants to. Girls fall for him all the time."

"Well, he can charm someone else besides a member of my family," Kenya said emphatically. "And where did he get a car from? For all Jasmine knows, she's been riding around in a hot car."

"Well, you're gonna tell Jasmine, right?" Marisa asked.

"You can count on it." Kenya noticed Jackie's look of discomfort. "What? You have a doubt?"

"Kenya, you know how smart Darius is."

"Diabolical, more like it," Kenya said. "He knows just how to fuck with people. How to get your goat."

"Yes, he does," Jackie agreed. "And Darius has been in the system long enough to know about client confidentiality rights. We have to be smart. If we go running our mouths to Jasmine and she tells Darius, we can find ourselves at the wrong end of a lawsuit."

Kenya brushed off that notion. "I doubt that."

"You put it past Darius?" Jackie asked. "You just got done telling me how diabolical he is. How vindictive he can be. And how will a breach-of-confidentiality lawsuit look for us in the eyes of the state next time we go to get funding for our home?"

As Kenya thought that over, their waiter came by and asked the ladies if he could get them anything else. When he left, Kenya spoke.

"You're right. But I have to do something, Jackie."

"We will," Jackie assured her. "If Darius isn't really that interested in Jasmine, just the fact that he knows I know her will scare him off. Why put himself through that headache when he can just find another girl?"

"True." Kenya agreed.

"And if he really is interested in Jasmine, then he will feel the need to tell her his side of things. He'll have to come clean to her about living in the group home, being a client of ours, and all the trouble he's been in. He'll want to get his version out there, for fear she's just getting ours." Jackie bit into a strawberry. "In fact, I bet he already has."

Kenya nodded. "Then he will have been the one who breached the confidentiality, not us."

"Exactly."

Jasmine's emotions were changing from confusion to irritation. "I told you, I don't know what you're talking about."

"So she hasn't told you anything?" Darius asked, still disbelieving.

Jasmine looked at the ceiling in exasperation. "Again, who is *she*?"

"Jackie."

Jasmine clutched the receiver tightly. "You know Jackie? How?"

Darius drew a deep breath. "She's been my caseworker since I was, like, thirteen," he confessed. "I lived in the group home that she runs for the past year, up until last month."

Jasmine sat down hard on her bed. "Her and Kenya's home?"

"You know Kenya, too?" Darius asked.

"She's married to my cousin," Jasmine answered.

Great, Darius thought. It gets worse.

Jasmine was trying to understand. "I thought you said you were down South with some relatives."

"Yeah, well, that wasn't the truth," Darius admitted.

Jasmine had a real issue about being lied to. She had already been lied to enough in her life by the person she loved the most. She was damned if she was going to put up with it from other people.

"What else have you lied about?" she asked edgily.

"Look, Jasmine, it wasn't out of a desire to get over on you. It was just because—it's embarrassing to tell people that you live in a group home."

Jasmine replayed the scene from yesterday in her mind. "How come you and Jackie didn't let on that you know each other? What was that all about?"

"She was probably waiting for me to make the first move," Darius explained. "She's not supposed to let people know our relationship."

Jasmine couldn't believe this shit. She remembered how stressed Jackie was in the car ride home. "So why all the secrecy?" she asked. "What are you? Some kind of mass murderer or something?"

"No, but I do have a past that Jackie . . . and Kenya know about." Darius hesitated. He was surprised that he was having such conversation trouble with Jasmine. He liked her more than he realized.

"I've been in trouble behind car theft—"

"What about the one you had me in?" Jasmine asked.

"No, that's really my cousin's," Darius hastened to explain. "I'm on the insurance and everything. He's gonna let me buy it from him."

Darius took Jasmine's silence as her desire for him to continue.

"I used to run around in a gang. Do stupid shit. I got a juvie assault charge. And a burglary." Darius tried to think of anything he might be missing that Kenya and Jackie would add. "I already told you about my problems in school. I've been told I have a bit of a temper."

"I don't believe this," Jasmine said wearily. All of a sudden Darius getting her phone number off the store receipt wasn't charming. It felt slimy.

"Look, Jasmine." Darius exhaled. "I know we just met

and all, but I really do like you. Have from the first day I met you in the mall."

"Yeah, well . . ."

"Well, what?" Darius pressed, his voice decibel rising. "I'm just asking you to give me a chance and form your own opinion."

Jasmine didn't say anything. Her thoughts immediately went to the stupid choices she had seen her mother make in men. She had long vowed that that would never be her.

"Those things are not me anymore," Darius insisted. "I haven't been in trouble in years."

"Except for getting put out of school, right?" Jasmine asked.

Darius felt a flare of anger. He felt Jasmine was just looking for a way out. "I told you the deal behind that, didn't I?" Darius asked.

"Yeah, *you* told me," Jasmine said.

"What? You don't believe me?"

"Well, you already lied to me once. Why should I?"

Darius wrung the receiver in his hands like it was a washcloth. This was all coming out so bad. He put the phone back up to his ear in time to hear Jasmine say she needed some time to think it over. Which he took as a nice way of brushing him off. Fuck that.

"Look, all we did was swap a little spit," he said harshly. "If you don't want to be down, I'll find somebody else. Believe me, it won't be a problem for me. I need someone who can think for herself, not some scared little girl."

Jasmine let out a sound of disgust. Not only was that unwarranted, it was unnecessary. "You know what, fine then."

"Peace."

Darius slammed the phone onto the kitchen table and stalked away. Ten seconds later, he went back in, picked it up, and began dialing Jasmine's number again, only to hang up before it connected. He held the phone to his temple and grimaced.

"Damn it."

Jasmine was sitting at the desk in her bedroom supposedly studying for a history test, but in reality thinking about Darius, when she heard a knock at the door. She figured it was one of the twins wanting to hang out with her.

"I'm studying, twin. I'll be done in a little while."

"It's me, Jasmine."

Surprised to hear Marisa's voice, Jasmine set her book down. "Come in."

Jasmine soon saw it wasn't just Marisa, but Kenya and Jackie, too. She immediately figured Darius was the reason behind this attention.

Jackie and Kenya sat down on her bed. Marisa shut the door and stood along the wall.

"What's up?"

"Jasmine, we want to discuss something with you," Kenya said.

"Yes?"

Jackie took over. "Yesterday, when I saw you in Camden, you were talking to a young man on the sidewalk in front of the shoe store. We know him."

"I know," Jasmine said.

"You know?"

"Darius told me."

"Did he?" Jackie asked, looking at Kenya.

"Yeah, he told me about his staying in y'all's facility."

"Did he tell you anything else?" Kenya asked.

Jasmine knew what they wanted to hear. "Yeah, he told me about all the trouble he's been in, the scrapes he's had

114

with the law, but that he hasn't had been in any real trouble for years."

"Define real trouble," Jackie said.

"With the law," Jasmine explained. She looked at Kenya and Jackie sitting on her bed. "Is that part at least true?"

Kenya conceded the point. "I believe it is." But she wasn't hardly there to sell positive points for Darius. She rose to her feet. "However, Jasmine—"

Jasmine interrupted her. "Don't worry. I don't think I'll be seeing him again. He's a jerk."

Marisa studied Jasmine. "What led you to that conclusion?"

"Dealing with him," Jasmine answered. "I've only known him for a short while. Only been out with him twice."

Kenya and Jackie believed that. Darius hadn't been out of the home long enough for it to have been a long-term thing.

Jasmine told Kenya firmly. "Don't worry, I don't need drama in my life."

The three ladies looked at each other. Each was thinking the same thing. But really, what choice did they have but to trust Jasmine?

"Good," Kenya said. "I'm glad to see you make a mature, rational choice without having to find out the hard way. Without getting into specifics about Darius' case, Jackie and I were gonna ask you not to associate with him, and hope that you valued our opinion enough to listen to it." Kenya put her hand on Jasmine's shoulder. "Is the fact that Jackie and I are asking you to stay away from him enough for you?"

Jasmine thought about what Darius had said. About her not being woman enough to make her own decision. She also knew what the ladies in the room wanted to hear.

"Yes," she said softly. "Are y'all gonna tell Aunt Peg?"

Jasmine could tell by their reactions they had already thought that over.

"If you're being straight with us, there's no need to involve her," Kenya said. She eyed Jasmine squarely. "Is there a reason to involve her?"

"No." Jasmine shook her head.

Marisa spoke up at last. "You know, Jasmine, successful people have years of experience for a reason. Fools, on the other hand, don't get very far in life. If you have older people around you who care about you, then you should use them as the valuable resource that they are. Adults don't come up with rules to make your life harder—they have rules to keep you safe. You put yourself in a potentially perilous position by acting grown in the first place. Being a grown-up means not just doing things adults get to do, but knowing what things not to do. Be sensible."

Jasmine nodded.

As they left, Jasmine hugged each of the ladies and told them she would be downstairs in a minute. She wanted to finish looking over the chapter she was working on in her history book.

As Jasmine turned her attention back to her studies, she couldn't escape what she was feeling in the pit of her stomach. She tried to brush it away. Told herself that it meant nothing. It was childish and stupid. And just because she was feeling it, she certainly didn't have to act upon it.

Yet it was there. An unmistakable gnawing.

A desire to see Darius again.

chapter 9

Saturday morning, Peggy stood in the kitchen, sipping coffee and looking out of the window. She was already dressed for work, figuring she would go into the salon early. Though she and Leonard worked in the same building—her salon occupying half, his barber shop the other—they didn't travel to work in the same car. Hadn't for years. One of a number of things they didn't do together anymore.

She remembered when the boys were young how the entire family would go together. The look of ridicule Amir would give Myles for wanting to be with her in the salon instead of with his father and brother.

She heard Jasmine coming down the kitchen.

"Good morning, Aunt Peg."

"Morning, Jasmine."

As Jasmine gave her a kiss on the cheek, Peggy held the cup away from her body so she didn't spill any. That was sweet, she thought as she and Jasmine exchanged smiles.

Jasmine opened the refrigerator, and Peggy eyed the jeans that she was wearing. She didn't recognize them, which meant she probably bought them when she was out at the mall with her friends. They were too tight for her liking, but she decided to let it go. She didn't feel like getting into a fight with Jasmine this morning. Besides, Kenya had pointed out to her that since it was now fashionable for girls to wear their jeans skin-tight, most stores didn't even sell them any other way. Peggy wished the look from a few years back would come back. The loose-fit jeans, print shirts, club shoes, hoop earrings, and those adorable little hats like Kenya used to wear when she and Amir were dating. She thought that the girls looked so cute back then. Now they all looked like hoochies.

"You going to the library again?" Peggy asked.

"Yeah," Jasmine said. "Can I come by the shop today later and get my hair done?"

"I think I'll have some free time in the afternoon," Peggy replied. "What did you have in mind?"

"Braids," Jasmine said nonchalantly as she peeled a banana.

"I said I had some free time, girl—not a free week."

"I'm just kidding, Aunt Peg." Jasmine sauntered over to the table. "I just want to add some length."

Peggy sighed. "Jasmine, I've done told you that that isn't gonna happen. At least not on my watch."

"C'mon, Aunt Peg," Jasmine whined. "Be reasonable."

"C'mon, Jasmine," she mimicked in the same tone. "I am being reasonable. No sixteen-year-old girl needs hair down to her butt. You trying to be Beyoncé? Or what's the name of that other child, who died in the plane crash?"

"Aaliyah. And I'm seventeen."

"Yeah, Aaliyah," Peggy said, taking another sip.

Jasmine put her palms on the table and tried another approach. "I'm not trying to be like anybody else. I'm just trying to be me."

"Well, *you* weren't blessed to be born with hair like Aaliyah's. So be *you* instead."

Jasmine fell back into her chair like a churlish child,

which she was, despite her attempts to alter her physical appearance otherwise.

"Why do you need hair that length anyway?" Peggy asked. "You playing Pocahontas in the school play?"

Peggy could tell that Jasmine wasn't exactly appreciating her attempts at humor. Plus, she sensed that something else was involved besides her request for a horse's mane down her back. She rinsed out her cup and then turned back to Jasmine, who was forlornly staring at the table, trying to elicit sympathy. It worked.

Peggy walked over to the table and began running her fingers through Jasmine's thick, shoulder-length hair. When she spoke again, her tone was softer and the teasing edge of before was gone.

"So, why do you want all that hair, niece?"

Jasmine shrugged her shoulders. "I just wanted it for the party tonight."

The stroking ceased. "What party?"

Jasmine realized she had misspoke and quickly went about trying to undo the damage. "Well, it's a sleepover—slumber party–type thing."

"Over at whose house?"

"Danae's," Jasmine said. She said it like she couldn't believe her aunt was playing dumb. "I asked you a couple of weeks ago—in the shop."

Peggy didn't remember. Though knowing Jasmine's manipulative self, she had probably picked a time when she had had a shop full of customers and was trying to do a million things at once.

"No, I don't remember," Peggy said. She walked over to the windowsill and inspected her plant. The soil was dry. "I do vaguely recall you coming in the salon with Teresa and asking about a sleepover."

"Exactly," Jasmine said, tapping her fingers on the table, "that was when."

Peggy filled a cup with water and poured it into the pot. "Well, if I said yes, it's because I thought you were asking about staying at Teresa's place—not Danae's."

"Well, I wasn't," she said, too fast.

"But that's what I thought."

"Well, you thought wrong."

"I'm thinking right now that you better watch your mouth. I hope you prove me wrong about that."

"So you're saying I can't go?"

"That's what I'm saying."

"Why? What's the difference? What's wrong with Danae's?"

Peggy felt the now moist soil of the plant and set the cup back in the sink.

There was plenty wrong. Peggy had noticed that Vanessa dressed far more provocatively than she should. Worse than that, Danae had come to see Jasmine in some stuff that made Peggy just want to throw a sheet and holy water over her. Why did young ladies think that was cute? To be walking around looking like prostitutes, garnering all the wrong kinds of attention. So what did a party at their house promise? Nothing good.

"Because I know Teresa's people. I don't know Danae's."

"What's that mean?" Jasmine said, exasperated. "Because they've only lived in this miserable-ass town for one year instead of their whole lives, they aren't credible?"

"Watch your mouth and stop yelling at me, Jasmine," Peggy said as she washed her hands. "You're not going."

"I hate it here!"

"Well, your alternative is a foster home," Peggy said evenly.

"It can't be any worse."

"I'd hate to lose you, though, because I love you."

Jasmine pushed herself from the table and stood up. "That's some bullshit!"

Peggy calmly finished folding the towel and set it on the counter. She walked over to where Jasmine stood and smacked her squarely in the mouth.

"Respect my house. Watch your mouth."

Jasmine rubbed her face. Peggy saw the shock of getting struck slowly fade from Jasmine's eyes. They were now awash with contempt. She knew something nasty was going to come spewing out, and prepared herself.

"You just wanna rule over me because it gives you something to do. Don't blame me because your husband don't want you!"

Well, she hadn't been prepared for *that*.

Peggy decided right then that Jasmine seriously needed her ass whipped, and she was just the person to do it. She also decided that maybe Jasmine would be needing a weave, after all, because she was about to snatch the child bald-headed.

Sometimes kids needed a talk. Or a hug. Or attention. And sometimes they needed a foot in the ass.

She again smacked Jasmine in the face and backed her against the wall. Jasmine, in raising her arms to defend herself, struck her aunt in the chin with an elbow.

This only fueled Peggy's rage. "Now I *know* you done lost your mind!"

She grabbed Jasmine by the shoulders and they spun into the hallway. Jasmine tripped over the runner and fell onto the floor with Peggy on top of her.

Peggy got up, lifting Jasmine up by the shirt with her and shaking her. "Who the *hell* do you think you're talking to? Huh?"

Jasmine tried to smirk to signify that she was unmoved by this display, but Peggy could plainly see the fear in her eyes. She had never seen her aunt lose it before.

"And don't you ever raise your hands to me again—you hear me, Jasmine?" Peggy hollered. She raised her hand to hit her niece one more time to reinforce that notion when she was grabbed by her arm and pushed away. She lost her balance and teetered into the kitchen doorway, hitting her head.

Startled, she glared up at her husband. Apparently, he had sipped from the same cup of crazy that Jasmine had.

Carlos had just gotten his regular Saturday morning cut and was lounging in Amir's office. "I'm thinking about catching the Woodrow Wilson–Moorestown football game later. You down?"

Before Amir could say anything, the phone on his desk rang. The last button on the bottom was flashing. The only people that had the private number was family.

"Hello? Wh-what—Mom—huh?"

Carlos saw Amir's face flash alarm, then confusion, then anger. Carlos began to get scared that something really horrible had happened. Amir was the coolest cat that he knew, and he never let his emotions betray him. But whatever his mother was telling him, he was having a hard time keeping it together.

"All right, I'll be right over." Amir hung up and stared at the phone numbly.

Carlos waited for an explanation. When none came, he asked. "What's wrong? Is everybody okay?"

Amir slowly turned his gaze from the phone to Carlos. "Apparently, my father has just lost his mind." He sprang to his feet. "I gotta go to my parents' house." Amir opened his desk drawer and began fumbling through it. "Damn." He abruptly stopped his search and closed the drawer. "I forgot that Kenya dropped me off this morning. My truck is in the shop."

"My car is right outside," Carlos offered.

Amir started for the door. "Let's go."

Darius pulled his Sentra up to the front entrance of the Camden County Library. He could see right away by Jasmine's face that she was upset. He had also heard it in her voice earlier when she called him.

"Thanks for coming to get me," Jasmine said as she slid in.

"No problem," Darius said. "Where we going?"

"I haven't decided yet," Jasmine replied.

"Okay, we can just drive," Darius said, pulling out.

"Thank you."

"What's wrong?"

Jasmine looked out the window. "My aunt done lost her mind."

Darius didn't respond. Jasmine turned toward him. "She put her hands on me," she explained.

Darius glanced at her to see if he could see any evidence of such. "Word? Aren't you a little old for that?"

"I certainly think so," Jasmine said disgustedly.

"What did you say to set her off?" Darius asked.

Jasmine shook her head. She didn't feel like getting into it.

"If you don't want to talk about that, lemme ask you something else," Darius said. "Why did you call me?"

"What do you mean?"

"Did you call me just because you're angry and you need a ride?" Darius asked.

"No," Jasmine said. "I was on my way to the library when my aunt went apeshit on me. Once I got here, I was gonna call you and asked if you wanted to come meet me."

Jasmine forgot about her problems and focused on Darius. "I've been thinking about you this past week," she said sweetly.

"Yeah?"

"Yeah." Jasmine slid her hand into his. It felt good seeing him again. She was glad that he had come. That he didn't hold a grudge over their last phone call.

"You happy that I called?" Jasmine asked.

"You hungry?" Darius asked.

"A little."

"Let's go get something to eat. We can go to Elgin Diner."

"You didn't answer my question," Jasmine said.

"Didn't I?"

Jasmine loosened the grip on his hand. "No, you didn't."

Darius pulled up to a red light and reclaimed Jasmine's hand, clenching it tightly. "I've been missing you all week. I'm glad you called."

Jasmine smiled. She leaned over and gave Darius a peck on the cheek. Darius turned so that she would meet his lips instead. Then they kissed again, deeper and longer this time.

The first time Jasmine had kissed Darius, she was surprised by how adept he was. She had kissed a number of boys who went right for cupping her breast and jamming a tongue into the back of her throat. But Darius was soft and tender as his mouth explored hers. And wasn't in a rush, as if kissing was just a necessary means to get to a further more gratifying end. Jasmine hated that.

Darius was in no such hurry; it was as if he relished the very sweetness of her lips. Jasmine couldn't help but think about how skilled he must be with other areas of the female body.

They leaned toward each other again. Jasmine closed her eyes as Darius kissed her top lip, sucked on her bottom one, before kissing her fully while exploring her more than willing mouth with his tongue.

Jasmine heard Darius let out a groan of appreciation; or maybe that was her, she couldn't be sure.

Before they separated, Darius turned his head slightly so that he could feel the softness of Jasmine's cheek along his. He sat back up and smiled at her.

"Jasmine," Darius asked, as the light turned green, "why does it feel like I've known you longer than I have?"

"Maybe because you've been waiting your whole life for me," she said, a little dazed. Kissing Darius had made her feel warm and fuzzy inside.

Darius grinned at that. He then let out an audible yawn.

"You tired?" Jasmine asked.

"Yeah. We worked all night at the garage," Darius explained. "My cousin was really backed up. When you called, I had just been home an hour. I grabbed a quick shower and came and got you."

Darius smelled like soap. He looked great, too. He was wearing black, FUBU jeans and matching jacket, and had an oversize, gleaming-white T-shirt on underneath. On his head was a white skull cap.

"Well, why don't you take a nap?" Jasmine asked.

Darius looked at her like he couldn't have heard right. "Where am I supposed to take a nap?" he asked.

Jasmine shrugged. "We could get a room somewhere."

Darius looked over at her again. Their eyes met. When Darius saw Jasmine's face, he knew there was no misunderstanding.

chapter 10

Myles' eyes were still stinging with anger as he turned off 295 onto the Lawndale exit. He had just made the trip up from Maryland in record time. He had listened to no music, made no stops. Nothing distracted him from his appointed mission. Which was to whip his father's ass.

Marisa hadn't been home when Myles received his mother's frenzied call. She was at a conference in the city calling for the end of the government's trade embargo against Cuba.

As Myles pulled up to his parents' house, he saw Carlos' car out in front. Though he didn't see Amir's truck, Myles assumed that he was there, too. What he didn't know was why, if Carlos and Amir were there, his father's broken body wasn't already splayed in the front yard. But that was a situation that would soon be remedied.

Myles burst in the front door. The first person he spied was the person he was looking for. His father was halfway up the steps.

Myles went straight for him. "You wanna put your hands on my mother?"

As he threw a punch, Amir appeared out of nowhere and

126

grabbed his shoulder, so Myles was only able to get a glancing blow that nicked his father's chin.

Leonard stood his ground. He hadn't flinched when Myles had lunged at him, and now met the rage in Myles' eyes dead-on with a cool stare of indifference.

Myles gripped the stairway banister and worked to free himself from his brother, who had him in a half nelson.

"Get off me, 'Mir!"

By now, Carlos had joined Amir. He pried Myles' hand loose from the banister, and they began pulling Myles away.

As Myles struggled to get at his father, Leonard turned and began walking up the steps.

"Where you going—? Get off me!" Myles said, trying to shake Carlos and Amir loose.

They dragged him through the family room—knocking over an end table on the way—and pushed Myles into the laundry room. Less stuff in there to break. Carlos closed the door behind him.

"Calm down!" Amir yelled.

Myles was ready to fight *them* for not beating his father down before he got there. "What the fuck is wrong with y'all?"

"Calm down and we'll tell you what happened," Amir said, still catching his breath. He looked at Myles wearily. "You're a big bastard to be dragging around."

"Myles, I was at the shop with Amir when your mother called. Your father didn't hit your mother. He was trying to break up your mother and Jasmine—"

"Jasmine?"

"—and in the course of him doing that your mother lost her balance and fell."

Myles didn't believe it. He looked at Amir. "Jasmine wouldn't hit Mom."

"Maybe she didn't," Amir replied. "You know how Mom used to black out on us when we pushed her too far. If we tried to move or raised our hands to defend ourselves, she would just get madder."

Myles remembered his short phone conversation with his mother. "She told me Dad hit her."

Amir shrugged. "Again, you know how Mom gets when she gets like that. In her mind, maybe she thinks he did."

Myles leaned against the utility sink and tried to gather his thoughts. After a couple of moments he turned back to Amir and Carlos. "Where is Mom?"

"In the backyard, I think."

Myles peeked through the blinds of the laundry room. He saw his mother sitting on the wooden bench of the picnic table. It was chilly to be sitting outside, but she seemed oblivious to her surroundings. Her face was fraught with worry. The portable phone sat on the table in front of her.

Myles was taken aback when he saw her lift a cigarette to her mouth. His mother had given up smoking many years ago.

"Where's Jasmine?" he asked, closing the blinds.

When neither of them answered, Myles knew the answer to this question.

"She jetted, right?"

"Yeah," Carlos answered. "We don't know where she went."

And neither did his mother, and that was probably the cause of the cigarette in her hands. That also explained the presence of the phone. She had probably been on it since Jasmine had left, trying to pinpoint her whereabouts.

"You guys wanna go look for Jasmine?"

"We were waiting for you before we could start," Amir said. "If your conversation with Mom was anything like mine, I figured you would try to kill Dad when you got here."

Myles shook his head. "I wonder why she told me Dad was abusing and disrespecting her. That seems a strange choice of words to use to describe this."

"She said that to you?" Amir asked.

"Yeah."

Amir and Carlos looked at each other. They were each thinking the same thing. Amir subtly shook his head as a signal to Carlos to keep quiet.

Myles looked at them. "Maybe I should apologize to him."

"No, I don't think that's necessary, Myles," Amir said. "I'm sure he knows you were only looking out for Mom."

"By attacking my father, though? I think I should."

Amir put his hand on Myles' chest and blocked his path to the door. "Maybe later. Let the situation cool down. Let's focus on Jasmine right now."

Carlos knew that Amir didn't want Myles anywhere near his father or mother for fear of what might come out. If Myles found out that his father was cheating on his mother, then that inadvertent push Leonard had given her earlier would take on a whole new context. And then ten Amirs wouldn't be able to keep Myles from whipping his father's ass.

"You don't think one of us should stay here?"

"No, we can cover more ground if all of us go," Amir explained. "Besides, Kenya dropped the girls off at the babysitter," Amir said. "She's on her way over here now."

"All right," Myles said, stepping back. He headed to the back door, next to the utility sink. "I'm gonna just check on Mom before we go."

"Okay," Amir said hesitantly.

When Peggy saw Myles approach her, she was relieved to see him. It was one more thing she had been worrying about,

Myles driving up from Maryland with the stress that her phone call had put on him. Knowing how emotional he was, she was grateful to see that he had arrived safely.

"You know, lady, no answers to any of your problems are gonna be found in that cigarette."

Myles kissed his mother on the cheek and sat next to her.

"I know, I know." She looked at Myles, her eyes brimming with tears. "I'm sorry to bring you up here for this."

Myles rubbed his mother's back. "No, don't be. If something goes on, I want to know."

"Marisa with you?"

"No, she's away at a conference." Myles saw the worry in his mother's eyes. "Don't worry, we'll find Jaz. Carlos, Amir, and I are about to go out looking for her."

Peggy gave a weak smile. "Y'all are some good boys."

"We should be—you raised us. Well, not Carlos, but he's freeloaded enough meals off you to qualify."

Myles and Peggy heard a car pull up out front. They both grew hopeful, until they heard the alarm activate. That meant Kenya. Myles stood up. "Kenya's here. So me and the fellas are gonna hit the road."

"Okay," Peggy said, looking up at him disconsolately. Myles saw his mother's eyes sparkle with tears.

"Don't worry." He leaned over and kissed her on the cheek again, then made his way toward the back door.

Amir could tell by Myles' placid demeanor that his mother hadn't told him anything about his father's indiscretion. Then again, Amir didn't know if his mother knew.

"Well, Kenya's here," he said. "How you boys wanna do this?"

Myles looked at his friend. "Yo, 'Los, you don't have to get further involved in this mess. I'm sure you got better things you can be doing."

Carlos snorted. "Like I can just go about my merry business knowing Mrs. M is stressing like this. Y'all know I'm her third son."

Myles smiled.

As they walked into the living room Amir said. " 'Los, you take the Echelon Mall. I'll start with the Deptford Mall. Myles, you hit the park and the rec center in town. Keep your cell phones on, so we can stay in contact. We'll hit other places as we go along, if she isn't at any of these spots."

Peggy looked down at the pack of Newports on the table. She had found them in the back of the cleaning supplies closet in the laundry room. Who knew how old they were. What she did know was that she shouldn't be smoking them. She was only making a bad situation worse.

She adjusted the gray cloth coat that Kenya had draped about her shoulders. Through the window she could see Kenya in the kitchen, probably making her some soup. This after finding someone to watch the twins because she thought Peggy might need some company. Kenya was such a sweet person. Peggy hoped Amir knew how lucky he was to have her. She remembered a conversation she and Amir had had many years ago when he and Kenya were still dating. She had tried to explain to her son how important it was for a woman to believe in her man. How nothing in the world tore at a woman more than being betrayed by a man that she loved.

Maybe once she was done with Amir, she should have had the conversation with her husband, too.

A breeze blew some of the scattered fall leaves through the yard. Peggy watched them join their brethren in a pile along the house. Suddenly she shivered violently. She should go inside before she caught pneumonia. She wouldn't have to look at her husband's face—he had left a half hour ago, going God knows where.

God knew where, but Peggy had a strong suspicion she knew what. She just didn't know with who.

She took one last drag and put out the cigarette along with her previous notion. Leonard was probably going into the barbershop. Hell, somebody might as well go to work today. Amir was missing work, and she had canceled her appointments for the day as well. Even Leonard wasn't brazen enough to pull any shit on a day like today.

Peggy was holding out hope that this distance between her husband and her was some later-life phase that he was going through, and needed to work out on his own. Maybe he feared death. Maybe he feared loss of time, opportunity.

Though she would never admit it to anyone else—halfway didn't want to admit it to herself—she probably could forgive Leonard if he slept with another woman. As long as sex was all it was. And provided it helped return her husband to her. She knew men were nothing more than little boys who shaved. And like little boys, they wanted whatever they didn't have. If an encounter with a younger woman was needed to make Leonard feel that he was still worthwhile, she *might* be willing to swallow her pride and endure that. Might, she thought, because no woman truly knows how she's gonna react until she's in that position. She did know that men are the vainest creatures on the planet. And nobody was vainer than an old man.

It's not like she was some ogre. She was still an attractive woman. She just wasn't thirty-five anymore. She had a few more inches on her hips. And though she no longer colored it, she kept her salt-and-pepper hair in a stylish taper cut. She made sure she kept herself looking sharp. For her, not for Leonard. Her hair and nails stayed done. She watched what she ate—got on a low-carb diet whenever she needed to drop a few. After all, while aging is inevitable, aging gracefully can be a beautiful thing.

So she told herself that if Leonard felt he had to prove his manhood by procuring a woman who had less birthdays, then so be it. She would try and endure it. As long as he was discreet, she didn't *ever* hear about it and it was somebody who was anonymous and wasn't misguided into thinking there was more to it than sex. After a short time, if Leonard realized that she was just a woman, just like the woman he had at home, then she would be patient.

It was awful to think about. Most women would rather stick their head in the sand than face the reality that their man was likely to cheat on them at some point. However, Leonard and she had been together nearly forty years. And never once, that she knew of at least, had Leonard cheated on her. So, if humping some young floozy could help ensure her another twenty years, Peggy would take it. At least she *thought* she could. He, of course, had better use protection, and get checked out afterward.

And guess what, Leonard? After all that, your ass is *still* gonna be old. Younger pussy will do nothing to alter that reality, except maybe remind your tired ass of that fact when you realize you can't perform like you did when you were young. And what the hell did you really accomplish? So bring your broken-down self home to a woman who at least loves your old ass. What, did he think she was immune to feeling the sense of time growing short? Of missed opportunities? Wouldn't it be better to work through these things together, of sharing your feelings with the person who knows you better than anyone else on the planet?

Peggy had had enough of the chill and walked into the house. She looked at the clock on the DVD player in the den.

It was only two o'clock, but if she knew her niece, she had no intention of coming back willingly. Jasmine would never make the first overture. She was far too proud. And that pride was precisely what was causing Peggy to be afraid. It could lead Jasmine into thinking any crazy, dangerous scheme was desirable over going back to the house where she got her face slapped. Peggy closed her eyes and said a prayer, asking for Him to keep Jasmine safe. She rubbed her temple and tried to think of who else she could call. She wanted to find this child before it got dark.

She had already called Danae's house. Had spoken to Vanessa, who had seemed far too nosy about her reason for calling. Although Peggy had tried to keep the concern out of her voice, Vanessa had sensed that something was amiss if Peggy couldn't account for Jasmine's whereabouts. All nosy and prying—had the nerve to ask, "Is everything all right? Did you have a fight?" Peggy found the woman's concern preposterous. Did Vanessa really think she was going to put her family's business out there to a woman she barely knew?

Hell, now that she thought about it, Peggy wouldn't put it past the woman's knowing where Jasmine was and just not telling her. As immature as she acted, she might be the type to choose to side with a child rather than an adult who is looking out for the child's well-being.

Jasmine sat at the small desk in the Route 130 motel room and channel surfed, clicking the remote angrily. The anger at her Aunt Peg had been replaced by anger at Darius. She was wearing only her bra and panties and hadn't envisioned sitting there watching stupid-ass infomercials when she had suggested the idea of getting a room to Darius.

She looked over at Darius. He was under the covers of the queen-size bed, with his back to her, apparently sleeping.

Jasmine shook her head in disbelief. When she had proposed to Darius that they go somewhere so he could "take a nap," had he really taken her literally?

Again, she buckled down and tried to figure out what the problem was. Think, girl. You're sitting here in your lingerie offering yourself to a man who isn't taking advantage of it. What's the holdup?

Gay?

Jasmine looked over at Darius' sleeping form. Not likely, she quickly decided.

Birth control?

When Darius had gone into the motel office to get the room, Jasmine had gone through his glove compartment. She had seen condoms in there.

Not attracted to me?

Jasmine dismissed that notion as well. Not the way he gets worked up when she's kissing him. And speaking of that, she rejected the "embarrassed by his little pecker" argument because she had felt it pressed up against her and it seemed to be of a more than adequate size.

And speaking of his dick, if there was the off chance that something was wrong with it, she didn't think that would prevent Darius from sleeping with her. Especially if they were gonna use condoms. While she had sat through enough health classes to know condoms weren't foolproof in preventing STDs, she also figured most boys were too selfish and too horny to care.

That just left the "scared of pussy" possibility.

Darius? Jasmine straightened in her chair.

If anyone should be scared to death, it should be her. She's the one who had to pretend that she knew what she was doing with nothing but remembrances of soft porn Cinemax movies as her guide.

Could Darius be a novice? She was sure that he wasn't. He was too fine, too confident, too cocky around girls. Like when they had first met in the mall.

Was it all a front?

She decided to take one more stab at seeing if she could get a stab.

Jasmine turned off the television and walked over to the bed. Darius was still facing the window. She slid under the covers and draped her arm around Darius' waist and began kissing his shoulders and neck.

"Do you really want to sleep?" Jasmine purred.

Darius didn't respond. Not vocally. But when she slid her hand down to his boxers, she felt what his body thought of her presence. She wrapped her hand around the circumference of his rock-hard penis and gave it a gentle squeeze. She wanted to see and feel it sliding inside her.

Darius reached down, gently removed her hand, brought it up to his mouth, and kissed the back of it. Jasmine snatched her hand away and stared at the ceiling. She sucked her teeth. "All the guys who would kill to be in this position with me . . ."

". . . put together don't care for you the way I do, Jasmine." Darius finished. "Know that."

Jasmine was beyond perplexed. She lay there silently for a good five minutes.

"Go to sleep, Jasmine," Darius said softly. "Don't stress anymore, okay? Trust me."

Hell, at this point, a nap didn't sound too bad, because her head surely hurt.

She rolled back toward Darius and draped her arm back over him. Darius clutched it and held it close to his heart.

*   *   *

Marisa set her cell phone down and concentrated on the road. She was on her way home following a long day spent at the End the Embargo conference. She then had stopped by her office to pick up some prep material for her next show and ended up running her mouth with Cassandra for a while. Before she knew it, it was eleven thirty. She was dead tired and normally would be looking forward to spending some quiet time with Myles, but when she checked her cell phone messages during a break at the conference she found out he was in Jersey. Marisa had just called him and he had just finished filling her in on the events of the day. She couldn't say she was surprised to hear what had transpired. Jasmine and Ms. Peg both had strong personalities. It was just a matter of time before they collided.

Still, she was surprised to hear that Ms. Peg had lost it like that. Marisa had noticed her moodiness lately.

And Marisa had noticed too many cutting looks, too many short breaths, too many bit tongues whenever Mr. Lenny was in her presence. Or that he always found some reason to leave whenever the family was gathered. Maybe because his wife was less likely to cause a scene in front of everybody? To press as to where he was really going?

Marisa tabled the notion. Maybe it was just her lawyer's intuition acting up. Myles always said that she was too mistrustful of people. Too ready to look for pretense in everything and everybody. He often asked her, "Do you ever find anyone to be genuine?"

Honestly? No. To Marisa, everybody had an agenda—that's human nature. Myles was the closest thing she had ever encountered to a kind, pure soul. That's part of the reason she loved him. But damn, if he wasn't infuriating sometimes with his perpetual optimism and good nature. Marisa often wondered, how did he survive for twenty-eight years before she had come along to look out for him?

So Marisa couldn't help but wonder if Ms. Peg's losing it today had anything to do with her husband. She hadn't brought it up to Myles just now on the phone primarily because it was none of her business. And besides, she doubted if Myles would put any credence in her supposition. She loved her husband dearly, but reading people wasn't his strong suit.

Right now, though, the concern was Jasmine. Marisa tried to think like a seventeen-year-old. Where Jasmine might go if she wanted to get away. Where she would go to find the freedom that she craved.

The ringing of her phone interrupted her thoughts. Marisa picked it up.

"Hello?"

"Hello, Ms. Marrero-Moore?"

"Yes, it is. Who am I speaking to?"

"This is Donald Bell of Chesapeake Security, ma'am."

The private security force for the gated community that she and Myles lived in. Damn, did somebody break into the house?

"Yes?"

"Yes, ma'am, I am very sorry to bother you. Normally, it's not our policy to contact our residents when visitors who aren't on their list come by. However, we have a young lady here at the north gate who says that she is a relative of yours—"

"What's her name?" Marisa quickly asked.

"—and it's only because of her young age that we decided to contact you—"

"I understand, Mr. Bell. What's her name?"

"Jasmine Taylor."

So it was her. Marisa didn't know whether to be relieved or alarmed. How in the hell did Jasmine get all the way to Silver Spring?

"Mr. Bell, yes I do know her. I'm on my way home. I'll be there in about half an hour. Is that okay?"

"Yes, ma'am. Would you like for us to keep them here at the station until you've arrived?"

Them? Marisa didn't like the sound of that. "Yes, that will be fine. May I talk to her?"

"Yes, she's in the outer office. I'll gather her."

Marisa had thought Jasmine was in the room with him. Seizing the chance, she asked another question. "Mr. Bell, before you get her, is the other person accompanying her a male or female?"

"A male, ma'am. Looks about eighteen, nineteen."

"Thank you."

Who the hell was this man that Jasmine had rode all the way to Maryland with? Don't even tell me it was Darius.

Marisa made sure she kept her temper in check. She wanted to keep the proper modulation in her voice so as to not alarm Jasmine. She wanted Jasmine to feel cool, at least until she had her in her sights. Then she could finish the job that Ms. Peg had started that morning.

Seconds later, Jasmine was on the phone.

"Hi."

"Hi, Jasmine, are you okay?"

"Yes."

Marisa decided to hold off on asking Jasmine who was with her. "I'll be home in about half an hour."

"Okay," Jasmine paused. "Are you gonna tell the family I'm down here?"

"We'll talk when I get there, okay, Jasmine?"

"Yeah," she said sullenly.

"Okay. Please put Mr. Bell back on the phone."

"All right."

"Hello."

"Mr. Bell, Jasmine is a relative of mine. My family has been very concerned about her whereabouts. Please don't allow her to leave."

"Okay, Mrs. Marrero-Moore."

"Thank you."

As Marisa hung up, she decided to fill Peggy in on the news first. She voice-activated Myles' parents home.

Peggy answered. "Hello?"

Marisa could hear the constriction in her tone. Like she was having trouble speaking for fear of what she might hear.

"Hi, Ms. Peg, it's Marisa."

Peggy exhaled. "Hi, Marisa."

"I have some good news. Jasmine is down here."

Marisa heard the sound of Peggy slapping a table with her hand. "Thank you, Jesus!"

Marisa heard Peggy telling Kenya the good news.

"How is she, Marisa?"

"She sounds fine, Ms. Peg. I haven't seen her yet. She's being held by the security force at the housing community."

"Wha-what? Security? Is she in trouble?"

"No, the community that Myles and I live in has a private security force. Remember coming through the gates when you came down here?"

"Oh, oh, yeah, that's right."

"She's waiting at the station for me to get home. I'm about twenty minutes away. I just spoke with one of the officers."

"How she get down there?"

Marisa decided not to tell her that Jasmine was with some man. Not yet. She would have a fit right there on the phone. Marisa wanted to wait until she found out who it was. "I don't know yet, Ms. Peg. Maybe she took a train? You know Jasmine's pretty resourceful."

"She's pretty re-something, all right. I'm just so thankful that that child is safe, Marisa." Peggy breathed deeply again. "You just don't know . . ."

Marisa heard her voice quaver. She knew her mother-in-law was releasing a well of emotions that had probably been bubbling within her since that morning.

"Teenage girls can be difficult, Ms. Peg."

"Ain't it the truth. My boys never gave me this kind of difficulty." Peggy was quiet for a beat or two. "I know girls are different, though . . . and Jasmine even more so. She is angry because her mother ain't around. Angry because her father never wanted her. . . . And I lost myself today—I'm supposed to be her rock. I'm supposed to be the rock for everyone I love. The person they can depend on, the one who keeps the family together. I always want to be the one where the people I love can go when they're troubled. The safe haven. Jasmine especially needs that with all the craziness she's seen in her life, ya know?"

Marisa was surprised that Peggy was sharing all this with her. Though she was sure that Kenya was listening as well. Maybe it was for her benefit, too.

Peggy saw the headlights from a car pull into the driveway. "One of the guys is home, Marisa. I don't know if it's Amir, Myles, or Carlos. They've been out looking for Jasmine. Kenya, will you see who that is?" Peggy returned to the call. "Marisa, you're gonna have Jasmine spend the night down there?"

"Yes, I think that will be best. It's kinda late to be driving to Jersey."

"Maybe your husband will stay up here tonight," Peggy said. "He's been running around all over south Jersey. He's probably beat. He doesn't need to be trying to make that drive tonight either."

"Yeah, that would probably be best, too." Marisa noticed that Peggy hadn't mentioned *her* husband. Was he home? Out looking for Jasmine?

Peggy chuckled. "Isn't that something that she ran down there to you?"

"Well, I don't know if it was to me. She knows Myles is down here, too."

"Uh-uh," Peggy said. "Myles ain't nothing but an extension of me as far as Jasmine is concerned. You know Jasmine thinks you're the cat's meow."

It was Marisa's turn to chuckle.

"No, I'm serious. She really admires you." Peggy paused. "I only hope she has your work ethic, your drive. When she gets older, if she accomplishes half of what you have, I would be thrilled."

Wow. That was out of left field. Marisa had always had the impression that Peggy thought she should spend less time working and more time having babies. Maybe it was the ebullience over the news of Jasmine's safety that brought that out, but it sure had sounded heartfelt.

Marisa didn't know what to say.

"Thank you, Ms. Peg."

"You're welcome. I sure hope someday that you have some children of your own."

So much for the happy feelings, Marisa thought.

"It's on my to-do list," she snapped.

"Don't misunderstand me, dear. I'm just saying that I believe you would be as good with your own kids as you are for Jasmine. I want you to experience that."

More like you don't want me to deprive Myles of being a father, Marisa thought. Or you of more grandchildren.

Marisa knew *her* fulfillment was way down on Ms. Peg's priority scale.

"Motherhood completes a woman," Peggy continued.

What kind of antiquated thinking is that? Marisa wondered. "Ms. Peg, I feel I'm already com—"

"Awww, is that my doodle! C'mere, Doodlebug!"

Marisa realized that CJ had arrived and that Ms. Peg wasn't paying her any mind. After all (as Ms. Peg had made sure she loudly proclaimed), a toddler was now in the house. Living proof that some women still procreated, though her "incomplete" daughter-in-law apparently couldn't be bothered.

"Here you go, Jackie. Marisa's on the phone."

"Hey, girl."

Marisa set aside her brimming anger at Ms. Peg. "Hey, Jackie."

"So Jasmine is down there, huh? After scaring everybody to death. Carlos, 'Mir, and Myles have been out all day looking for her—Kenya, do the guys know that she's safe yet?"

Kenya took out her cell phone. "I'm calling them right now to tell 'em to come on home."

"Tell Carlos I'm over here," Jackie said.

"All right." Kenya walked into the living room where the reception was better.

"Well, I'm not done being scared yet," Marisa said. "Don't tell Ms. Peg, but Jasmine came down here with some man."

"What?" Jackie said in a harsh whisper. "Don't even tell me it's Darius."

"I don't know yet," Marisa said. "They're waiting for me at one of the security stations at my complex."

"I'm'a hurt that girl myself," Jackie said.

"Take a number. Line forms to the left."

*   *   *

"This is a nice place you got here, Marisa." Darius peeked into Marisa's piano room, nodding his head.

Darius and Jasmine had both used the bathroom and had gotten something to drink. They were all now gathered in the living room.

Marisa had been giving Jasmine the once-over since they had entered the house. She seemed okay. She found herself looking at Jasmine's hair to see if it was tousled. Whether her clothes were rumpled. Marisa made eye contact with her to see if she could stare a telltale look of embarrassment out of her, but none was forthcoming.

Marisa felt like her aunt Esther. She used to give her the evil eye whenever Marisa came home a second past when she was supposed to. Marisa wondered if she was making Jasmine feel the way her aunt Esther used to make her feel. Like the devil had a private suite in the fifth ring of hell with her name already engraved on the door.

In any case, Darius wouldn't be staying. Marisa had told the security people to stop back in twenty minutes and if Darius' car wasn't gone by then to knock on the door.

"Darius, I would like to thank you for bringing Jasmine all the way down here from New Jersey."

"No problem," Darius said.

Jasmine knew that Marisa was upset that she was with Darius. She was debating on whether to ask Marisa for a moment alone so she could talk to her.

"Well, Darius"—Marisa picked up her purse—"I want to thank you again for bringing Jasmine to me." She took out two hundred-dollar bills. "Please take this for gas, tolls, and your time."

Jasmine looked at Marisa like she was crazy. "Why can't he stay here tonight and leave in the morning?"

Marisa pulled out another hundred-dollar bill. "He can get a hotel room nearby. I want to talk to you alone." She laid the three bills on the end table and sat down on the couch.

Jasmine sucked in a sharp breath. She was about to say something else, but Darius spoke first. "Marisa, I know you care about Jasmine, and I can respect that. I care about Jasmine, too. I know you would have no way of knowing that, nor do I know what you have heard about me, but . . ." Darius caught himself and exhaled. "You can keep your money."

Darius and Marisa exchanged unblinking stares. Finally, he turned toward Jasmine. "Don't worry, J, I'll be close by. Just give me a call on my celly in the morning if you need anything."

He walked over to where Marisa was sitting and extended his hand. "Nice meeting you."

"Likewise," Marisa said. "Excuse me."

Darius backed away so that she could stand up.

Marisa noticed that Darius had that cocked sideways grin that celebrities like Eve and Kobe Bryant had perfected. He gave Jasmine a wink and nod before he headed out the room.

As Jasmine and Marisa walked him to the foyer, the light from a Chesapeake Armed Response cruiser pulled into the driveway and flooded the window.

Darius gave Marisa a smirk over his shoulder. "You must've left something at the station."

Marisa had been busy looking down at the scuff marks that Darius' Timberlands were leaving on her floor. She saw the cruiser.

Marisa said innocently, "Must have. Or maybe they came to get something from me."

Jasmine just stared at Marisa with her mouth open. Marisa could tell she was losing cool points with Jasmine at a record pace.

"Well, good night."

"I'll call you in the morning, Darius." Jasmine turned around and stalked into the living room.

Marisa could deal with that. Stalk all you want, as long as it's in the house. This character was still leaving.

After Darius had pulled out and Marisa had had a brief conversation with Officer Bell and his partner, she took a deep breath and readied herself for her showdown with Jasmine.

When she walked back into the living room, Jasmine was sitting on the couch petting Winston. "You remember me, pupper?" Jasmine asked while she stroked his neck.

Before Marisa could say anything, the phone rang. She picked it up off of the coffee table. "Hello? . . . Yeah, babe, she's here . . . yeah, she's fine . . . Your mom?"

Marisa saw the look of discomfort on Jasmine's face. "Tell your mother we'll call her first thing tomorrow morning, okay? Jasmine's tired."

Jasmine looked relieved.

"All right, bye, babe." Marisa clicked off the phone.

"Thanks," Jasmine said.

Marisa stood in front of her. She in fact did look tired. Marisa decided the talk she wanted to have with Jasmine could wait until the morning. She motioned for Jasmine to follow her.

"C'mon, let's go to bed. I'll get you some pajamas."

Peggy stood at the entrance to her bedroom. Her husband was sitting on the edge of the bed taking off his socks.

"So, Jasmine went all the way to Maryland, huh?"

Peggy walked into the room, raising her eyebrows in mock shock. "Oh, so you do care about the events of the day? What goes on in this family?"

Leonard stood up and diligently folded his socks before addressing his wife. "I was looking for Jasmine, too."

"Oh." Peggy sat in the reading chair and faced him expectantly. "Between beers at Starks you asked the boys had they seen her?"

Leonard walked over and closed the bedroom door, then faced his wife. "I didn't go to Starks today," he said in a collected tone. "I went to the police station and told Butch about Jasmine. He told me that while it was far too early to issue a missing-persons report, he would keep an eye out for her. He also called a few of the neighboring vicinities and asked that they do the same since I was able to tell them what she was wearing when she stormed out of here." Leonard opened the bureau. "Then I drove around to some places that I thought she might be. After that, I went to work, figuring I could ask the young brothers that came in had they seen her anywhere around town. More eyes that way, ya know?"

"That explains why you're not getting home until midnight? You were cutting hair by moonlight?"

"After I closed the shop, I called Amir on his phone. I knew Jasmine hadn't come home yet. I went back to the police station and updated them—seeing if they could press the issue because it was now dark. Then I got in my car and drove around some more, looking for her. When Amir called me and told me that she was in Maryland, I came home."

Peggy was a little embarrassed by her husband's thoroughness. "Well, it was your fault that she stormed out of here in the first place."

Leonard looked up at the ceiling and snorted. "Ha."

"No, I mean it, Lenny. I had the situation well in hand—"

He looked over his shoulder. "Is that what you call it?"

Peggy ignored him. "—before you threw me like a bale of

147

cotton. That's what really frightened the child." She walked over to him. "Not me giving her a much-needed ass whipping."

"Peggy, I done told you that I was sorry about being so rough—"

"And how come you didn't let the boys know that you went to the police station and all? Coordinate your efforts with them?"

Leonard finished putting on his pajama top and snorted again.

She hated when her husband did that stupid, condescending snort. Like everybody around him was dimwitted and he was brilliant.

"You mean with my son that had just attacked me because he thinks I'm abusing his mother?" Leonard brushed past her on the way to the bathroom. "Myles could barely look at me downstairs just now."

"You are," Peggy said quietly.

chapter 11

Marisa opened the door to the guest bedroom. It was still early, but she wanted to talk to Jasmine before the family started calling from Jersey. To her surprise, Jasmine wasn't sleeping, but lying in bed staring at the ceiling.

"Good morning."

"Morning."

Marisa and Winston came into the room. Marisa sat on the bed while Winston sniffed along the perimeter.

"You had a lot of people worried yesterday, Jaz. Was that your intention?"

"My intention was to get away from my crazy aunt." Jasmine faced Marisa with an angry pout. "She attacked me."

"Why did Ms. Peg hit you?"

"Because she's psycho. Needs to be locked up somewhere."

"So, just for no reason she woke up and said, 'I think Jasmine needs her ass kicked today.'"

"Yeah," Jasmine answered, her eyes widening, "crazy people don't need a reason."

Marisa gave her a "you know better" look.

Jasmine sighed. "Well, we kinda had words first. But

that's no excuse for her to launch herself on me like something out of *The Matrix*."

"I agree," Marisa said, picking a piece of lint out of Jasmine's hair and letting it fall to the floor. "So tell me, what did you say that caused such a reaction?"

Jasmine flushed with embarrassment and turned away.

Marisa tapped her shoulder. "Um, I'm over here. Surely, you don't mind repeating it—since it was nothing that could've possibly warranted such a response from Ms. Peg."

Jasmine drew a deep breath and turned back to Marisa. "Well, a while back Aunt Peg told me I could stay at Danae's house Satur—last night."

"Okay."

"Well, anyway, yesterday morning she acted like she didn't say it. Saying she"—Jasmine mimicked her aunt's voice—"thought I asked if I could stay at Teresa's house."

"Well, maybe she did."

Jasmine brought her hands out from underneath the comforter. "What's the difference?"

Marisa shrugged. "I suppose the answer lies in the difference your aunt has in her comfort level between Teresa's house and Danae's house." She noticed Jasmine's eyes drop at that statement. "Is there a reason for that?"

Jasmine sat up in the bed. "She thinks there is. Danae's mom is mad cool. She's just a new face in that incestuous, nosy, backwater town."

Marisa stifled a laugh. She wondered if Jasmine even knew how sharp she was. She was going to have to remember that description the next time Myles bragged about his historic hometown.

"Aunt Peg's problem is that she's old," Jasmine said dejectedly. "Danae's mom is only thirty-two."

"First of all, fifty-nine isn't old," Marisa corrected. "Second of all, living long enough to be considered old isn't 'a problem'—it's a blessing."

"Yeah, well, it is if you distrust any and all things younger than you," Jasmine said, refusing to yield.

Marisa curled her lip at the suggestion. She wondered if in her slick way, Jasmine wasn't also referring to her rough condemnation of Darius. "I wanna tell you a quick story." She patted Jasmine on the knee and stood up.

"When I was fifteen, I was in a position similar to you," Marisa said as she walked over and picked up Jasmine's jeans off of the floor. "I was without my parents and was being raised by my aunt Esther and uncle Eli. To be more specific, they were my great-aunt and great-uncle, so they were a great deal older than me."

Jasmine reactively flung her fingers in the air. "So you know my pain? My struggle?"

"Oh, I know more than that." Marisa draped the pants on the back of a chair. "So anyway, one time I asked my aunt Esther if I could go with my friend Sharon's family to their cabin for the weekend. I didn't see how it was going to be a problem. Sharon's family—the Gables—were active in our church. My aunt Esther knew them well. And in fact, when I asked her, she did say yes."

Jasmine brought her knees up to her chest. Marisa sat back down on the bed.

"Now, what my aunt didn't know was that there was a family with a couple of cute teenage boys a couple of cabins down that Sharon was going to introduce me to." Marisa scrunched her face up and shook her head. "I didn't feel my aunt needed to know all that."

"I wholeheartedly agree," Jasmine said, nodding.

"So you *know* I was looking forward to it. You think Ms. Peg is strict? Shoot, she runs a country club compared to the prison warden that was my aunt Esther. I'm talking serious lockdown."

Jasmine allowed herself a chuckle.

"I'm glad you think it's funny, wasn't nothing about it humorous to me then, believe me. Well, anyway, the day of the trip, I was packed and raring to go. When the Gables—Mr. and Mrs. Gable, Sharon, and her younger brother, Samuel—came by to get me . . ." Marisa looked at Jasmine. "Do you know my aunt came out of her house and told them, 'Marisa isn't going.' "

"What?"

"Yep. She said . . ." Marisa closed her eyes as she tried to recall the exact words, "that an emergency had arisen and that I would have to stay behind." Marisa opened her eyes and smiled at Jasmine. "The only emergency I could think of was me going into cardiac arrest."

"You know," Jasmine agreed. "Why did she do that?"

Marisa shrugged. "She never told me why."

"Shoot." Jasmine kicked the covers off and threw her legs over the edge of the bed. "She would have had to tell me *something*."

"She didn't have to tell me anything." Marisa paused a few beats. "I was too grateful when the news came that the Gables' car had gone into that ravine and that my friend and her family were all dead."

The color left Jasmine's face. Marisa nodded to let her know she was telling the truth.

Marisa stood up and looked at Winston lazing by the foot of the bed. "Maybe my aunt smelled alcohol on Mr. Gable's breath. Saw something suspicious. Maybe just intuition, I don't know—we never talked about it." She leaned against the dresser and folded her arms. "Maybe Ms. Peg has her reasons, too."

Jasmine twisted her mouth and stared at the wall.

That was an interesting reaction, Marisa thought as she studied her. "You wouldn't know of any possible reasons, would you?"

Jasmine raised and dropped her shoulders.

"Is Danae's father around?"

Jasmine shook her head. She stood up abruptly and put on the bathrobe hanging from the bedpost. "Do you have a toothbrush I can use?"

"In the medicine cabinet in the guest bathroom. What does Jasmine's mother do for a living?" Marisa asked.

Jasmine tightened the belt, not answering.

"Is it that incriminating?" Marisa asked.

Jasmine stuffed her hands in the robe's pockets. "She's an entertainer."

"Ahh, the plot thickens."

"Why? She isn't doing anything illegal."

"Nor did I say she was," Marisa said. "I just want a clar-ification. By entertainer, do you mean like lead cellist for the Philadelphia Philharmonic? Performing artist? Mime?"

"C'mon, Marisa, you know what I mean."

"And if she's a dancer, then just who was going to be the adult supervision in that house last night? Or is she the only stripper in the world who doesn't work Saturday nights?"

Jasmine opened her mouth to mount a defense, but de-cided that trying to offer a response would only make matters worse. "Sometimes I forget you're a lawyer," she grumbled.

"You're a trip," Marisa said, shaking her head. "You al-most had me feeling sorry for you."

"Mari—"

"And what exactly did you say to set your aunt off yes-terday?" She saw the hesitation in Jasmine's face. "You might as well come clean with it now. Don't make me ask Ms. Peg."

Jasmine shut her eyes. When she spoke, her voice was subdued, "I told her that she shouldn't take it out on me just because her husband didn't want her."

Marisa gasped. She hadn't been prepared for that. Marisa felt like popping Jasmine herself. She recovered, though, and stepped to the side, pointing to the bedroom door.

"Leave my house immediately."

Jasmine looked up to see if Marisa was serious. When she saw how impassive her face was, she began tearing up.

Marisa let Jasmine suffer for a couple of more seconds before she brought her to her and gave her a hug. Jasmine was really crying now. If Marisa's suspicions about the rift between Mr. and Mrs. Moore were correct, she could imagine how much Jasmine's comments had stung her.

"I know I was wrong," Jasmine said, sobbing.

Marisa held her for a while longer and tried to soothe her. She then led her over to the nightstand and picked up a couple of tissues. "Wipe your face off, Jazzy."

Jasmine took the tissues and began drying her tearstained cheeks. She sat back down on the bed. Marisa sat Indian-style on the rug in front of her.

"There's another matter I want to discuss with you, and that is this Darius person."

Jasmine sniffled. "I figured that."

"I thought you were gonna leave him alone," Marisa said. "Isn't that what you told me, Kenya, and Jackie in your room last weekend?"

"Yeah."

"So what happened?" Marisa asked. "You needed a ride and forgot about your agreement?"

"No," Jasmine said defensively. "I really care for him."

Is that supposed to make me feel better? Marisa thought. She'd rather Jasmine was just using him for a ride.

"And you know you care for him already?" Marisa asked like the notion was absurd.

"How long did it take Myles to realize it with you?" Jasmine rejoined.

Marisa ignored Jasmine's question. "So you lied to us, then?"

"Marisa, it's not right for them to twist my arm not to see someone because they don't like him."

"They know him a lot better than you do, Jasmine."

"And even they admitted he hasn't been in trouble in years," Jasmine responded. "How long are we supposed to hold someone's past against them? He was just a child."

"So you know more than Kenya and Jackie?" Marisa asked.

"Did Kenya know more than her mother when she advised her to dump Amir back when they were dating?" Jasmine asked. "Did Myles listen when people were telling him to forget about you when y'all were dating?"

Touché, Marisa thought. "But Myles and Kenya were a lot older than seventeen."

"Yeah, and they still had people trying to tell them what to do," Jasmine said. "Me being seventeen doesn't make me wrong and Kenya and Jackie right."

Marisa conceded that. "No, it doesn't." She also realized that she needed to change her approach. Jasmine was too filled with resolve.

"I tell you what," Marisa said. "If you care about Darius, then you should come above board with him."

"What do you mean?" Jasmine asked.

"No more sneaking around. Present him to the family. Have him meet your aunt and uncle, and Amir and Myles."

That thought stopped Jasmine dead in her tracks. "What about Kenya and Jackie?" she asked slowly.

155

"Cut them off at the knees. Prove that their opinion of Darius is based on his past not his present. Show the new Darius."

Jasmine nodded. "Intriguing. Give me some time to do it?"

"Okay, I'll give you a couple of days, but that's it." Marisa paused. "Jazzy, understand something. You know all of us love you, but you scare us because you have just enough sense to get yourself into some real trouble."

Jasmine digested those words before speaking. "Maybe I can come live with you and Myles."

"Why? Because you think you can get over on us?"

"No." Jasmine scratched her arm reflexively. "Because Aunt Peg doesn't want me."

"Doesn't want you?" Marisa said. "Myles told me that she's been trying to get custody of you since you were five years old, Jasmine."

"Only because she thinks that's what she's supposed to do, because she's a goodhearted person. But she doesn't want me."

Marisa scrutinized the teenager, who was feeling sorry for herself. "Listen, Jazzy, do you believe that? Or is that just something you thought to say that might elicit the wanted response from me?"

Jasmine opened her mouth to protest, but fell silent instead.

"Stop being manipulative," Marisa insisted. "You know full well that your aunt loves you, so spare me."

Jasmine shifted her weight. "So your answer is no?"

"Jasmine, you know I love you to death. This room and this house is waiting for you. For when you go to Georgetown, Coppin State, Howard, University of Maryland, or whatever college you want to go to in this area, should you choose to do so. Myles and I will even let you have use of one of the cars, should you prove responsible enough—which I fully expect you will. But right now you need your aunt, and as outlandish as it might sound to your ears, I believe your aunt needs you."

Jasmine looked at her strangely.

"You're a bright girl. I trust you'll figure it out." Marisa looked at Winston strolling out of the room. He probably needed to be let outside.

"Let's go downstairs."

After letting Winston out into the backyard, Marisa and Jasmine watched him run down the steps of the expansive wooden deck, frolic around in the chilly morning air, then lift his leg against a tree to do his business.

"So are you gonna call Darius at the hotel and tell him you won't be needing a ride back to Jersey?" Marisa asked.

"I called him late last night," Jasmine said. "No need for him to be spending money on a—a hotel room." Geesh, Jasmine thought, that was close. She had almost said "on another hotel room."

"Um, speaking of Darius," Jasmine said, sidling up to Marisa, "there's no reason to tell the Moores how I got down here, is there?"

Marisa laughed harshly and headed for the kitchen. Jasmine was in hot pursuit.

"Come on, Marisa," Jasmine said, nudging her with her elbow like they were old bar buddies. "Why upset Aunt Peg needlessly?"

Marisa took two glasses out of the cupboard and set them on the granite top island. "Don't worry, I won't tell Ms. Peg."

Jasmine relaxed a bit.

"Because you're going to introduce him to the family anyway," she said, opening the refrigerator and taking out a pitcher of orange juice. "But I am gonna tell Myles about how you got down here."

Jasmine stamped her foot. "Marisa," she whined.

"Why shouldn't I?" Marisa asked. "Surely you're not asking me to keep secrets from my husband."

"Myles doesn't know everything about you."

"Sure he does," Marisa said, taking a sip.

"He knows everybody you've ever been intimate with?"

Marisa stifled a chuckle and put down her glass. "Right there is an example of you knowing just enough to say just the wrong thing, to get yourself in trouble."

Jasmine pushed her glass aside and hopped onto the counter. "Marisa, I just want you to know, regardless of Darius, or anybody else, I don't plan on being a fool for no man. If Darius doesn't come correct, he will be cut loose."

Marisa nodded as she took a sip.

"Nor am I trying to emulate Vanessa—"

"Who?"

"Danae's mom. The exotic dancer. She's flashy and jiggles in all the right places, and has a wardrobe straight from a music-video set. She knows men fall down over her, and she uses her looks to get what she wants from them. I certainly wouldn't choose that as a lifestyle like she has. I see her make a fool of men, but it comes at a price. Her self-respect. And my whole life, I've seen men make a fool of my mother, and she's paid dearly. Still is."

Jasmine gazed at the floor. Marisa waited for her to finish.

"Neither is the path I want to choose. I want to be fly as hell—but not make money using my body. I want to be able to entice men—but not need their money. I want to be smarter than men, richer than men, more successful than men. Not need them for jack, other than to love me *if* I so decide I want to be loved. Or amuse me if I so decide I want to be amused." Jasmine looked up. "Like you."

Marisa's mouth came agape. "Like me? I don't know whether to be flattered or insulted."

Jasmine smiled. "You married Myles 'cause he amuses you."

"You should quit while you're ahead." Marisa sighed, tapping the rim of her orange juice glass, thinking over what she wanted to say. "Listen, Jazzy, here's what I want from you."

Jasmine gripped the edge of the counter and girded herself.

"*A*. No more antagonizing your Aunt Peg by pretending you don't have any sense. For instance, you know you're going to college, as do I, so cut it out. Okay?"

Jasmine chuckled. "Agreed."

"*B*. Continue to make the honor roll in school. No slippage allowed."

Jasmine blew on her nails. "I can make the honor roll in my sleep."

"*C*." Marisa's face turned serious. "Tell the family about you and Darius."

Jasmine nodded. There was silence in the room as her heels softly bounced against the island.

Marisa admired the way Darius had handled himself last night, refusing to take the money and all. Still, she could see why Kenya and Jackie would have reservations. He had a definite assholeness about him.

"You hear me?" Marisa repeated.

"Yes," Jasmine said, looking up and meeting her gaze.

"Now, this is me you're talking to now." Marisa walked over close to her. "Don't try and play me, Jasmine. I'm somebody that you want to keep on your side. We understand each other?"

Jasmine nodded again.

"And if you do that, then maybe you can spend the summer down here with me and Myles. Give your Aunt Peg a much needed break from you."

Jasmine grinned.

Marisa smiled with her. "We'll have a ball, shopping, going to movies, restaurants, plays . . . just keep up your end of the deal."

"No problem," Jasmine assured her.

Winston barked from the deck.

"Oh, and I didn't mention you apologizing to your aunt Peg for what you said and dutifully accepting whatever punishment she administers," Marisa said.

Jasmine hopped off of the island and put her hands up. "Tut-tut, you didn't mention it because you didn't have to mention it."

"Thata girl," Marisa said, smiling.

Winston yapped again.

Marisa gave her a hug. "Let's go out to eat," she suggested.

"Cool by me." Jasmine sighed. "Though I was looking forward to the maid serving me breakfast in bed."

Marisa laughed. "The maid only comes two days a week and she doesn't serve breakfast in bed."

"The cook does?"

"Sometimes, when I can talk him into it. The cook is Myles."

"What?"

"Hey, Myles can burn."

"It's just that I thought you people were down here living *large*," Jasmine said.

"Well, we do plan on bringing someone in to cook us breakfast in bed every morning."

"Yeah, when?"

"Next summer when you come down to stay with us," Marisa said casually.

"Really?" Jasmine asked.

"Yep. And just so you know, I like my eggs *tightly* scrambled."

Jasmine leaned her head back and cackled. "No, you didn't just tell me how you liked your eggs."

Marisa joined her in laughter. "Uh-oh, I can see right now that you don't wanna work."

Jasmine stopped and put her hand on Marisa's arm. "Thanks. For listening, for everything."

Marisa smiled. "You're welcome." This child had no idea how much she reminded her of herself.

"Come on," Marisa said, draping an arm over her shoulder and leading her out of the kitchen. "Let's go let the other male I keep around here to amuse me back into the house."

chapter 12

Sunday morning, Peggy sat down next to her husband as he ate the breakfast she had prepared for him. She had just returned from the early-morning service at Bethel Baptist, where she had given thanks to Him for keeping Jasmine safe. She had asked her husband if he wanted to go, but he mumbled that he was too tired. His ass was tired, all right.

Sometimes she felt guilty for complaining. Leonard had provided everything he had promised when they were courting, save for Etta James. He had given her two wonderful sons, a great house, a successful business, and a lifestyle a thousand times better than her mother had had, God rest her soul.

When the boys were children, they had had some wonderful times. Family vacations in the summer. Weekends in Wildwood.

But she didn't realize that in their golden years Leonard would go his way and she hers. She had assumed that everything would remain the same, they would just be doing things as a pair now. And would still occasionally do things as a family, with the grandkids filling the roles once occupied by their now-grown children.

What bothered her more than anything was that Leonard apparently wasn't bothered by the distance between them. He went about his daily business like nothing was wrong.

How much poker could a man play? How many fight nights? How many must-see football, basketball, and baseball games should take precedence over one's wife? How much time did a man Leonard's age need to spend with "the boys"? She feared that he simply didn't find her interesting anymore. Wasn't interested in her thoughts, her feelings, or in having a conversation of any length with her.

So bearing all that in mind, she was starting to dislike the sex that she and Leonard had recently been having. She had assumed it would be accompanied by an overall return of intimacy. A recommitting of their partnership. An evolving of their relationship to the point when they could grow old together. And not just living together, but *together*.

But as she watched her husband reading his *Sunday Inquirer* and devouring his fried egg and bacon sandwiches, she knew she was fighting an uphill battle. In his way of thinking, they were spending quality time with each other now. Why complicate matters by having an actual conversation?

"Myles already left, huh?" she asked, taking a sip of her coffee.

Leonard nodded.

"Are you gonna go with me to Philly to pick up Jasmine?"

Leonard grunted. Peggy had long ago realized that was his not-so-endearing way of saying that he had heard her and the answer was yes.

She couldn't believe that he was acting like everything was status quo. Like nothing traumatic had happened yesterday. Not even reminding him that Jasmine had run all the way to Maryland had moved him from his newspaper.

"Is it possible for you to put that newspaper down for

three seconds?" Peggy asked. "I feel like I'm talking to a caveman."

Leonard sighed like he was dealing with a spoiled child, which aggravated Peggy to no end. "Peggy, if you see that I'm reading the paper, then why are you trying to talk to me?"

She glared at him. "And whatever is in that paper is more important than anything I could possibly have to say, right?"

"I didn't say that. . . ."

"And if you're not reading the paper, then you're watching TV and don't want to be interrupted—though, then at least I have a shot of catching you on the way to the bathroom during commercials," Peggy continued angrily. "Most of the time you aren't even home."

"You're overstating it a bit, aren't you?"

She rose from her chair and put her mug in the sink with a clang.

Leonard set the newspaper aside. "What do you want to talk about? I know, let's talk about whether Jasmine is eating enough. That's always a favorite of yours, right? Let's go over all her meals from the past week."

This sarcasm pricked her more than he knew. It went directly to her fear that she wasn't interesting enough to him. She folded her arms across her chest.

"Go to hell, Leonard."

"Oh, someone is full of Christian fellowship," Leonard said. "Is that what the good righteous doctor reverend taught you in service this morning?"

Peggy regretted that she had been considerate enough to cook him breakfast after service. She also thought about how good it would feel to take a fork and poke him in his smug, balding pate.

But she wasn't getting into it with Lenny's ignorant self today. She had to change clothes.

"No," she said crisply, "he taught me that the Enemy comes in many forms, sometimes from those closest to you."

"Uh-oh." Leonard chuckled with bemusement. "I guess the rev better keep his eye on his limo driver, then."

Keep laughing, jackass, Peggy thought. You'll wish it was just my fork when Ol' Slewfoot is jabbing you in the ass with his pitchfork.

Peggy decided not to let Leonard upset her any further. She needed to go upstairs and get out of this dress. She walked over to the table and calmly scooped up the newspaper.

"What are you—"

Peggy snatched the section he was reading out of his hand. It tore, leaving him a three-inch piece of print in his hand. She decided to let him keep it.

She stuffed the newspaper in the trash can. Then poured bacon grease all over it lest he get any ideas.

"Real nice, Peggy, real nice. What's wrong with you?"

Oh, *now* he wants to talk.

She walked out of the kitchen without a word.

Myles entered the den to see Marisa and Winston watching a rerun of *Law & Order*. He came up behind the couch.

"Hey, pretty girl," he said, smiling.

Marisa leaned her head back with her lips puckered. Myles bent over and gave her a kiss. He lovingly wrapped his hands around his forearms and gave her a hug.

As Myles released her, Marisa shifted on the couch and patted the leather. "Come sit next to me."

Myles came around and motioned at the TV. "Did I miss Detective Briscoe's wisecrack yet?"

"Yeah," she said as she leaned her body into Myles, "but don't worry, you'll catch the next one. TNT is running a marathon."

"Oh, boy," Myles said derisively, knowing what a fan Marisa was of the show.

She snuggled closer to Myles, burrowing her head into his chest. "Sorry if it doesn't have the same panache as one of your Steven Seagal flicks. We can try to find one of those so you can watch it for the billionth time."

"Don't sleep on Seagal," Myles said. "The man says more with a squint than most actors can with a soliloquy. I don't know why the Academy keeps overlooking his many fine efforts."

"An oversight, I'm sure," Marisa said. Reaching over to the small TV table, she picked up the remote and turned the television off.

"Why did you do that?"

"I've seen that episode before," Marisa said. "Let's talk."

Myles kicked off his shoes and lay more supine on the couch. He slid his hand underneath Marisa's sweats and started rubbing her behind.

"Yeah, this isn't bad at all."

"I said talk."

Myles brought his hand out and placed it on her hip. "I don't think I could muster up any acts of perversion today anyway. Not after yesterday's drama."

"So fill me in what happened yesterday?" she asked.

"What do you mean?"

"When I got the message that you were driving up to Jersey, I could tell you were pissed off. What happened when you first got there?" Marisa asked.

"I took a swing at my dad."

Marisa sat upright. "Are you serious?"

"I thought he had hit my mother," Myles said defensively. "When my mom called down here yesterday, she made it sound like he had just dragged her down Warwick Road by her hair."

"Really?"

"Yeah. All he had done was pull her off Jasmine . . ." Myles shrugged. "I don't know why she exaggerated so much."

Based on what Jasmine had said, and her own suspicions, Marisa had an idea.

"So before this could be explained, you went in and roughed up your father?"

"I thought—you didn't hear the phone call from my mother," Myles said, more than a little embarrassed. "Amir and Carlos stopped me anyway."

"Lord. Carlos was there?"

"Yeah, he had been getting a haircut in Amir's shop, so when my mom called Amir with her tale of woe, Carlos drove him over. 'Los helped us look for Jasmine, too. Where is she anyway?" Myles asked sitting upright as well. "She's the one who started all this nonsense yesterday.

"I put her on a train back home."

"I wish you had waited until I got here. I wanted to talk to her."

"I think she was precisely trying to avoid that," Marisa said, taking a sip of her iced tea. "Don't worry. I had a long talk with her. I told her she could stay with us next summer if she kept on the straight and narrow. Is that cool?'

"Yeah, it's cool by me." Myles just hoped his mother didn't have a problem with it. "How did she get down here, anyway?"

"She rode down with Darius."

"Who is Darius?" Myles asked suspiciously.

"A guy Jasmine has been seeing."

"What?" Myles asked. "I've never heard of any Darius."

"She's seventeen years old, Myles," Marisa said. "You don't think she dates boys who can drive? Don't worry, you'll be meeting Darius soon. Jasmine and I spoke about that."

Myles grumbled, but couldn't say much.

Marisa changed the subject. "So after you found out the truth about what happened between your mom and dad, did you apologize to your father?"

"Yeah, this morning before I left." Myles playfully kicked at Winston, who had sauntered over. "I could barely look him in the eye."

"Because you were embarrassed about hitting him?" Marisa asked.

Myles thought it over. Though his father had told him he forgave him, Myles could tell he had been hurt that Myles had not given him the benefit of the doubt before assuming the worst of him.

"Yeah, I guess that was it."

Peggy watched Jasmine come up the steps of the platform at Thirtieth Street Station. When Jasmine caught sight of her aunt, she paused and shifted her knapsack from one shoulder to the other. She sauntered over to the big wooden bench where Peggy was waiting. "Hi, Aunt Peg."

"Hi, baby," Peggy rose from the bench and studied her. "You unhappy to see me?"

Jasmine shrugged, keeping her eyes on the floor. "No, just surprised. Marisa told me that it was gonna be Kenya or Amir."

"I wanted to come instead—is that okay?"

Jasmine twitched to signal it was all right.

Peggy suppressed a smile. "Nice outfit."

"It's one of Marisa's."

"I figured as much. It's nice," Peggy said as she inspected the gray and maroon Ralph Lauren warm-up suit. "But you and I both know that Marisa can't pull it off like you, though."

Jasmine looked up strangely. Then smiled. Then laughed. She walked into her aunt's outstretched arms and gave her a hug.

"I am not that vain, Aunt Peg."

Peggy chuckled and continued squeezing her niece.

"Aunt Peg, I'm sorry for what I said."

Peggy released her. "Did Marisa tell you to say that?"

"Yes," Jasmine admitted, "but I really am. I can't afford to be evil to one of the few people in the world who does care about me."

Peggy cradled Jasmine's face and wiped away her forming tears with her thumbs, then brought her back close to her. "Jazzy, I can't tell you how worried I was." She wiped away a tear of her own. "I love you so much."

"I love you too, Aunt Peg."

"Listen, I can't promise there will never be a time when I won't get angry with you, but I certainly don't want to black out again like I did. I used to be able to pop Amir and Myles when they were your age, but I'm getting too old for all that now."

Jasmine smiled. Peggy gave her a tissue.

"You won't have to," Jasmine said. " 'Cause I'm getting too old to say just anything out of my mouth."

"Wipe your face, baby," she motioned to the food-court area. "You hungry? We can go to Delilah's for some ribs."

Jasmine nodded.

"We need to grab them to go," Peggy said. "Your uncle Lenny is out front waiting in the car for us."

Peggy thought Jasmine's face hardened at the mention of Leonard's name.

As they continued to stroll, Peggy checked out Jasmine's

outfit again. "I can't believe you and Marisa wear the same size. With her little self."

"Yep," Jasmine said, "and I'm looking forward to raiding her closet this summer. She said I could stay with her and Myles."

Peggy's eyebrows lifted. "Did she now?"

"Provided I keep my grades up and don't give you a hard time."

Peggy concealed her disappointment. Just that morning she had pondered the idea of them going down South in the summer so Jasmine could visit family. Jasmine hadn't been to Georgia to see her kin since she was seven. Maybe they could hit somewhere else, too, before they came home.

But she could see how excited Jasmine was about the prospect of staying with Marisa, and she didn't want to dampen her enthusiasm.

"So what else did you and Marisa talk about?" Peggy asked as they approached the food court.

"How she keeps Myles and Winston around for the same purpose—to amuse her."

Peggy stopped in her tracks as she thought that over. Jasmine laughed at her aunt's strange expression.

"You know, Jasmine," she said as they got in line at the Delilah's stand, "I wonder how far from the truth that statement really is."

chapter 13

Jasmine walked into the kitchen, already dressed for school. "Aunt Peg."

Peggy was sitting at the table, enjoying a cup of coffee and thumbing through the latest issue of *Essence*. "Yes?"

Jasmine sat down at the table. "There's something I need to talk to you about."

When Peggy saw the seriousness on Jasmine's face, she closed the magazine. And girded herself for the worst.

Jasmine stared at the fruit-bowl centerpiece as she said, "I met this new boy, and I like him." She lifted her eyes to Peggy's. "And I want you to meet him."

Peggy exhaled. That didn't seem so bad. She took a sip of coffee, "Really? Where did you meet him? At school?"

Jasmine shook her head. "No, at the mall. He's eighteen. He's done with school. He's studying to be an auto mechanic." She paused and smiled. "Though I am trying to talk him into going to college. He's too smart not to."

Peggy nodded. Again, it didn't sound so bad. Jasmine was now seventeen. Of course she was interested in boys. And Peggy appreciated the fact that Jasmine wanted to bring him to meet the family. It also solved the mystery of why Jasmine was spending so much time on the phone lately.

Yet Peggy's body was still tense, waiting for some other shoe to drop. "That sounds fine, Jasmine."

Jasmine palmed an orange and placed it on the place mat in front of her. "There's something else."

I knew it, Peggy thought.

Jasmine spoke fast, wanting to get it all out. "The guy's name is Darius. He's a former client of Jackie and Kenya's. When he was younger—years ago—he got into trouble. Burglary, fighting, getting expelled"—she cast a worried glance at Peggy—"but like I said, that was years ago, when he was a child. Kenya and Jackie still have a negative opinion of him, though. All I want is for you to give him a chance and judge him for yourself. It's not like we're getting married or anything, but I do like him, so I want you to meet him." Jasmine ended with a big intake of breath.

Peggy tried to digest the torrent of information. When she saw Jasmine's hopeful face, she wanted to make sure she kept her cool.

"Well, if he—what's his name?"

"Darius."

"If Darius is a former client of Jackie and Kenya's, then that means he's had some problems with his home life as a child, right?"

"He didn't have a home life," Jasmine said. "Not once his grandmother died."

Peggy nodded. "I understand. So I can understand his acting out at that point." She eyed Jasmine intently. "You say he's stopped doing all the negative stuff, right?"

Jasmine nodded emphatically. "Even Jackie and Kenya will vouch for that—and they don't particularly care for him."

"Why not?" Peggy asked.

"Well, the thing that Darius still carries from being kicked around so much is he's quick to become defensive. It's his mechanism because he's scared to be vulnerable and open up to people. So rather than expose himself to getting hurt, he'd rather play the role of jerk or tough guy. I believe he thinks Kenya's and Jackie's minds are already made up about him—slanted toward the negative—so he doesn't care to expend the energy to try and change their opinions. Plus, he's probably a little uncomfortable that they know all his business. From talking to him, though, I can tell he likes both of them and appreciates all they've done for him." Jasmine chuckled. "He'll never tell them that, of course."

Listen to Ms. Amateur Psychologist, Peggy thought. It's ironic that she can't apply the analysis to herself.

Peggy shrugged. "I believe in forming my own conclusions about a person. I look forward to meeting him."

Jasmine smiled.

"I'm sure your uncle would like to meet him, too."

Jasmine's smile dropped.

"What?" Peggy asked. "Is that a problem?"

"I guess not," Jasmine said forlornly as she rose from the table. Putting the orange back in the bowl, she picked up her book bag and slung it over her shoulder. "I'll let you know when, okay?"

"All right."

Jasmine headed down the front hallway. "Bye."

"Bye, baby."

Jasmine stopped at the front door. "Oh, Aunt Peg, no fair calling Kenya or Jackie until after you meet him. You can't properly form your own conclusions if your judgment is clouded."

Peggy laughed. "You think you know me, don'cha child?"

Jasmine laughed. "I do. Promise me you won't talk to them about Darius."

"Go to school, girl."

After she left, Peggy wondered if she really was upset with the way Leonard had grabbed her Saturday. She had barely spoken to him since she got back yesterday.

The phone rang. Probably one of Jasmine's friends trying to catch her before she left. Peggy walked into the den and picked the receiver up off the sofa.

"Hello?"

She heard breathing and then a dial tone.

She clicked off the receiver. This was becoming a more frequent experience. She needed to break down and get Jasmine her own phone line. She didn't have time for this silliness.

She heard Leonard rustling upstairs. He had gotten up an hour earlier, when she did, but went back to bed.

"You want breakfast?" she yelled.

"Yeah."

"Me, too. Come down here and make us some." Peggy chuckled to herself. After he showed his ass yesterday when she cooked him breakfast, he was tripping to think he was getting it today.

Five minutes later, her husband entered the family room. She looked down at his worn leather slippers. "Why don't you wear the slippers the twins got you for Christmas?"

"Too frilly." He put his feet on the ottoman. "These right here are a man's slippers."

"You might as well be walking around barefoot with how raggedy they are." Peggy eyed them scornfully. "When did you get those anyway? When Carter was in the White House?"

"No, I believe it was during the Nixon administration," he said after giving the matter some thought.

"You're probably telling the truth."

Abruptly Leonard got up and came over to where she sat. He stopped in front of her. Through his open bathrobe, poking out of his pajamas, was his erect penis.

"Tricky Dick," he growled at his wife as he opened his bathrobe wider. "Do you want some of my tricky dick?"

Lord have mercy. What the hell is he doing with an erection?

"I don't need to see that first thing in the morning—put that thing away, Lenny." Peggy turned and made sure she had closed the blinds behind her.

He bared his teeth. "Tricky Dick, Peggy."

"It's more like a one-trick pony, isn't it?"

"What?" Leonard backed up, adjusted his pajama bottoms and tightened his flannel bathrobe. His erection was still evident underneath his clothing. "For that crack, I'm not gonna cook you breakfast."

"I don't want your nasty self cooking me anything anyway," Peggy replied. "And what the heck are you doing aroused? You got some nasty magazines under the bed?"

Lenny snarled, "You do something to me, woman."

"I'm'a do something, all right," she assured him, "like get you neutered. You're getting to be ridiculous around here lately."

Offended, Lenny walked into the kitchen. Soon she heard him washing his hands in the kitchen sink.

"What are you still doing here anyway?" he called out sharply.

Peggy knew why he was asking. On Monday mornings she usually went to the Willow Glen Retirement Community to do some of the residents' hair.

"I didn't have any appointments today."

*　　*　　*

"See ya later," Vanessa said.

"Bye," added Stacy.

Vanessa and her friend stepped out of the salon. A chilly breeze invaded the shop before the door was closed behind the ladies.

Good riddance, Peggy thought as she shampooed one of her clients' hair. She didn't know what she had done to incur the wrath of Vanessa's friend, but she had felt her stare (whenever she thought Peggy wasn't looking) the whole time Stacy was having her nails done.

She searched her memory. It was that same funny-looking woman she had seen Vanessa with at the supermarket, but what was her beef? Was she a girl who had dated one of her sons before they were married? If so, it was likely Amir. Lord knows, he had probably done more dirt than she cared to think about and had done more than a few women wrong. Probably considerably more than a few.

If that was the case, then what exactly was this girl's problem with her? She was never one to excuse either of her sons' negative behavior. In fact, Peggy despised parents like that. Ones that didn't hold their children accountable for anything because they felt they could do no wrong. Their kid could set a forest fire and the parents would blame the timber for being so damn flammable.

Peggy began rinsing her client's head. Well, whatever the child's issue was, she had better things to do than to worry about it.

Jasmine and Darius were sitting on the top bleacher at the Highland High School gym. They were watching the boys basketball team get blown out by Camden High.

"These guys are butt," Darius said, laughing. "It makes a brotha like me want to suit up."

Preoccupied, Jasmine didn't hear him. She wanted to return to the topic they had been discussing earlier. She searched Darius' face.

"Are you cool with meeting my family?" she asked.

Darius mulled it over for a second, then nodded. "Hell, I already know half of them anyway." He smiled as he thought of something. "Kenya's husband, Amir, I met him a few times. I always appreciated that cat's sense of style."

Jasmine smiled. "Yeah, I think you'd like Amir."

"Dude looks like a playa to me," Darius said.

"He's retired," Jasmine replied firmly.

Chuckling, Darius put his arm around Jasmine's shoulder. "I'm just glad that you like me enough to want me to meet them."

Jasmine sucked her teeth. "I wanted to show you Saturday in that motel room, what I felt about you."

"Is that what you really wanted to do?" Darius asked.

Jasmine furrowed her brow. "Huh?"

Darius smiled. "Don't think I didn't want to, but I like you too much to have slept with you then."

Jasmine crinkled her nose. "Huh?"

"I wasn't sure why you wanted to sleep with me," Darius explained, "especially considering what you and your aunt had just went through. And if you slept with me for the wrong reasons, I was scared you would resent me, want nothing to do with me later if we did it. Now, that would be cool if all I was interested in was just hitting it." Darius gave her a sideways grin. "But I kinda like you, and I want to keep you around me for a while. The way I see it is, if it's right, and meant to be, you will offer it to me again. And it will be perfect."

Jasmine swore she felt her heart flutter. How sweet. She leaned into him. They cuddled like they did on Saturday.

"Why didn't you tell me that then?" Jasmine asked.

"Because you would have spent the next five hours telling me that you weren't stressing over your aunt. That you were in your right frame of mind to make the decision to be sleeping with me. Then after you failed to convince me, you might have really lost your mind and started calling me a punk or a fagboy and shit." Darius shook his head. "I don't think I could have handled all that."

Jasmine laughed.

"So I figured it was better to not let you know the reason," Darius concluded.

Jasmine purred contently. "Ahh, you really love me, don'cha?" she teased.

Darius blushed. "Just watch the game, girl. Watch the game."

chapter 14

Peggy struggled to open the door of the salon while holding two bags of beauty supplies she had picked up at a hair show in Philadelphia the day before. One of the bags began to rip, and she made a desperate lunge with her thigh to trap it against the door.

"Leonard!"

It was early, so she and Leonard were the only ones in the building. He had driven his car over earlier that morning.

She leaned her body into the bag and held it against the door while she waited for her husband to come.

"Leonard, come help me!"

Again, she waited. Again her husband failed to emerge.

She decided to make a go of it. Reaching her hand around the rip, she righted the bag in her arm. As she tried to quickly negotiate the ten or so paces between the door and the first chair, though, the contents of the torn bag fell though the tear, sending bottles of shampoo, conditioner, and relaxer rolling in every direction.

"Damn it!"

Peggy's agitation at having to get on her knees to retrieve items that had rolled under the hair-dryer chairs was increased by her husband's failure to help her. She knew he was in the shop. She had seen his Lincoln in the parking lot when she pulled up.

After finally recovering all the wayward products, she stood up and brushed her knees off. It was then that she noticed that one of the buttons was lit up on the phone.

"He'd better be talking to the president to ignore me like he did," Peggy grumbled. She threw the ripped bag away and violently stuffed it into the trash can. Then she began putting the products on the shelves behind the register.

After she was finished, she noticed the phone was still lit. Though she did her best to ignore it, she was compelled to walk toward it. She slowly picked up the receiver.

"You know you like the taste of my asshole, Mr. Lenny."

"Girl, I don't know what you're talking about."

"Well, somebody that looks like you had his tongue in my ass yesterday."

"Did you call the police, Stacy?"

"What am I gonna show them for evidence? My wet behind?"

"If they lucky, you will . . ."

"What the hell!" Peggy took the receiver and banged it against the counter as if it was their heads. The battery door popped off. "What the hell is this—who is this?"

"Oh, shit!" Leonard hung up, ran down the small hallway that separated the barber shop and the salon, and appeared at the rear entrance of the salon.

"Peggy."

"Oh, you heard me that time, didn't you?" Peggy hurled the receiver at him. "You sonofabitch!"

Leonard ducked under the whirling phone and tried to think of something to say, but he wasn't sure how much his wife had heard.

Peggy was so angry, hurt, and frustrated that she was trembling uncontrollably. Felt like she was on the verge of passing out. But her fury wasn't about to allow that to happen.

"I can't believe the filth I heard on that phone." Peggy's eyes blazed with rage. "You put that same mouth on me, you nasty muthafucka?" She reached down on the counter and picked up a pair of shears. "I will kill your black ass!"

At first Leonard only backpedaled as his wife approached. Then he turned around into a full trot when she got too close. He scooted out the back door into the gravel parking lot.

"I want you out of the house! You triflin', janky-ass bastard."

"Peggy."

"Out!" she screamed. "Go live with your whore!"

Leonard realized that she wasn't going to listen to anything he had to say.

"I need my car keys."

"Nigga, walk!" Peggy slammed the back door shut and locked it. She leaned against it, holding the doorknob. Her legs felt like they were going to give. She took a deep breath and managed to stagger into her office, where she closed the door and had a long cry.

Amir came into the room still toweling himself off from his shower. Kenya was sitting at her vanity table talking on the phone. One look at how tight her face was, and Amir knew it was bad news. He hoped Jade wasn't fighting at school again. He didn't feel like visiting the school before going into the shop. Amir grabbed the lotion off of his dresser and sat on the bed.

"That's right, Ms. Peg," Kenya said. "You gotta be strong . . ."

The bottle of lotion froze in midshake. Amir hoped his mother was all right.

"We'll find out . . . okay. I'll stop by later after work," Kenya continued. She looked at Amir in her mirror. "Amir's out the shower now, do you want to talk to him?" Kenya asked. "Okay . . . okay, I'll have him call you later, bye now."

Kenya turned off the phone and exhaled.

"What's wrong with my moms, babe?"

"Nothing. Something is very wrong with your dad, though."

"What is it?"

"He's been cheating on your mother. She caught him on the phone talking to some nasty-behind hooker."

Amir stood up and let out a snort of disgust. Taking off his towel, he walked over to his dresser, where he slipped on a pair of boxer shorts.

Kenya watched him in the mirror as she applied her lipstick. "You certainly don't seemed too shocked. Why is that?"

"Maybe it's because I'm not." Amir sat back down on the bed and began putting on a pair of socks. "She put him out, right?"

"Of course." Same place you would go if you pulled the same shit, Kenya thought. "I wanna know why you're not surprised."

Amir ignored her. He got up and headed into their walk-in closet.

"I guess you didn't hear me," Kenya said, swiveling around in her chair. "I asked you why you aren't surprised."

"Okay, I'm shocked. Flabbergasted," Amir said from the closet. "What the hell is the world coming to?"

"You're not funny." Kenya got up and when Amir came out buttoning his shirt, she blocked his path.

"You knew, didn't you?" She studied his face, daring him to lie.

Amir tucked in his shirt. "I had a suspicion."

He sidestepped her as he adjusted his belt and walked back over to the bed. Kenya was right on his tail and sat down next to him.

"Based on what?"

Amir leaned over and pulled a pair of boots from under the bed. He decided not to drag Carlos into this. "A friend of mine said they saw him in Camden with another woman."

"What?" Kenya rose from the bed. She faced Amir with one arm on her hip. Uh-oh, he thought. That was her optimum arguing position.

"You knew your father was messing around on your mother and didn't say anything about it?"

"First of all, I didn't *know* anything."

"Don't hand me that bullshit, man. How much proof would you have needed if someone told you they had seen Jasmine, or one of our daughters, doing something?"

"They're children," Amir said incredulously.

"Or me," Kenya added.

"You're my wife."

"And that's your *mother*."

"Second of all," Amir continued, "who says I didn't say anything?"

Kenya took a step back, dropping her chin. "Who'd you tell? You didn't tell your mother. You didn't tell me."

Amir finished tying his shoes and stood up. "I talked to my dad."

Kenya laughed harshly.

"What?"

"*What?*" Kenya mocked. "Lemme guess." She shut her eyes tightly and rubbed her temple like she was in deep thought. She opened her eyes. "He said no?"

"Yep."

"That's like asking a murderer did he kill a man, him saying no and the judge moving on to the next case."

"I'm not my father's judge." He began to move around her.

Kenya put a palm on his chest. "But are you your mother's son?"

Stopped in midstride, Amir sighed. "What's that supposed to mean, Kenya?"

"Why were you so quick to let it go? Would you have let it go as easily if it was your mother accused of being out there?"

He brushed off her hand. "Whatever, Kenya. I have a double standard."

"Or maybe it's just one standard." Kenya maneuvered to block his path again. "One where it's permissible for a man to fuck around on the side as long as he's handling business at home."

Amir had taken all the interrogating he was going to take. "Kenya, that's unfair. I have never cheated on you since we've been married."

She wasn't letting him go, however. "Why not? Because you fear getting caught? Maybe you were waiting to see how well your old man pulled it off."

Seeing his face immediately shut down, Kenya regretted saying that. It wasn't called for. She slid her hand into Amir's. "I apologize."

Amir nodded. Kenya rested her head on his shoulder.

"I could've done more," he admitted.

"The thing is, Amir, your mother was *out* there." Kenya stroked the back of his hand. "How many people knew what was going on? How many low-class hoes were laughing at her behind her back?"

Amir winced.

"Not to mention the possibility of your father bringing home some disease to your mother."

Amir's face went from discomfort to revulsion. "Jesus." That notion was too much for him to bear.

Jasmine trudged upstairs to her room. When she reached the landing, she heard noises coming out of her aunt and uncle's bedroom. She peered into the doorway and saw her uncle Lenny packing. Two open suitcases and a bag were laid out on the bed. His face was lined with stress. When Jasmine saw the perspiration beading on his forehead, she had a good idea what had happened.

"Going on a trip?" she asked.

Leonard was startled. When he saw it was his niece, he relaxed a little. He headed into the bathroom.

Jasmine leaned against the doorjamb and repeated the question. "Going on a trip? I hear Paris is lovely in the fall."

Leonard threw some deodorant and other toiletries into an overnight bag. Without looking at Jasmine, he responded, "Your aunt and I are going through some problems. I'm going to be away for a little while."

"Oh, no, Uncle Lenny," Jasmine said. "Is there anything I can do?"

"No, there isn't."

She kept up her pretense of innocence. "What sort of problems are you and Aunt Peg going through, Uncle Lenny?"

Leonard glared at her. He was pretty certain she was being a pain on purpose. "Nothing you need to concern yourself with. It's grown folks' business."

"Oh"—Jasmine straightened up—"well, since I'm on the verge of adulthood, maybe I can learn from an adult such as yourself."

Fuming, Leonard emptied out his sock drawer.

"Did these 'problems' you and Aunt Peggy are having occur when your pants were on or off?"

"Mind your own goddamned business, child!" Leonard barked.

"My aunt is my goddamned business!"

"Get out of my sight before I smack you, Jasmine."

"Gladly. I can think of a lot better things I'd rather be looking at."

chapter 15

That evening, Peggy sat in her car in the salon parking lot, alone with her thoughts for the first time since the morning. She gripped the steering wheel and drew a deep breath. Despite her shock at what she'd overheard, she had been able to keep all her appointments that day. Even if she was hardly herself, she reasoned that she would rather be at work than at home with Leonard, who had better be packed and gone when she got home. With his nasty, sorry ass.

She had thought about unburdening herself on Joyce, one of her stylists and a dear friend of hers, or calling her sister Roslyn in Michigan. But she had decided against it, at least for the time being.

Peggy had told the boys that she put their father out the house. She called Kenya and Amir first, then Myles. Her younger son offered to drive up, but she told him that there was nothing that couldn't wait until the weekend. She still had to tell Jasmine. Though, if Jasmine was home when Lenny was gathering his things, she already knew.

She wondered where Leonard would go. Would he move in with that tramp he was fooling around with? What was the name he had used on the phone? Peggy put the key into the ignition and started up her car. Stacy. It wasn't a familiar name. She didn't know any Stacys, so at least it wasn't one of her friends. She was probably some skank he had picked up at a bar. Kenya told her that they would find out who it was. Not that it mattered, since Leonard's ass was history anyway, but Peggy still wanted to know.

She had a lot of questions. How long had it been going on. The frequency of it. How discreet they had been. In short, how long, how often, and how openly Lenny had been disrespecting her and playing her for the fool.

When she got home, the house felt different to her. Too sterile and bright. As she hung up her coat in the hall closet, she heard Jasmine coming down the stairs.

"Hi, Aunt Peg," she said, appearing in the vestibule. Her voice sounded more adult than usual.

"Hi, baby." Peggy saw the look of concern on Jasmine's face. She finished hanging her scarf and gave her a weary smile. "How was your day?"

Jasmine walked over to her aunt and wrapped her arms around her waist. "Don't worry about my day. How are you feeling?"

Peggy didn't respond as she stroked her niece's hair and gave her a kiss on the forehead. She tried to talk, but any words were stymied by a lump in her throat. Peggy felt that if she forced her voice past it, a whole flood of emotions were sure to follow, so she chose to say nothing instead.

Jasmine didn't press the issue, but took her hand and led her into the kitchen. "Sit down, Aunt Peg," she said, holding out one of the chairs. "You look spent."

Peggy sat down wearily.

"Do you need anything?"

After swallowing hard, Peggy said. "Just a glass of water, baby, and then I want you to sit next to me."

As Jasmine retrieved a glass and got cold water out of the refrigerator dispenser, Peggy noticed the smell of cooking. A covered skillet was set on the stove.

"Did you cook dinner, Jasmine?"

The girl handed her the glass of water as she took a seat. She smiled sheepishly. "It's just Hamburger Helper."

"Mm, that's my favorite," Peggy affirmed. They both smiled.

Peggy took a long sip of water. Obviously, Jasmine was already aware of the situation, so there was no point in beating around the bush. "Were you here while your adulterous uncle was packing?"

"Yes," Jasmine answered, startled by her directness.

"Why the look of surprise?"

"I thought you would try to soft-pedal the situation to me," Jasmine explained.

"I thought about it," Peggy said as she distractedly fingered the edge of a place mat, "but you're old enough to be told the truth. You got too much sense to be lied to anyway." Peggy looked at her. "Besides, I need someone to talk to."

Jasmine gave her a tight, proud smile. One that said, you can rely on me, Auntie.

"Did you happen to notice how many bags he was carrying when he left?"

"I saw him walk to his car from my bedroom window." Jasmine leaned back in her chair and closed her eyes to replay the scene. "He had a suitcase—no, two suitcases and a shoulder bag."

Good, Peggy thought. She'd wanted Leonard to take her seriously. If he had thrown an outfit or two and a shaving kit in a gym bag, that would have been told her that he expected this to be a passing storm that would blow over in a few days when her crazy ass calmed down and realized that she *really* didn't want him gone. It was good that Leonard knew that she meant business.

However, the finality of what he'd done struck Peggy hard. Leonard hadn't packed for a hotel. He packed like a man who had somewhere to rest his head already lined up.

She wished that she didn't care, but she did. Thirty-eight years with a person tends to do that. But she did feel she made the right decision. She could not let Leonard stay and still be able to live with herself. And right now *she* was going to be her primary concern.

"Aunt Peg, did you have any suspicions?"

Peggy cocked her head. "Is that your polite way of asking me how come I didn't know when you did?"

"No, I didn't know—"

"But you had serious doubts, right?"

"Well," Jasmine nervously played with her hair, "didn't you?"

Peggy stared at the flowery place mat border as she mulled over that question. She decided to be completely honest with Jasmine. Maybe this experience could be instructive for her. The last thing she wanted to do was to show her niece weakness. She had already seen enough of that watching men play her mother for a fool.

"I asked your uncle point-blank if he was messing around on me—months ago," Peggy said slowly. "He denied that he was."

"But for you to have asked the question in the first place meant you had doubts, right?"

"Indeed," Peggy continued. "After his denial, though, he started showing me more attention, and maybe I really started to believe nothing was going on."

She noticed Jasmine's gaze dropped to the table.

"What? You're not buying that?"

Jasmine was clearly ill at ease.

"It's okay, Jasmine. I want you to be honest," Peggy assured her.

Jasmine was still trying to gain her footing here. She was having her first adult conversation with her aunt in which her opinion was respected.

Jasmine rested her elbows on the table. "Aunt Peg, don't you think you asked him so that he could have the opportunity to stop? Hoping that if Uncle Lenny knew you had suspicions, he would stop what he was doing on his own? Then you wouldn't have to pursue it any further."

Peggy rubbed her chin thoughtfully. Jasmine had learned from her mother's mistakes.

Jasmine further pointed out, "If you really wanted to know if he was doing something, why would you let him know you suspected anything and give him the opportunity to clean up his affairs? No, instead you would've investigated and tried to catch him in the act."

"What was I gonna do, Jaz? Call that show, *Cheaters*, to follow him around? Take him on *Maury* for a lie-detector test?"

Jasmine shrugged. "Why not hire an investigator? You wanted the truth, right?"

"Because when people have been together nearly forty years, you tend to give your spouse the benefit of the doubt before you go outside the marriage with your problems."

There was a pause. Then Jasmine spoke again.

"But didn't Uncle Lenny choose to go 'outside the marriage' first, Aunt Peg? You would have just been reacting to his breach."

"I didn't know that for sure, Jasmine." Peggy reconsidered that statement as she leaned her body back in her chair and exhaled loudly. "I don't know . . . I probably did. I just didn't want to know."

"If a woman has suspicions her mate is cheating, nine times out of ten, he is."

Peggy eyed her niece. "Jenny Jones?"

"No," Jasmine said smoothly. "Kenya Moore."

Peggy emitted a soft chuckle. "She's probably right." She reached over and patted the back of Jasmine's hand. "Well, it looks like it's gonna be just you and me around here, kiddo."

Jasmine nodded.

Peggy gripped her hand. "I mean for good, Jasmine. Your uncle's not coming back, ever."

Jasmine's eyebrows lifted in surprise. "You can't make such an definite statement like that so early on, Aunt Peg. . . ."

"The hell I can't," Peggy said, straightening back up. "And I'll tell you why. You helped me realize a truth here at this table. When I went to that man and asked him was he messing around on me, I *was* giving him the opportunity to clean up his act. A chance to . . ." Peggy bit her bottom lip to conceal its quiver, but couldn't stop a tear from rolling down her cheek. "For him to think so little of me—or so much of *her*—to dismiss that chance and still be doing what he was . . ." Peggy shook her head resolutely. "That I cannot forgive. Ever. I know me, I never will be able to—and why should I lower myself like that?" Her lips pinched together sternly. "Just so I can say that I have a husband? What the hell would I be married to if there's zero trust?"

Jasmine handed her aunt a tissue, then came around the table and gave her a hug. "I love you, Aunt Peg."

Peggy smiled through her tears. "I love you, too, baby."

"Babe," Myles called out.

"Hm?" Marisa replied, coming to the doorway.

"My parents are splitting up."

"What?" Marisa hurried over to sit beside him.

"Yeah," Myles said, "she caught him cheating."

"Wow." So she had been right. Mr. Lenny was running around on his wife.

"How do you know they're gonna split up?" Marisa asked.

"Well, my mother has already put him out of the house," Myles explained. "And unless it was a one-time thing where my father slipped on a patch of ice and some woman came along after him and fell on top of his dick, then my mom isn't gonna be able to let it go. Especially with what she heard."

"What do you mean?"

"My mom heard them talking on the phone—my father and the chick he's been running with. My father was talking about . . . things he and the woman did . . ." Myles squirmed recounting what his mother had told him. If Myles knew anything about his mother, she *definitely* wasn't going to forgive him.

"Like what?" Marisa asked.

"Sexual acts."

"Oh." Marisa let out a soft whistle. "And your mother overheard it?"

"Yeah."

"How bad was it?"

Myles widened his eyes to the size of baseballs. "Pretty damn bad."

They sat quietly for a good half minute. Marisa knew she shouldn't, but she couldn't help herself.

"What—"

Myles cut her off. "I'd rather not say. It's not important."

Marisa leaned onto his shoulder. "I know—I know it isn't, but I want to know." She did want to know, not only because of curiosity, but so she could compare it to how she'd react.

Myles groaned. He realized she wasn't going to be able to let it go. "My father and the woman was talking about how much he enjoyed putting his"—Myles exhaled; there was no turning back now—"tongue up her ass."

The words jolted Marisa to her feet. She let out a torrent of curse words in Spanish, far too fast and too many for Myles to make sense of.

Winston scampered for cover behind a chair. Myles leaned away from her. "You said you wanted to hear it."

"I thought you were gonna tell me he was getting oral from her or something like that—not no foul shit like that!" Marisa's face contorted menacingly. "He sat at his wife's table eating her cooking with *that* mouth, kissed his wife with *that* mouth . . . he needs his old ass kicked!"

Myles nodded in agreement. She had a point there.

Marisa whirled on Myles. "I will hurt you if you pull any bullshit like that on me. Believe that!"

Myles recoiled. He didn't doubt her crazy ass. "Marisa, how did this get about me?"

"You just see that it doesn't." Marisa started walking out of the room, but stopped at the entrance and looked over her shoulder. "I've seen too many sons who grow into their fathers."

Myles listened to her cursing, stomping, and snarling all the way up the stairs.

Jasmine and Peggy had just finished eating a dinner of Hamburger Helper and salad.

Kenya and Amir had called while they were eating and asked Peggy if she would like for them to come over. Peggy had told Kenya that she didn't have to bother with bringing the girls over when they were doing homework—that they could wait until tomorrow when Myles and Marisa would be here as well. She didn't want Kenya and Amir to have to go right back out after they had worked all day or bother with bringing the twins over on a school night. Besides, Peggy was enjoying the time she was spending with Jasmine.

"That was delicious, Jasmine," Peggy said. "I thank you for dinner—and the conversation."

Jasmine beamed.

The phone rang.

Jasmine looked at her aunt, then got up and answered it.

"Hello? . . . Yeah, hold on."

"It's Jackie." Jasmine handed Peggy the phone.

"Hello? . . . Thank you, Jackie, I don't need anything. . . . No-no, you don't have to do that. . . . No, your buddy and Myles are coming up tomorrow, do you have to work? . . . Can you stop by then? . . . Great, give CJ a kiss for me. . . . Bye now."

Peggy handed Jasmine the phone.

"So Jackie knows now?"

"Kenya probably told her," Peggy replied.

"You don't mind people knowing your business?" Jasmine asked, hanging the receiver back on the wall.

"Jackie isn't people—she's like family," Peggy answered. "Besides, I don't have anything to be ashamed of or that I need to lower my head about. Your uncle and his mistress do."

Jasmine slid back into her seat. "Do you know who the woman is, Aunt Peg?" she asked. "Or whether it was more than one?"

During the entire day, while she had been preoccupied with the morning's developments, Peggy had never considered the possibility of multiple partners. She wondered if Lenny had gotten equally as nasty with all of them.

"Well, the one I heard on the phone was somebody named Stacy." Saying the name, Peggy got up abruptly to put the plates in the sink. "I don't know her."

Jasmine shrugged. "The only Stacy I know is a friend of Danae's mom."

A ceramic plate crashed against the edge of the countertop and shattered on the floor below. Jasmine looked at the broken pieces scattered on the tile and then at her aunt. She was leaning against the counter, clutching another plate against her chest.

"You okay? Aunt Peg?"

Peggy was busy connecting the dots. The looks in the shop and the supermarket. The name she had heard Leonard use on the phone. The woman on the phone's snotty voice.

"That heifer's name *is* Stacy, isn't it?" Peggy uttered more for her benefit than Jasmine's. "It wasn't because of Amir that she was looking at me funny. It was because of Leonard."

Good grief.

Lenny was driving his Lincoln Town Car along Marne Highway, thinking about the events of that day. Was it wrong for him to sleep with another woman? Yes, of course. Had Peggy seriously overreacted? A resounding yes.

If a man has been married forty years, shouldn't he be allowed a pass? Hadn't he earned it? *One* pass? Hell, if every woman flew off the handle like Peggy had, no one would be married. That's her problem, he thought. She's too fucking emotional.

And knowing Peggy, she had probably already made the mistake of running her mouth to the family. Like to that snotty-ass Jasmine. Who the hell is that child to question me? I take you into my home, feed you, put clothes on your back, and you got the nerve to show your ass to me?

Naw, Peggy didn't have the good sense to keep it between them. She'd rather solicit sympathy instead of thinking things through. *Look at poor Peggy. Ain't it a shame what her no-*

good louse of a husband put her through? The real shame was that because of her big mouth, Peggy was now going to be a sixty-year-old woman with no man and no prospects for getting one. She couldn't reconcile with him now because she would lose too much face.

"Dummy," Leonard muttered.

He was gonna be fine. He was a sixty-two-year-old *man*. He could find somebody. He had a little loot behind him. He would have no trouble finding a woman, if he had to, which he didn't, because he already had a thirty-something-year-old woman waiting for him. Leonard remembered that Stacy had already asked him to move in, and had gotten rid of her roommate. She was gonna be thrilled that Peggy had acted so impetuously. Her loss was gonna be Stacy's gain.

After a good deal of exertion, Leonard walked up the flight of stairs to Stacy's condo, holding his two suitcases and his overnight bag. Leonard rang the doorbell. He knew Stacy was home because he saw her car in the parking lot.

"Who is it?" Stacy asked.

"It's some dick," Lenny said lasciviously.

"Who?" she asked again

"It's Lenny," Leonard said.

Stacy opened the door. "Mr. Lenny," she said, surprised. Her eyes immediately went to the suitcases. "What's up?"

Leonard lifted his suitcases up. "Your wish has come true."

Stacy wasn't following. "Huh?"

"I've come to live with you, girl," Leonard said. "Come on now—these bags are heavy."

Flummoxed, Stacy stepped aside. Leonard walked into the living room of the condo and put his suitcases down on the carpet and his shoulder bag on the chair. He couldn't have put his things on the sofa even if he had wanted to because there was a thin light-skinned young brother sitting there. Looked to be in his mid-twenties. And mighty comfortable.

Leonard turned back to Stacy for an explanation.

"Lenny, this is Marlon. Marlon, Lenny."

Marlon nodded toward Leonard.

Before Leonard could get some explanation on who Marlon was, Stacy headed for the closet.

"What are you, Stacy's father?" Marlon asked.

Leonard scowled. "No, I ain't her father."

Stacy came back with a coat. "Marlon was just leaving."

Apparently Stacy had regained her bearings and decided that old dick and money won over young dick and broke.

Marlon looked at Stacy, at Leonard, and back at Stacy again. "Oh, shit," he said, laughing. He rose to his feet, walked over to Stacy, and grabbed his jacket.

On his way out of the door, Marlon paused and looked over his shoulder. Leonard was eyeing him, daring him to say something stupid.

"Oh, *shit*," Marlon repeated, looking at Stacy again before closing the door. Stacy and Leonard heard peals of laughter all the way down the stairs.

Leonard sat down on the sofa and gave Stacy a jaundiced eye. "Who was that idiot?"

Stacy couldn't believe that Leonard thought *he* was due an explanation. She sat down on a stool at the breakfast nook. "What are you doing here—with bags?" she asked.

Stacy's reaction wasn't nearly what Leonard had expected. Never mind that Marlon fellow's presence and behavior.

"Stacy, you act like you don't know what happened today," Leonard said. "You know my wife overheard us talking."

"Yeah," Stacy said, adjusting herself on the stool. "You should be more careful."

Leonard was stunned. "More careful? Stacy, my wife put me out."

"I'm sorry to hear that, Mr. Lenny."

"You're sorry to hear that?" Leonard leaned forward with his elbows on his knees and sputtered. "I thought you'd be pleased."

Stacy could not believe this fool had taken her seriously when she used to bad-mouth his wife. When she stroked his ego about her desire that he live with her, that was just shit talking. Part of the game. She stroked his ego, he greased her palm. Hell, if she wanted to live with an old man who loved her, she'd move in with her grandfather.

Lenny couldn't be this stupid, could he?

One look at his dumbfounded expression told Stacy that he indeed was.

She couldn't very well put him out. Not right away. He was too good a meal ticket.

chapter 16

Myles and Marisa sat in the living room of his parents' home. It was a quarter past one on Saturday afternoon. They had just made the drive up from Maryland and were alone in the house.

"Okay, thanks, Joyce." Myles hung up the phone. "Well, my mom isn't at work."

"Did you try her cell phone?" Marisa asked.

"Yeah, there's no answer."

It was an overcast afternoon, the sun hidden behind a blanket of gray. Marisa scooted closer to her husband on the couch.

"She's probably out with Jasmine somewhere." She leaned her head onto Myles' shoulder. "Sorry for snapping at you like I did last night. I know you're not your father."

Myles leaned back, bringing Marisa back with him. "That's okay. You can spaz out on me all you want if the reward is what you put on me this morning."

Marisa smiled. "I did work you, didn't I?"

"You did more than that—with your lewd self," Myles teased. "I wonder if you violated any obscenity laws."

"I noticed you weren't exactly looking to call the authorities." Marisa saw people approaching the door. "Jackie and Carlos are here."

They got up to greet them.

"Hey, boopty!" Marisa said, picking up CJ as soon as he entered the house.

"Dang, Marisa, let the boy get in the house." Myles took off CJ's Yankees knit hat. "What's up, slugger?"

The three of them headed into the living room, leaving Carlos and Jackie standing in the entryway.

"Can we come in, too?" Jackie called after them.

Ten minutes later, Kenya, Amir, and the twins arrived. There was still no sign of Peggy, however. The adults congregated in the living room, while Deja and Jade played with CJ in the den.

"You spoke to Dad?" Myles asked Amir.

Amir shook his head. "I don't even know where he's staying. On the way over here we stopped by the shop. His car wasn't out there."

"What's that gonna be like? He and Ms. Peg working in the same building?" Jackie asked.

"Good question." Myles shrugged his shoulders. He looked at his brother and smirked. "Maybe he could go work for you, Amir. Cut hair in your shop."

"Yeah, imagine that," Amir said sarcastically.

"How's your agency doing?" Marisa asked Jackie and Kenya.

They looked at each other. Kenya spoke first. "Well, we had to fire our overnight supervisor, but other than that things are going smoothly."

"I don't know why you guys waited so long to cut that *pendejo* loose," Carlos said.

"Me neither," Amir agreed. "Carlos and I offered way back to come up there and tell him to hit the bricks."

"Oh, and wouldn't that just look great?" Jackie said with derision. "We have to get our husbands to do our dirty work."

"I can understand you not wanting your husbands involved," Amir said. "But we could've put in a call to Hakeem and Rashahn."

Carlos and Myles began laughing heartily.

"Who are Hakeem and Rashahn?" Jackie asked.

"A couple of crazy, thugged-out brothas from north Jersey," Myles said. "We never met them, but one of Amir's customers, Ibn, is always telling us stories about them."

"Apparently, they specialize in the problem-removal business," Carlos added, still laughing. "What did Ibn tell us their motto was?"

Amir grinned. *"No problem too big or too small to be fixed, no ass too big or too small to be kicked."*

The men laughed again.

"Every day is a party at that barbershop, isn't it?" Jackie asked.

"Maybe you should hire them to deal with your father," Kenya said.

Myles ignored that comment. "How is Mom handling it?" he asked. "Did anybody see her yesterday?"

"I called," Jackie said. "She told me that she was fine and that she would see me tomorrow."

"Same here," Kenya said. "She seems to be handling it well."

"That's just shock," Myles said. "She put in nearly forty years with Dad. I can't imagine her not being devastated."

Marisa wavered on whether to say what she wanted to say, then decided to go ahead. "I'm sure she's hurt. I'm not so sure she's shocked."

"Come again?" Myles said.

"How do you know she didn't have an inkling that some-thing was up?" Marisa asked.

"Because if she did, she would have . . ." Myles fumbled.

"Would've what?" Marisa asked.

Myles couldn't think of anything to say.

"Like you said, they lived with each other for almost forty years," Marisa continued. "She doesn't know him inside out?"

"Good point," Jackie said.

"Haven't you guys noticed that lately every weekend, when the family was together, he found some reason to leave?" Marisa asked.

"Yeah, I did notice that," Kenya said slowly. "Always when there was a roomful of people."

"There you go."

"Well, I didn't notice anything," Myles said. "Why didn't you guys speak up?"

"And say what?" Kenya asked.

"If you had told me," Myles said, "I would've approached Dad about it."

"It wouldn't have worked," Kenya said. "Amir tried that. He told your father point-blank he was spotted in Camden with another woman—"

Carlos raised an eyebrow. So Amir *had* told Kenya about his motel spotting.

"—and your father denied he was having an affair," Kenya ended.

"What!" Myles looked at Amir. "You didn't tell me about it?"

"Sorry, bro," Carlos said. "Blame me. I should've told you the night when I saw him at that motel."

Oh, shit. Amir closed his eyes.

"What!" Jackie, Kenya, Myles all yelled in unison.

Jackie and Myles were like a pair of stereo headphones shrilling on Carlos' ears. "You keep that from me? . . . I'm supposed to be your wife . . . What the hell is wrong with you?"

Kenya turned on Amir. "How come you didn't tell me it was *Carlos* who saw your father in Camden? Or that it was a motel? Huh?"

Marisa left the squabbling to join the kids in the other room. She wanted to make sure they stayed in the den.

Just then, Jasmine and Peggy walked in the front door. They peered into the living room. They had heard the yelling before they hit the door.

When the combatants in the den saw Peggy arrive, they stopped. Their faces were all knotted in various degrees of lividity, and their chests heaved as they caught their breaths.

Peggy looked at Jasmine. "Maybe I should join y'all for that other movie."

Who is "y'all"? the combatants wondered.

Darius appeared behind Peggy and Jasmine, carrying two bags from Bed Bath & Beyond.

"Thank you, Darius," Peggy said. "You can put those on the kitchen table for me."

Amir turned to Kenya, "Isn't that the kid from . . ." He didn't have to finish his thought when he saw the look of consternation on her face.

Myles, Carlos, and Amir were lazing in the den, their stomachs densely packed with Peggy's chicken. Everyone else in the house was in the dining room, where tense negotiations had been going on for the past several hours.

Jasmine and Darius finally emerged into the den.

"We're on our way to catch the new Seagal flick," Jasmine said.

Myles perked up. At the very least, Darius had good taste.

"It was nice meeting you all," Darius said to the trio of men.

"All right, Darius," Carlos said.

Myles got up and shook his hand. "We look forward to getting to know you better, Darius."

"A lot better," Amir said, rising as well.

Darius nodded. "Cool. I understand."

Amir liked the way Darius kept eye contact.

Jasmine rolled her eyes. "Come on, Darius."

The two of them left.

Carlos looked over at Myles. "You still mad?"

It was a little difficult to summon up fury when you feel like a beached whale, Myles thought as he sat back down. "Naw, forget about it." He extended his fist and gave him a pound. "Please, next time, don't decide for me what I need to know."

"Fair enough," Carlos said.

Myles looked at Amir. He nodded in agreement as well.

"Did you get a good look at the woman, Carlos?" Myles asked.

"Not that great," Carlos said. "I didn't know her. She was short, young."

"Young?" Myles repeated.

"What," Amir interjected, "you think sixty-year-old men cheat with sixty-year-old women?"

"How young?" Myles asked.

"Like I said, I didn't get a good look at them," Carlos answered. "But she was too spry to be but so old."

"You think your mother will ever take him back?" Carlos asked.

"Highly doubtful," Amir said.

"Really?" Carlos got up and peered into the dining room to make sure the coast was clear. Marisa, Peggy, Jackie, and Kenya were still discussing Darius and Jasmine. He then made sure he sat close to Amir and Myles so he wouldn't have to speak loudly.

"A lot of women won't leave their men over sex," he said. "I've even heard some of my female colleagues say it's stupid to break up a good relationship over just sex—especially if there are kids involved—because the next man you get with is just as likely to cheat on you as the last one. But may not be as good a provider, or as good a man, period."

"I agree with that," Amir said.

"You do?"

"Yeah, to a point." Amir shifted around so he was facing the other two. "Lemme give you a hypothetical. Do you think if Kenya found out I fucked some grad student two years ago, she would divorce me? Break up the family—have the girls grow up in a house different from their father over some inconsequential shit like that?"

"Probably not," Myles said. "But she would put you through such hell, you'll probably wish she left you."

"No doubt," Amir said, "but Kenya knows I'm a good man. Not perfect, by any means, but I'm a man who loves my wife and adore my children. And I bust my ass to give them the best lifestyle I can. If Kenya left me, it would be akin to letting that little coed become so significant that she could break up her family. She wouldn't let some little tramp have that kind of power over her life."

"So why do you think your mother's situation is different?" Carlos asked.

"Because me and Myles are grown," Amir replied. "Because my father's shit wasn't inconsequential—it was a full-blown affair. Because she doesn't need him financially. Because she's at a point in her life where she can afford to think of herself first."

"And because of what she heard him tell that trick on the phone," Myles said, contorting his face in disgust.

Amir was about to reply when Kenya and Jasmine came back into the den.

Carlos checked his watch. "It takes less time for America and Russia to agree on antiballistic missiles."

"Yeah. Why are y'all giving that kid such a hard time?" Myles asked. "He doesn't seem that bad to me."

"Because we've known him for years, and you've known him for hours," Kenya said before sitting next to Amir.

"Still, it's gonna be easier dealing with Darius now that we don't have to deal with him professionally," Jackie admitted.

"He certainly seems to be making an effort," Kenya said. "Jackie, didn't you expect him to get up from the table at some point and just say fuck it, I don't have to sit through this bullshit?"

Jackie laughed. "Yeah, I did. But he's too smitten with Jasmine to do that. That's what is so surprising."

"Why?" Carlos asked.

"Because Darius gets a lot of attention from girls," Kenya explained, "but I've never see him care too much for any *one*."

"Well, he knows he's strictly on a probationary period," Amir said. "I have an extra ticket to the Sixers-Lakers next week. I'm gonna see if he wants to go. I wanna get to know this guy personally if he's gonna be dating Jasmine. I wanna know what color drawers he wears."

"That would be nice," Jackie said. "I think you'll like Darius. He can be rough, but there's a lot of potential there."

Kenya concurred. "However, it's the 'rough' that worries me," she added.

"It must not worry you too much," Myles said, "look at who you married."

*   *   *

Darius and Jasmine had just returned from the movie. They were sitting parked in his car about half a block down from the Moore home.

Jasmine put her hand around the back of Darius' head and gave him a long, wet kiss.

"Thank you again for enduring that inquisition," Jasmine said, running her fingernails along his scalp. "I swear, I thought Jackie and Kenya were trying to provoke you."

Darius leaned closer to her, closed his eyes, and rolled his neck slowly. Jasmine's stroking felt good.

Jasmine continued. "Just so they could tell my Aunt Peg, 'see I told you so.'"

"That may have been part of it," Darius agreed. "But I kept cool because I know that they're just looking out for you." Darius opened his eyes. "So, I kept my eyes on the prize."

Jasmine smiled. "I'm a prize now?"

"No doubt," Darius said, straightening up. "And I also know that deep down, Jackie and Kenya like me."

Jasmine gave him a disbelieving look.

"Deep, *deep* down." Darius said, half-chuckling.

Honestly, he hoped that over time when they saw how much he liked Jasmine they would come around. After they saw how responsible he was, how well he treated her, and how happy he made her. If not, then so be it. Ultimately, the only person in the family that had to like him was sitting beside him in the car. Though her aunt would be a nice ally to have as well.

"Well, at some point expect the family to send you an emissary to talk to you about attending college," Jasmine sighed. "Probably Amir."

Darius leaned over and gave her a kiss. "See, right there, that's what I like about you."

"What, that I warn you about my family?"

"No, that you use words like 'emissary.'" Darius flashed a toothy grin. "You know a brotha appreciates a brainy girl."

Jasmine was on her way upstairs to call Darius on his cell phone even though they had just parted ways five minutes ago, when the receiver she was holding rang.

"Hello?"

"Hey Jaz, what's up?"

Jasmine rolled her eyes. "Yeah?"

"Where you been all day?"

"Out with Darius," Jasmine said evenly.

Danae sucked her teeth. "You still seeing him? He ain't worth all that."

Jasmine recognized sour grapes. Danae wasn't ever going to take to Darius because he hadn't chosen her.

"I been seeing a college guy from Rowan named Stanley," Danae said. "I showed his friend your picture. He wants to meet you."

"What do you want, Danae?" Jasmine said, bristling.

"Dag. What's your problem?" Danae asked. "Why you acting so funny? And why are you giving me the cold shoulder in school?"

Jasmine closed the door to her bedroom. "Don't play dumb with me, Danae."

"I ain't playing. Why are you throwing me all this shade?"

Jasmine shifted the receiver from ear to ear in irritation. "You know what, you probably ain't playing. You are a dumb chick."

"Oh, shit. And you're supposed to be my friend. You know what? Fuck you, Jasmine."

"No, fuck you, *bitch*. You and your hoey-ass mom."

"My moms?" Danae sputtered. "She's better than your drug addict of a mother."

"If you say so. Even where my mom is, she's still probably hanging out with a better class of people," Jasmine snapped. "Your hoey-ass mom is the one hanging out with people who think it's cute to sleep with sixty-year-old married men."

"Wh-what?" Danae exclaimed. "What are you talking about?"

Acting definitely wasn't Danae's strong suit.

"Cut the shit, Danae," Jasmine said, losing patience. "I know your hoey ass knows what your hoey-ass mom and her hoey-ass friend have been up to."

"Who you calling a ho?"

"You're lucky that all I'm doing is calling you names," Jasmine said. "If I didn't think it would cause my aunt more grief, I'd be putting my Iversons in your ass."

"Yeah, right. Whatever."

"Oh, it ain't too late for me to throw you a beatdown, bitch," Jasmine warned. "So you better not try me."

"Go right ahead and blame me for something that Stacy did, then. I don't care."

"I never told you it was Stacy," Jasmine said. "If you're so innocent, how did you know it was her?"

Danae sputtered, "You—you said it was my momma's friend."

"What, your momma only got one friend?" Jasmine shook her head in disgust. "How did it happen, Danae? Did my uncle come by to pick me up one day and Stacy saw his Lincoln? Did she and your mother start conversating about my uncle having a little loot? How he might be vulnerable to attention from a younger woman. Did Stacy decide right then to start hanging out at Starks Bar and throw a little ass my uncle's way?"

"I don't know—"

"Stop lying. I know you know, Danae. You're their little 'hit' girl. Ho-In-Training."

"I ain't no ho in training."

"You're already a full-fledged ho?" Jasmine mocked. "Congratulations. Your momma must be proud."

"It ain't Stacy's fault if your uncle don't want your aunt," Danae said. "If he don't want her, he don't want her. Get over it."

"That's just what a ho would say," Jasmine said bitterly. "Don't call my house anymore."

Jasmine clicked off the phone.

Later, Jasmine did the ladies a favor and shepherded Deja, Jade, and CJ upstairs so they could lie down and the adults could talk freely. They were impressed that she did so without being asked.

"She's turning into quite a lady, isn't she?" Kenya asked. She came out of the kitchen and joined the ladies at the dining room table, where they were drinking coffee. She looked at Peggy. "Do you remember how grown she was when she was small?"

Peggy took a sip of her coffee and rolled her eyes. "Do I."

"I remember when I was first dating Amir," Kenya continued. "Jasmine was up on all the latest fashions, designer names, too. When she was seven years old."

"Get out of here," Jackie said, disbelieving.

Kenya raised her hand, "If I'm lying, I'm frying. Homegirl used to check the tags on my clothes."

Jackie and Marisa chortled.

"And would tell me if something looked cute on me."

Jackie tossed her head back. "No, she didn't."

"Girl, I was grateful for those times," Kenya said. "Have you ever had a seven-year-old girl look you up and down, crinkle her nose, and tell you, 'You don't need to be wearing that?' It's not a pleasant experience, trust me."

All the ladies fell out over that. When the laughter died down, Peggy looked at Marisa. "She sure is looking forward to spending the summer down there in Maryland with you and Myles."

Marisa quickly realized that with the events of the past week, Peggy was going to be alone. "You're welcome to join her."

"Thank you." Peggy smiled. "Maybe for a week or two, but actually, I'm thinking of taking me a nice, long cruise this summer."

Peggy noticed the looks of surprise around the table.

"I've been thinking about doing so for a while now, taking a short cruise somewhere. But now I think I'll make it a nice, long one."

"What about the shop?" Kenya asked.

"It'll be there when I get back."

"I mean having to see Mr. Lenny there every day," Kenya said.

Peggy shrugged. "As long as he stays over there on his side of the building, I'll be fine." She noticed the cutting looks. "Look, I've been with Leonard nearly forty years. I haven't been with Leonard for nearly two days. I think I'm allowed a little time to be angry, be in denial, stew, make light of this serious situation, whatever I need to do."

Peggy gathered her thoughts.

"I know at some point, I—we, myself and Leonard—are going to have to make a lot of decisions regarding a lot of things. Home, shop, marriage, bank accounts . . . I'm not ready to deal with all of that, or deal with him."

"You don't have to," Kenya said. "When you're ready to, if you need any help, we're here for you."

"Yeah, Ms. Peg," Jackie added. "I know a good lawyer"— she nodded subtly at Marisa—"and she's a real shark."

Peggy smiled. "Besides, I'm sixty years old. It's almost

time for me to hang up my curling iron for good anyway. I'm not working myself to death like some washerwoman. I'm almost done with work—period."

She looked around the table. "Anybody want to buy a salon?"

Carlos, Amir, and Myles were at the video store to rent some DVDs.

"You staying for the movie, Myles?" Carlos asked. "Or are you and Marisa driving back tonight?"

"We're staying, 'Los," Myles replied as he browsed the foreign-film section, "Neither I nor Marisa has anything to do tomorrow."

Myles perused the selections some more, then asked, "Do you guys know any short, elfin-looking women named Stacy?" he asked. "That's who Mom thinks the woman is that Dad has been running around with."

"Really?" Amir asked.

"Yeah, Mom must've told them when they were all in the dining room after dinner," Myles added, "because Marisa told me. Y'all know her?"

After giving the matter some thought, both Carlos and Amir shook their heads.

"Apparently she's a friend of Danae's mother," Myles said.

"Who's Danae?" Carlos asked.

"One of Jasmine's friends." Myles picked up a Spanish film titled *Hable con Ella*.

"Geesh," Carlos said, "that'll put a little strain on the ol' friendship."

"You know," Amir said. He thought about it some more. "No, I don't know a Stacy who looks like an elf. I'll put the word out, though. If she's local, someone in the barber shop is bound to know her."

Amir suddenly became aware of his surroundings. "Where the hell you got us, Myles? Let's go get an action flick. Forget this artsy-fartsy nonsense."

"I heard this is a good film," Myles protested.

"I don't want to see a 'film,' I want to see a *movie*." Amir snatched the box out of Myles' hands. "What the—what the hell is *Hable con Ella*?"

"It's Spanish," Carlos said. "It means 'Talk to Her.' "

"Talk to Her?" Amir was incredulous. "The reason I'm getting the DVD is so I won't have to 'talk to her.' "

Stacy brought her empty bowl out of the bedroom. She had been eating ice cream in there because Leonard was monopolizing the television, watching sports in the living room.

Even if he was watching something she was interested in, she wouldn't have stayed in the living room. She was tired of Leonard's hands being all up her shirt, cupping her ass, and down the front of her pants. It seemed like her condo had become too small for her to turn around without coming into contact with his erect dick.

Stacy went to put her bowl in the sink, but there were a dozen chicken wings floating in water.

"Where did this chicken come from?" she asked.

"I picked it up earlier when I went out. I thought you'd want to cook for your man," Leonard said, smiling from the couch.

Stacy bit her tongue. She placed the bowl on the counter and leaned against it.

Leonard came into the kitchen. He was wearing a T-shirt, light blue boxers, dark blue dress socks. He reached into the refrigerator and grabbed a Heineken. Before he left the kitchen, he grabbed Stacy's ass.

"I got two heineys," he said, laughing.

Stacy watched his spindly legs carry him back into the living room. He rubbed his stomach, sat down, and took a sip of beer, then set the bottle on the coffee table. Right next to a stack of coasters.

Stacy willed the edge out of her voice before she spoke. "Lenny, can you please use a coaster?"

"Oh, sure, babe." He smiled at her as he put his bottle on a coaster. "It sure feels good to be able to open a fridge and see ice-cold beer in there."

He was ahead of her, Stacy thought, because she was now scared to open the fridge. It had become inhabited with the most disgusting products she had laid eyes on. Head cheese. Liverwurst. Pig's feet.

Thirty seconds later, Leonard was up and headed to the bathroom. That had really become a disaster area for Stacy. As if the Preparation-H, Ben-Gay, and other medications weren't clutter-forming enough, she about had a fit when she saw his partial denture swimming in one of her good glasses.

And her plan to turn her spare room into an office was for naught. He had all his shit spread out in there. His personal shit. His shit for the barbershop.

It was like having a roommate all over again. Except she was supposed to fuck this one whenever he wanted some.

And how was Stacy supposed to entertain men—real, viable, long-term-option men—with Leonard squatting here?

Stacy heard a disgusting hacking sound emanating from the bathroom. What was he doing? Dying in there?

Gold mine or not, she wasn't sure how long she was gonna be able to endure this.

chapter 17

That Saturday, Amir was in his usual spot, behind the first chair in his barbershop. It was early evening, and the pace of customers had slowed considerably. He was contemplating leaving Willie in charge and knocking off to take his family out to dinner and to the drive-in movie in Delaware.

As he stretched and yawned, the bell on the door sounded.

"Close your mouth, nigga. No one needs to see all that."

"Leave him alone, frat. You know that's how dogs sweat."

Amir looked as Mike and Ibn entered. Amir realized that he hadn't seen Mike since he had tied the knot. "Yo, Mike, congratulations on getting married," Amir said as the pair settled in chairs.

Mike beamed. "Thanks, man."

"I hear you overachieved," Amir needled. "A doctor, no less."

"And he better treat her right," Ibn chimed in, "or he will be needing her services."

Mike pointed his thumb at Ibn. "This guy . . ."

"You know," Amir agreed. "Say, Ibn, when are you going to make someone an unlucky woman?"

"Ha-ha," Ibn said. His face turned solemn. "Truth is, I

don't know if there is any *one* woman who can handle me. It wouldn't be fair to put that kind of burden on one sista." He spotted the looks he was getting from the other people in the shop. "I'm serious."

Amir and Mike exchanged head shakes. "On that note." Amir picked up the smock, "Mike, you ready?"

Mike climbed into the barber's chair. Ibn picked up an issue of *Vibe* and began thumbing through it. "Just keeping it real," he grumbled.

"Same as usual, Mike? High and tight?" Amir asked.

"Yeah, natural hairline." Amir fastened the smock around Mike. As he turned on his clippers, he decided to ask these two about Stacy. Amir wasn't expecting much. He hadn't gotten anywhere all week with any of his other customers.

"Do you guys know a Stacy, lives in Willow Run in Collingswood?"

When Amir saw Ibn's head snap up from the magazine, he knew they did. Ibn slowly rose to his feet and trained his ear so he could hear Amir better over the clippers.

"Yeah, we know her," Mike said. "What about her?"

Though he didn't know their opinion of her, or the extent of their relationship, Amir decided not to beat around the bush.

"She's messing around with my father."

"What!" Ibn leapt onto the row of chairs like he had just seen a rat. He lost his balance and went tumbling over onto his side, splaying his body across four chairs. When he finally came still, he lay on his back staring at the ceiling, hyperventilating and mumbling incomprehensibly.

All activity in the shop had stopped. Willie had just finished up his customer. They were both frozen at the sight of Ibn. The other barber, Durango, who had been talking on the phone while waiting for an appointment to come in, stood with his mouth agape.

"Isn't your dad married, Amir?" Mike asked.

Amir shrugged. "He was. Now they're separated because of this."

"Oh . . . Jesus Christ . . . ," Ibn groaned.

Amir looked at Mike. "I'm guessing you brothas don't think highly of her."

Mike lifted his brow, "Yeah, well . . ."

Ibn's moaning interrupted him. He was still lying flat on his back, looking at the ceiling, deeply pained. When he spoke, he could only get a couple of words in at a time because he was gasping for air. "Bitch . . . nearly . . . broke up my boys . . ."

Mike translated. "Stacy was the former longtime girlfriend of one of our boys, Colin. She caused so much stress on our friendship, it was ridiculous. Ibn and Colin even stopped speaking for a while."

". . . bought . . . her . . . stank ass . . . a Benz."

"Stacy pressured Colin into buying a Benz," Mike said. "She's one of those women who feels she's always entitled to the best, regardless of whether her man can afford it or not."

Amir immediately thought of the Escalade his father told him that he had just purchased. He wondered whose idea that really was.

". . . skank repaid him . . . by getting caught . . . with her titties out . . . with the dude . . ."

Everyone in the shop looked to Mike.

"Stacy cheated on Colin with the same salesman he'd bought the Benz from."

An uproar rose from the other men in the shop.

". . . peddlin' . . . her ass . . . for a . . . luxury auto . . . ," Ibn moaned.

Mike continued, "Colin walked in and found them on the couch in their condo." Mike leveled a wry look at Amir. "The condo in Willow Run."

". . . pissy attitude having . . . Keebler-looking . . ."

"Stacy has always had a nasty demeanor," Mike explained. "She only seems to derive joy from sucking happiness out of everyone else. As far as her appearance, she's very short in stature, with a sharp nose and chin."

". . . opportunistic . . . exploitive . . . sneaky . . . money-hungry leprechaun . . . where's me pot o' gold, where's me pot o' gold . . ."

"Watch your pop, Amir," Myles warned. "Stacy will suck him dry if he lets her. She's the type who will sit pious in church on Sunday and the other six days be the most underhanded, backstabbing, self-promoting person you never want to meet. She's ruthless, for real. My guess is that if your dad isn't coming out the pocket heavy yet, he soon will be."

Amir nodded.

"Now . . . she's fucking old men . . . breaking up homes . . . where does it all end . . . you tell me . . . where does it all end . . . ," Ibn lamented.

Willie placed a cold towel on Ibn's forehead.

Mike looked at Amir in warning. "She really is bad news."

"I believe you," Amir cast a glance at Ibn. He was still asking no one in particular "Where does it all end?"

"Is there anything you can do?" Mike asked. "Will your dad listen to reason?"

"I'll try," Amir said. "But he's been acting so nutty lately that I don't know." He turned his clippers back on. "One thing I know I can do is protect my mother's future. If my dad is gonna be an idiot, let him do it with his own money. He isn't dragging my mother down with him."

Myles and Amir pulled away in his Land Cruiser from Thirtieth Street Station.

"So Dad is living in Collingswood, huh? You got the address?" Myles asked as he buckled his seat belt.

"Yeah."

Myles looked out the window at rush-hour Philadelphia's bustle. "What did he say when you talked to him on the phone?"

Amir lifted and dropped his shoulders. "That he was living in Collingswood. That we could come by and talk to him around six o'clock tonight, and that he wasn't in the mood to be lectured to by people he brought into the world."

Myles turned toward Amir. "He really said that?"

Amir nodded.

Myles was really startled by his dad's attitude. This whole situation of his parents was weighing on him. But he had resolved on the train ride up that he wasn't going to be the only one wallowing in sentimentality. If his dad didn't give a damn, why should he? He was going to be stoic, like Amir.

Myles let out a snort of disgust. "This cat is really feeling himself, isn't he?"

"Yep. He got rid of his Town Car."

"Huh?" Myles was almost too scared to ask. "For what?"

"An Escalade EXT."

"The pickup?" Myles was astonished. "What is he, a rapper now? I swear if that man is wearing a Rocawear hoodie and Timbs when we get there . . ."

"What are you gonna do?" Amir deadpanned. "Hit him again?"

"It might do him some good," Myles muttered. "Knock some sense back into him."

Amir turned onto I-676.

"Has he been back to work yet?"

"Why?" Amir asked. "Are you worried about him supporting his mistress?"

Myles stared at him. "I was wondering if he and Mom have been coexisting at the shop."

Amir checked his watch. "I think they both went in today. Mom is probably still at her salon. They don't have to see each other, so it shouldn't be a problem."

"It's about time for them to think about retiring anyway," Myles said. "Selling the shop and the salon—the whole building. That's just become more complicated, though."

"True." Amir slowed down as traffic backed up. "But I was wondering, do you think Mom will want to stop working now? Maybe she will want to stay busy."

"The hell with that," Myles said. "There's more to her than being Dad's wife. There are numerous things she can do to occupy her time besides standing on her feet all day working herself like a government mule. I'll be damned if Dad's stupidity is going to cause *that* to happen. He's done enough damage as it is, but he isn't going to take away my mother's health, or make her think she's less than what she is," Myles said with resolve. "Even if I have to go in there and yank the smock off her myself."

Amir smiled. "Well, *you* could do that. Seeing how you could just fill in for Mom, anyway."

Myles laughed. "Really, why don't you just admit that when we was growing up, you should have learned how to do female hair like I did."

"No, thank you, Ms. Thing."

"Yeah, okay." Myles sneered. "Do you have any idea how popular I was with the ladies in college because I could do hair?"

"That's the difference between me and you," Amir said as he approached the Ben Franklin Bridge. "I was popular with the ladies without having a marketable skill. They were more interested in doing for me."

"Whatever, pardner." Myles shook his head. "I grieve for you. You don't know the sensual joy that is derived from doing the hair of the woman you love. The erotic pleasure of washing and drying, massaging and oiling, combing and brushing, braiding and curling—"

"Yeah, yeah, yeah," Amir said disinterestedly.

"—the hair of the woman you love. It's an excellent form of foreplay." Myles put his hand on his brother's forearm. "Oh, I'm sorry. There I go 'bigwording' you again. Foreplay is the activity before intercourse designed to—"

"I know what foreplay is, cockmeat," Amir said. He sighed loudly. "I do believe that I've stepped into the bizarro world. My dad is acting like a teenager, and my no-pussy-getting younger brother is lecturing me about sex."

They drove in relative silence until they got to Collingswood.

"Do you have the address?" Myles asked.

"I know where it is," Amir replied, "Willow Run Condos off Haddon Avenue."

So that's where my father has chosen to lay his head, Myles thought as Amir turned onto Haddon Avenue. After being with my mother for nearly four decades. Willow Run.

They pulled into the complex. It was broken up into four different courts. The first two contained two-story town houses clustered in groups of six. In the rear were the condos. They were three-story brick buildings with four condominiums located on each floor.

Amir had the unit number written down on a piece of paper in the glove compartment, but they didn't need it. Not when they saw the shiny, new, black Escalade sitting prominently in the parking lot. Amir pulled into a visitor's spot alongside it.

"Come in," Leonard said, opening the door of the second-floor unit for his sons.

The sight of their father jarred the boys a bit.

He was completely clean-shaved, now sporting a baldy. Leonard was wearing a blue T-shirt and black jeans. Myles caught himself looking down at his footwear. He was wearing the black Reeboks he wore when he cut hair.

"Have a seat."

Myles and Amir followed him into the living room. They sat on the couch together while their father sat in a chair.

"Can I get you guys something to drink?"

"Yeah, a glass of ice water," Amir said.

Leonard looked at Myles.

"No, thanks."

Their father retreated to the kitchen. Seconds later, he brought Amir his glass of water.

"Thanks, Dad."

"How are the twins?" Leonard asked.

Amir took a sip. "They're fine. They're fine."

Amir set the glass on the coffee table.

"Son, make sure you use one of those coasters," Leonard said, pointing to a set of round, cork coasters on the end of the table.

Hearing that pissed Myles off. For years it was no small source of aggravation for his mother that his father refused to use coasters and was constantly leaving rings on her furniture. But here he was, in this whore's house, and he respected her enough to do so?

Biting his tongue, Myles got up and walked to the balcony door. Dusk was beginning to fall, and Myles watched the lights in the courtyard below come on.

Leonard's eyes followed his son, but he didn't say anything.

Amir recognized one of his dad's suitcases standing in a corner.

"You still haven't unpacked yet, Pop?"

"Huh?" Leonard took his eyes off of Myles and followed Amir's gaze. "Yeah, I—no, I don't need all those clothes in there. . . . But anyway, I'm only staying here temporarily anyway."

"Why?" Myles asked. "Aren't you welcome in her home? Or is your girlfriend only good at wrecking homes?"

"No, I'm welcome for as long as I want to stay," Leonard assured him, though not with much conviction as far as Myles was concerned. "I just want my own place." Leonard eyed his younger son. "And as far as wrecking homes, your mother and I have been drifting apart for years, so she didn't wreck nothing."

"If that's the case, you should've just told Mom you wanted out," Myles said. "Instead of all this duplicity, sneaking around."

"Yeah, that's how it's usually done," Leonard said dryly. "Men just go up to their wives of thirty-something years all the time and say 'I want out' whenever a little distance comes in between them."

"Well, isn't that better than what you've done?" Myles asked.

"Maybe. What I did is what's usually done," Leonard said. "I just got caught."

Myles winced.

"Don't believe me, then," Leonard said, "Come back to me in thirty years and we'll see if Marisa is the only woman you've been with in all that time."

"Is Stacy the only one?" Amir asked.

"How do you know her name?" Leonard asked.

Myles spoke up. "Mom heard you say it on the phone. When you were talking about eating her ass out."

Leonard glared at him. "What's your problem?"

Myles shook his head. "No problem here." He smiled wide. "In fact, I'm happy for you. I just wanna know, is she gonna be our new mommy?"

"Myles." Amir gave him a "calm down" look.

"No, let him speak his mind," Leonard said. "It's something to see a son disrespect his father so openly. After all, I only fathered him, watched him breathe his first breath on this planet, fed, clothed, and provided for him twenty-something years, put him through school, taught him to drive, taught him how to cut hair. . . . He's more than justified disrespecting me now."

Leonard stood up and walked toward Myles. Once he was in front of him, he continued. "If you ever have a child, I hope you never fall short in his eyes." Leonard narrowed his eyes. "It's really something to know that all those years can be undone so quickly."

Myles twisted his face. "What do you want from me? Respect? You left my mother to shack up with a woman my age." He looked at his father with disdain. "Your new truck, your clothes—you look to be on some ridiculous quest to reclaim your long-lost youth. I'm supposed to pretend I respect that?"

"I'm not asking you to like what I'm doing, I'm asking you to respect what I've *done*," Leonard said. "What's me and your mother's relationship got to do with you?"

Myles was going to say something, but instead just stuck his hands in his pockets and looked back out onto the courtyard.

Amir asked. "Is this thing here serious?"

"What do you mean?" Leonard asked.

"Is this woman going to be your woman?"

"Well," Leonard shot Myles one more look before coming back over to the living room area and taking a seat, "she is my lady. But if it wasn't something serious, your mother certainly made it so."

Amir scowled. "What do you mean?"

Leonard rubbed his newly shorn head. "Well, let me first say that I'm glad that things turned out the way they did. I'm looking forward to this new chapter of my life—as your mother should be, too. In fact, we probably should've parted company years ago. As I said before, we've been drifting apart for quite some time."

Listening to him, Amir couldn't help but think that his father was trying to convince himself.

Leonard continued. "The way the whole thing went down—I can certainly understand her being upset. But she didn't have to make a big production out of it. That was her choice."

Myles turned and cocked his head, as if he couldn't believe what he had just heard.

"Dad, how was it her choice?" Amir asked. "She didn't tell you to go out and sleep with this woman."

"No, she didn't. But once she found out, she made the decision to broadcast her business to everybody." Leonard rested his elbows on his knees. "So now she's forced to do something or she'll lose face."

Myles looked over at Amir, as if he needed verification that he had just heard that right.

"Let me get this straight," Myles said. "You expected Mom to just swallow what you did, keep it under wraps, like *she* did something wrong? Like she had something to be ashamed of?"

"Women do it all the time," Leonard said nonchalantly. "You keep it in house. Your husband assures you he will leave the other woman alone, buys the wife a new fur or a new piece of jewelry, and it's done with."

"Who do you think Mom is? Carmela Soprano?" Myles snarled. "You get to have the dutiful wife, the home-cooked meals, the clean laundry, all while you get to hump any piece of ass you want on the side? What makes you so entitled?" Myles asked, his tone full of incredulity. "You know what, Amir. He doesn't think he's a rapper, he thinks he's a don. El Negro Mafioso."

"You know what, Myles—," Leonard said, rising.

"I meant no disrespect, Don Corn-y-one," Myles said, bowing.

"You should leave," Leonard said firmly.

Myles shrugged. No skin off his nose. He headed to the door.

Leonard's gaze followed him. "When you're ready to deal with the reality of this situation like an adult, we can talk then."

"I'll be waiting in your truck, Amir," Myles said ignoring his father. He opened the door, but paused and turned around for a parting shot.

"Don Corn-y-one," he added in a mock Italian accent, "may you and Stacy's first child . . . be a masculine child."

"Get out."

"You can be its daddy and its granddaddy."

"Get out!"

Myles closed the door. Amir and Leonard could hear him laughing all the way to the parking lot.

"Asshole," Leonard grumbled.

"Maybe," Amir said, rising to his feet, "but you should hear how you sound, Dad." He motioned with his hands at the surroundings. "How this looks. You haven't made your case very well."

"I shouldn't have to 'make my case' to my own sons," Leonard said emphatically. "Or is unconditional love a one-way street? Parent to offspring, not vice versa?"

Amir didn't answer.

"Whether or not you guys agree with what I've done, I'm still y'all's father. Whether or not I'm doing right in this situation, you know that I've always done right by you." Leonard shifted his weight from foot to foot as he searched for his next words. "Me and your mother are long done raising y'all," Leonard continued. "It's my time now. Let me be happy."

Amir looked his father square in his eye. "You're happy now, Pop?"

Leonard nodded. "Oh, I'm happy. That you can be sure of." He paused. "It's still early on in this transition, but I see good times ahead."

Amir nodded, said his good-bye, and left.

As he walked down the stairs and toward the parking lot, Amir was only sure of one thing. His father was a fool.

Four months later . . .

Peggy Moore was sitting in the den watching a Braves-Phillies game when she heard a knock at the front door.

She was expecting Leonard. They had just completed their last mediation session earlier that day, and all remaining issues regarding assets had been resolved. It hadn't been overly contentious. Peggy could've tried to take him to the cleaners because of his infidelity, but she chose not to. As long as she got the house, there was more than enough to support both of them comfortably. No need to go to war and end up shelling out to lawyers all that they had saved. They had worked hard for four decades to build their nest eggs for these golden years. Of course, the thinking had been that they would spend these years and their savings together, but it hadn't worked out that way.

So after they had the business independently appraised, Leonard had bought her out at fair market price. He had found another lady to manage the salon for him. Some of Peggy's old employees had chosen to move on, but enough had remained so the transition had been relatively seamless.

Peggy's thought was that they should just sell the building and both businesses. How much longer was Leonard planning to work? Now matter how young he liked to pretend that he was, he was still in his sixties.

But Leonard wasn't her concern anymore. If he wanted to cut hair until they pried the clippers from his dead, cold hand, that was his business. Besides, Peggy figured that Leonard needed a steady cash flow if he was intent on squiring young women around. Why else would they want to be with an old man unless he was capable and willing to commit wanton acts of financial generosity on their behalf? It certainly wasn't the force of Leonard's personality.

But let him learn the hard way. Her future was secured.

She opened the door and let Leonard in.

"Hi, Peggy."

"Hi."

There was an awkward pause in the foyer, which was finally settled by Leonard giving her a peck on the cheek.

"It felt strange having to knock on the door," he said as he entered the den and sat in a chair.

Peggy didn't know how to respond to that, so she said nothing.

"Maybe one day you can come see my apartment."

Why would I want to do that? Peggy thought.

"I rented a loft unit in that new building on the Camden waterfront," Leonard continued. "It has a great view of the Philadelphia skyline."

"I know," Peggy said. "Deja told me."

Leonard smiled. "Kenya brought the girls by last week. I took them to the Aquarium and the Children's Garden. It's within walking distance from my place, you know."

Peggy was about to ask him if she could get him something to drink but decided against it. In this setting, together in the den, it would be too much like the thousands of times she had got him something to drink when they were married.

Leonard noticed the game on the tube. "Who's winning?"

"Phillies. Thome just hit a homer."

"That's great." Leonard stretched his legs. "You know, I have a partial season ticket plan this year. If you ever want to go to a game, just let me know."

Peggy nodded in acknowledgment. She tucked her feet underneath her on the couch.

"Is Jasmine home?"

"She's spending the summer at Myles and Marisa's place. She left last week after school let out."

"You agreed to that?"

"Why not? My only stipulation was that she read a book a week and that she commit at least one day a week to doing something positive for the benefit of others. Whether that be work in a soup kitchen, or read stories to the blind at the library, or volunteer at a hospital, whatever. Myles and Jasmine both assured me that she would. The rest of the time she will spend shopping, going to concerts, plays, and whatever else Marisa and she have planned."

Peggy continued, "This is one of Jasmine's last summers to just be a child, so I want her to enjoy it. I also wanted her to be around Marisa so that she could see the benefit of what education and hard work can get you. If Jasmine wants the nice cars, the designer wardrobe, the gazillion pairs of shoes, the jewelry—you know about the fabulousness of your daughter-in-law, Lenny—then maybe Jasmine will work as hard to get it, ya know?"

Leonard smiled. "Yeah, that seems like good thinking." He looked at Peggy. "So you're gonna be home alone all this summer?"

"Hardly," she replied. "This weekend I'm going down to Maryland, too. I'm gonna spend a week and a half there, then I'm off."

Leonard waited for her to finish. "Off where?"

"Roslyn and I are going to Africa."

"Africa?"

"Yep, for a month. We're gonna see it from tip to tip. The pyramids in Egypt, go on a safari at Masai Mara in Kenya, Victoria Falls, the Cape . . ."

"What?" Leonard was taken aback. "You know you better sit your old butt down."

"No chance of that happening," Peggy assured him. "When we get back, I only have a couple of weeks before I'm going on a cruise to the Caribbean with Joyce."

Leonard just shook his head in disbelief.

"Speaking of doing more than our age would allow," Peggy said, "I found a vial of Viagra on the closet floor. Any idea how that got there?"

Leonard turned beet red.

"I guess that explains your newfound energy so late in life," Peggy said mockingly.

"Naw, I barely used them . . ."

Peggy smirked.

"Listen," Leonard said, rising to his feet, anxious to change the subject, "are you doing okay?"

Peggy digested that for a moment. "What do you mean?"

Full of anxiousness, Leonard stuck his hands in his pockets, then took them out again. "You know, with the new arrangements."

Peggy shrugged nonchalantly as she turned the channel. "Yeah, why not?"

"It's nice to see you taking forty years together so seriously."

Peggy set down the remote. "You got more nerve than a toothache, Lenny. It was your ass that threw away the forty years when you started frolicking with tramps."

"There was no tramps," Leonard protested. "It was just one tra—woman."

"I don't know that."

"I'm telling you it's the truth," Leonard said, sitting back down on the couch, closer to Peggy this time.

"Okay, it's the truth," Peggy said. "So only one woman out there can say you licked her booty."

Leonard waved his hand in exasperation.

"What do you want from me, Lenny?" Peggy asked. "To fall apart? To cry myself to sleep every night? I'm just reacting to *your* actions. We're in this position because of *you*."

"Don't put it all on me, Peggy," Leonard said. "We've been drifting apart for years."

"I see," Peggy said, feigning deep contemplation. "And in your infinite wisdom, you thought that sleeping with some trollop was the best way to bridge that distance?" Peggy found her blood starting to boil, but she caught herself. What was she getting worked up for anyway?

"You know what? Then it's all for the best, isn't it?" she said casually.

Leonard stared at the rug. "Maybe it is, maybe it isn't." He looked up at Peggy. "I don't know—maybe we should try again."

Oh, this is rich, Peggy thought.

"What happened?" she asked soothingly. "Did your little girlfriend break up with you."

"Why do you have to be so cynical?"

"Oh, I can't imagine why. I'm funny like that, I guess," Peggy said. "So where's your friend, Stacy?"

"We're not seeing each other anymore." Leonard noticed Peggy's bemused reaction. "It was a mutual decision."

"I bet." Peggy nodded. "She told you to hit the road and you agreed to do so. Mutual decision."

"You don't know what you're talking about, Peggy. You—" Leonard caught himself. "Why does it matter anyway? It was all a big mistake."

"You got that right, buddy."

"It was a big mistake . . . and I'm sorry."

"You got that right as well," Peggy added. "And I'd have to be pretty sorry to buy this. When you were with your girlfriend, you didn't give a damn as to how I was doing. Now that she doesn't want you—or has bled enough money out of you to satisfy her for the time being—I get to have you back? So not only do I play second fiddle to your childish whims, she gets to dictate to me as well? No, thanks. I think better of myself than that, even if you don't."

Leonard turned his palms up. "What can I do now?"

Go to church. You need Jesus. "I suggest you get on with your life. I certainly plan to."

"It's that easy for you?" Leonard asked. "After all these years together?"

"What choice do I have?"

"I'm giving you a choice now."

Peggy couldn't believe Leonard was approaching her about a reconciliation. She had assumed the purpose of his visit tonight was for a simple clearing of the air.

"I don't know who you think you are, or who you think I am, but you do not have the right to treat me like some damn yo-yo," Peggy said, almost yelling. She knew that there was no calming down now. "You caused me to alter my life once." She held up her index finger. "Once. I'm not fool enough to give your crazy ass the opportunity to do so again."

"I am still the man who you've been married to for forty years of your life." Leonard squinted with irritation. "Why are you giving more weight to a mistake of a few months than all those years?"

Peggy glared at him. "Why do you want me back?"

"Because I *love* you, Margaret Eva Moore."

Peggy knew he was saying that because he thought it was what she wanted to hear. It sounded so rehearsed. Like he had practiced it on the ride over.

She didn't doubt that he loved her. It was hard to live with someone for two-thirds of your life and not have some attachment to them.

But what Leonard missed was the convenience of having her around more than loving her. Peggy sized this situation up real quick. Stacy was probably a selfish young thing who grew tired of Leonard's neediness real fast—if she ever really wanted him in the first place. So now he had to wash his own clothes, shop for his own groceries, do his own cooking, pay his own bills, and everything else. Leonard had been spoiled. He had never had to worry how toilet tissue got in the house. He just knew that when he went to wipe his ass, it was always there. Now, if he didn't remember to buy it, he was shit out of luck.

"I want my life back," Leonard said. Realizing how selfish he sounded, he quickly added, "And I want to give yours back."

"Why would you want it back?" Peggy asked. "I thought you said we were drifting apart anyway."

"Well, we can work on that."

"No, jackass." Peggy rose to her feet. "We could've worked on that *before* you did what you did. That option is no longer available to you." She put her hands on her hips. "I look at you, trendy new vehicle, trendy new wardrobe, clean-shaven to hide your gray—why are you doing all this? Because you think it makes you look more attractive. Because you are concerned with your appearance. How you are perceived?"

"Okay, so?"

"Well, setting aside the fact that you look like an idiot trying to be so damn young, are you so self-centered that you don't think anyone else should care about how they look? How they are perceived?" She pointed an index finger at the window. "You humiliated me out here running around with that whore of yours. How many people at that bar, in this town, knew what was going on and were laughing at me behind my back while they were smiling in my face? Do you know?" Peggy leaned forward. "Do you care, Lenny?"

"Yes, I—"

"Shut up, man." Peggy put up both her hands to shush him. "You don't care, because it doesn't involve *you* looking like a jackass. If we reconciled, it would again be me looking ridiculous and you're more than comfortable with that being the case. You would look like your dick is so strong that I can't get enough of it no matter how badly you disrespect me. Maybe you would get to brag to your drinking buddies down at Starks Bar how your dumbass wife ain't going nowhere because . . ." Peggy hitched her pants up. " 'Heh, heh, heh, she can't get enough of this good stuff.' "

Leonard rolled his eyes, but Peggy continued.

"By the way, if you were as young and as vigorous as you think you are, you wouldn't need that little blue pill. Because despite your misguided thoughts to the contrary, Lenny, your ass is still old. You're just an old fool. And that's the worst kind of fool to be."

"Oh, is that a fact?" Leonard said.

"Yes, from where I stand, it is. Anyway, like I said, I'm an option that is no longer available to you," Peggy said with as much finality as she could.

Fear crossed his face. "Do you mean that?"

"Yes, I do, Leonard. I really do. I don't want you anymore." Peggy headed to the foyer.

Leonard soon realized that was his signal to leave. He exhaled, stood up, and shook out the creases of his tan, linen slacks.

From the moment she saw them, Peggy had known that a woman had picked them out for him.

Leonard walked past her to the front door. Peggy turned her back to him. She heard the door open.

"Peggy."

She turned and faced him.

"There's no reason to tell the boys about this conversation."

Unbelievable. It's still all about how he looks. Even to his own sons.

"Lenny, get the hell out of my house."

chapter 18

Jasmine and Darius were lying in a double bed at a Rodeway Inn on the outskirts of Baltimore.

"Do you think your family knows we're not going to the harbor every Saturday afternoon?" Darius asked.

Jasmine shrugged. She had a pretty good idea that Marisa knew what was up. She had accompanied Jasmine and Kenya to the doctor when they put Jasmine on the pill. And that was months ago, right after Kenya found out that Jasmine was seeing Darius. Jasmine figured Jackie also knew she was on the pill, but didn't think anyone else was aware of it, including her Aunt Peg. Well, at least, if she was savvy, she hadn't let on to Jasmine that she was.

Darius didn't know either. Jasmine had promised Kenya that she would wait a year before she told Darius. If, in that time he didn't fuck around on her with anybody else, then she could feel safer to let him go bareback. Seemed like a good idea to Jasmine, so she had went along with it.

The pill had caused her ass to become a little fuller, which Darius loved. He just thought it was a result of Jasmine putting on a few pounds. He kept bragging about how he was responsible for putting those hips on her.

"If you're tired of the motel life," Jasmine offered, "my aunt, Myles, and Marisa are going to a baseball game tomorrow night. We'd have the place to ourselves."

"I gotta work tomorrow. Besides, I wouldn't want to disrespect their house like that," Darius said.

"Sheesh," Jasmine said playfully as she got out of the bed. "I'm still waiting for an appearance of the 'bad boy' that Jackie and Kenya warned me about about."

"Ha-ha," Darius said dryly.

"Shhh, Boy Scout. Lower your voice," Jasmine teased. "You don't want to disrespect the people in the next room, do you?"

Jasmine felt Darius' eyes on her as she slipped into her bra. He propped his head up with a couple of pillows and folded his arms behind his head. He was wearing nothing but his boxers and a broad grin.

"What are you cheesing at?"

"Perfection."

Jasmine smiled, and tried to figure out how she should pout her butt to look even more alluring.

"So get out of the way, because you're blocking my view of the mirror," Darius continued.

Jasmine gasped, ran over to the bed, and pounced on top of him.

"Whoa, whoa!" Darius said, turning away protectively.

Jasmine felt why brushing up against her calf. She had very nearly jumped on an erection.

"You nearly right-turned my dick," Darius said.

Jasmine threw one of her legs over Darius penis and slid down his body so that it rubbed against her behind. She bit at his nipples.

"You sure are hard for a man who wasn't looking at me." Jasmine said as she licked his chest. His penis writhed against her backside. "Feels like you're ready for another go-round."

"Oh, okay—if you insist." Darius quickly reached onto the nightstand and began opening another condom.

Myles was running on the treadmill in the exercise area of the second-floor sunroom and watching *SportsCenter* on the wall-mounted television. He decided he'd better do a little extra cardio this morning because he, Marisa, Jasmine, and his mother were going to an Orioles-Yankees game that evening, and there was nothing he enjoyed more than pigging out at a baseball game.

After his programmed thirty minutes was finished, Myles grabbed his towel and moved over to the pectoral machine to do some flys. The seat on the machine afforded a view of the backyard and pool.

When Myles saw that Jasmine and his mother were already lounging by the pool, he smiled. They looked like matching divas lying on the lounge chairs, wearing their bathing suits, shades, and straw hats. Both were reading books while they soaked in the rays.

Myles looked at his watch. It wasn't even nine thirty. They must have gotten an early start. Not as early as Marisa, however, who had left the house at the crack of dawn on some mysterious jaunt.

Myles saw Mrs. Myers make an appearance poolside carrying two glasses of iced tea and lemon. She was the lady who, along with her sister and niece, owned the service Marisa and Myles had hired to come to the house three times a week. Monday, Wednesday, and Friday they cleaned, ran errands, and cooked dinners to either be consumed or frozen for the next day's use.

Myles watched Mrs. Myers hand a glass to Jasmine and the other to his mother. Jasmine thanked her, took off her hat, and put down her book. Myles couldn't make out what she was reading, but he knew it was one of ten classics of American literature that he had bought for her to read that summer. Twain, Hemingway, Melville, Hurston, Dickinson, Fitzgerald, Wright, Ellison, and a few others.

Darius had driven back to Jersey late yesterday evening. He and Marisa had agreed to let Darius come down there on weekends when he was off work. He stayed in a spare bedroom, of course. Myles had really grown fond of Darius. And really admired his taking the time to read the same books that Jasmine was reading that summer.

Jasmine walked to the edge of the pool, set down her glass, got in the water, and climbed onto the portable chair raft. She then picked up the glass, put it in the chair's cup holder, and pushed off into the pool.

Myles chuckled as he watched her leisurely float like she didn't have a care in the world—like living large was the most natural thing in the world for her. Ever since she was a toddler, Jasmine had always appreciated the finer things in life.

Myles watched Mrs. Myers walk back into the house. When Marisa had first approached him with the idea of hiring the service, Myles had thought it was unnecessary. They already had a lady coming by twice a week to clean; surely they could fend for themselves as far as meals.

But Marisa had reminded Myles that when school started back up in September, he wouldn't have time to do much cooking. And they both knew that Marisa rarely had the time (or the inclination) to stand in front of a stove, so Myles relented.

Myles had also relented as far as giving his dad such a hard time. Whenever he went to New Jersey, he made sure he stopped by his father's place in Camden.

The way Myles saw it, his father had come out the loser in all this. Sure, he had hurt his wife, too, but his father had really made a mess out of his own life. And he didn't have the solace of blaming anyone other than the man in the mirror.

Of course, when Myles went to see him, his father never let on that he regretted anything. Oh, he *loved* the bachelor life. Fancied himself a distinguished older gentleman, a prize any lady would want. He and Stacy cooling down? That was a mutual decision. See, he didn't want to tie himself down to just one woman. Not when there were so many just dying to be on his arm.

Yeah, right, Myles thought. His dad had more bullshit than a pasture in Wisconsin.

Before he left, his father would inevitably find a way to ask Myles about his mother. All while pretending to show casual interest, of course. One of these times, Myles was going to lie and tell him that Mom had moved some strapping buck into his old spot, one who apparently didn't need the aid of Viagra to get the job done.

His father had taught him a lesson. Amir, too. And that was to appreciate what you had. If you're fortunate enough to have a good woman love you, don't let the passage of years and the familiarity that time breeds cause you to forget that she is a blessing.

The phone rang. Myles got off the machine and answered it.

"Hello?"

"What's up?"

"Hey, 'Los, what's going on?"

"Nothing much, man, just enjoying summer break."

"As if you do anything during the school year," Myles teased, "Mr. Guidance Counselor."

"Yeah, you're one to talk," Carlos said. "Listen, I just now saw the weirdest thing, while I was at the light at Warwick and Mouldy."

Myles could tell that Carlos was on a cell phone. "What happened."

"I saw Ibn yelling at a woman outside Church's Chicken," Carlos said, laughing, "cutting a real fool."

"What?" Myles laughed. What was that nut up to? "What for?" he asked.

"I don't know, man," Carlos said. "I see him coming out of the place with his food, and about to get in his car, right? So, as I'm about to honk my horn and wave to him, Ibn spots this short woman getting out of her car and walking toward the restaurant door."

"Yeah?"

"Yeah," Carlos continued, "so Ibn just runs over to the woman and says, 'What are you, a cannibal, you chicken-head?' "

Myles laughed. "You serious?"

"Yeah, and then he starts cursing her out right there in the parking lot."

"What the hell?" Myles said in disbelief. "Why?"

"How should I know?" Carlos said. "All I heard was him yelling 'Where does it all end, ho? Tell me, where does it all end?' The woman ran back to her car and left. Forgot all about getting her chicken."

Myles shook his head. "That's some strange shit."

"Myles!"

"Yo, 'Los, let me call you back later, Marisa's calling me."

"All right, bro. Later."

Marisa wouldn't tell Myles her news until they had gone outside and joined his mother and Jasmine.

Once they were by the pool, Marisa spoke.

"I just want to tell everyone that my TV show was re-newed for another season."

Myles hadn't been aware there was a doubt.

"Congratulations, dear," Peggy said.

"Thank you, Ms. Peg," Marisa said. "You're the first one to congratulate me on joining your ranks."

Myles drew his head back, puzzled. "What ranks are you talking about? My mother isn't a talk show host."

Marisa turned to face Myles and wrapped her hand in his. She drew a deep breath. "She is a mother."

Myles' mouth fell open.

"I love you," Marisa whispered.

Peggy clapped her hands together. Tears welled in her eyes.

Myles drew Marisa close to him and looked at her cautiously. She smiled and nodded.

Myles put both fists in the air and looked skyward. "Yes!"

"Myles is gonna be a father?" Jasmine asked. "Lawd."

Marisa hugged Myles. He hugged his mother. His mother hugged Marisa. All three of them were having difficulty reining in their emotions.

"Marisa, congratulations on your impending motherhood," Jasmine said as she continued to float, "but how are you gonna be fly-fabulous if you're a mommy?"

"Don't you worry about that, mermaid," she said. "Ms. Marisa gonna *stay* fly-fabulous, girlfriend," Marisa said, snapping her fingers in the air for emphasis. She then paused and cocked her head. "Does Versace make maternity-wear?"

She and Jasmine cackled.

Myles shook his head and looked at his mother. "What can I do with her?"

Peggy smiled and held her son's hand. "You can love her for a lifetime—that's what you can do. Love her for life."